I0760320

Clavis Carmesina

The Crimson Key

The Complete Collection

This is a work of fiction.

Clavis Carmesina

The Crimson Key

-The Complete Collection-

By Simon S. Steel

Dedication

For the dreamers who dare to unlock forbidden doors,
for the curious who never stop asking what if,
and for every reader who craves stories that awaken the body as much as the mind.
This book is for you.

Acknowledgements

My deepest gratitude goes to those who inspire me to write boldly, without apology.

To my close friends who encouraged me to take this leap into the erotic and the explicit — your laughter, your curiosity, and your honesty kept me going when the pages felt too daring.

To the many readers of my earlier work — thank you for your messages, your feedback, and for letting me know that there is always an audience hungry for more.

And finally, to you, holding this book in your hands: thank you for stepping through the door with me. Without your willingness to explore, these pages would remain empty.

About the Author

Simon S. Steel is the author and creator of Clavis Carmesina

-*The Crimson Key* series, exploring power, pleasure, and punishment across the world.

Also by Simon S. Steel

Clavis Carmesina – The Crimson Key: Dubai
Clavis Carmesina - The Crimson Key: Rome
Clavis Carmesina - The Crimson Key: Marrakesh
Clavis Carmesina – The Crimson Key: Maui
Clavis Carmesina – The Crimson Key: Acapulco
Clavis Carmesina – The Crimson Key: Tokyo

'Deep Blend'
'Deep Blend 2: Ecosexation'

'She Grew It All Away'

'For Those Who Hold The Key.'

Dubai
Prologue

Ten years. That's how long it had been since a man had touched me. Ten years since I'd last felt the weight of someone's body pressing mine into the mattress, the heat, the mess, the unravelling.

It wasn't that I'd stopped wanting. Not entirely. Desire had simply been buried — under meetings, flights, boardrooms, and the sheer grit it takes to build a business from nothing. You learn to silence your body when the rest of your life screams for attention. Eventually, silence becomes habit.

Then came the envelope.

It was lying on my desk the morning after my retirement dinner, placed carefully between the leftover cards and a bouquet of roses. Black, heavy to the touch, sealed with velvet. No note. No sender. Inside, a single object: a sleek deep crimson key card, threaded with a thin black velvet ribbon. Embossed in gold letters was the name of a hotel in Dubai. No instructions. Just a date.

At first I assumed it was some kind of promotional gift. A luxury stay, perhaps. A retirement perk from a supplier. But the moment I held that key in my hand, memory stirred.

Years ago, in Geneva, after too much champagne, an old business acquaintance had leaned close and whispered about parties for the elite. Not conferences. Not clubs. Hidden gatherings behind hotel doors. "The key," he'd said, lowering his voice, "is crimson. If you ever see one, you'll know."

I'd laughed it off at the time. Some urban legend of the rich and bored. But here it was. In my hand.

For a moment, I felt absurd. Fifty-eight years old, ten years celibate, imagining secret sex parties in Dubai like some wide-eyed twenty-year-old. But the longer I stared at that crimson card, the more my body betrayed me. My pulse quickened. My stomach flipped. And deep between my thighs, an ache I thought had long since died began to stir.

Could it be genuine? Could this be that crimson key?

I told no one. Not friends, not family. This secret was mine.

I slipped the card back into its velvet envelope and placed it in my handbag. I told myself I'd forget it. I told myself it was ridiculous.

But the truth was simpler.

For the first time in years, I wanted.

And curiosity, I knew, would be enough to put me on that plane to Dubai.

Dubai
Chapter One

The heat struck me first. Heavy, perfumed, and laced with spice, it clung to my skin as I stepped out of the taxi onto the marble forecourt of the hotel. Even for Dubai, this building was something else. A seven-star palace of glass and chandeliers, its entrance polished to a shine that made me feel smaller, more fragile, as though I were walking into another world entirely.

I smoothed the front of my dress, my palm brushing the velvet envelope in my handbag. My heart was pounding harder than I liked to admit. For days I had told myself this was nothing more than a gift, a retirement perk from some faceless sponsor. But the moment I walked into the lobby, the hush, the sidelong glances, the subtle perfume in the air — I knew better.

The concierge looked at me, and then, as though he could already sense it, his gaze dipped to the velvet envelope. "May I?" he murmured.

My hands trembled slightly as I placed it on the counter. He touched it with the kind of reverence most men reserve for relics, then gave the smallest of nods. "Of course, madam. Please, this way."

I hadn't felt wanted in years. Worse, I hadn't felt alive. But standing in that lobby, clutching a velvet envelope as the concierge's eyes flickered knowingly, something low and hidden inside me stirred.

He led me to the elevator with a deference I had forgotten men could show. No questions, no forms, no small talk. Just quiet respect, as if he understood what that envelope meant better than I did.

Inside the lift, velvet walls seemed to press close around me. My reflection caught in the brass panel: a woman of fifty-eight, neat dress, silver at the temples, lipstick just bold enough to fake confidence. But behind the gloss, my chest was rising too fast, my thighs already pressed together.

When the masked hostess guided me into the suite, her voice rich and warm, she told me only one thing: *"Tonight you rest. Tomorrow you play."*

Rest. My body had no intention of resting.

The suite was decadent: crimson sheets, chilled champagne, soft lights that caressed rather than revealed. I poured myself a glass and drank greedily, then sank onto the bed. That's when I saw the garment bag — draped like a secret on the armchair — and for the first time in years, my nipples tightened without warning.

I undressed slowly, each piece of clothing feeling more like an unnecessary barrier than a comfort. Naked, I lay back on the bed. The sheets were cool against my skin, the champagne fizzing still on my tongue. My hand hovered at my stomach, as though nervous, as though I hadn't done this a thousand times in my youth.

Ten years. Ten years of nothing. And now here I was, aching.

I let my fingers trail lower, past the softness of my belly, to the heat between my thighs. The wetness startled me — thick, eager, already waiting. I groaned softly, shame flickering with the sound, but it only pushed me further.

I spread my legs wide across the crimson sheets and touched myself properly for the first time in a decade. My clit pulsed under my fingertips, swollen and demanding, as though furious I had ignored it for so long.

The image of the hostess's masked face floated before me. '*Tomorrow you play.*'

I pressed harder, faster, my hips rolling against my hand. My other hand found my breast, squeezed, tugged at the nipple until I gasped aloud. The ache became unbearable.

When I came, it was violent, shuddering, my thighs clamping around my hand, my cunt clenching and spilling against my palm. I cried out, raw, half into the sheets, half into the empty air of the suite.

For a long while after, I lay panting, trembling, wetness cooling on my skin.

I hadn't just remembered desire. I had remembered myself.

Tomorrow couldn't come fast enough.

Dubai
Chapter Two

I woke with sunlight pouring across the bed like honey. The crimson sheets were tangled around my legs, damp where I had soaked them the night before. For a moment, I lay still, stretching, letting the memory of last night play across me — the trembling release, the muffled cries, the startling wetness of a body that had been ignored for too long.

I showered, the water hot and relentless, sluicing over breasts that still tingled, over thighs that quivered with a secret soreness. My clit pulsed when I ran the sponge between my legs. It was like it had been waiting all these years, buried under stone, and now, in one night, the stone had been split open.

Breakfast came on a silver tray. Coffee, pastries, ripe fruit that glistened like jewels. I ate little. My eyes kept straying to the black garment bag still draped over the chair. It sat there like a lover waiting to be unwrapped.

I finished my coffee with shaking hands and finally unzipped it.

The sound was loud in the silence, a zipper cutting open expectation. Inside, folds of black lace slipped free. I lifted the garment out slowly.

It was not modest. Not discreet. It was lingerie so sheer it would show everything — my nipples pressing through, the curve of my stomach, the dampness between my thighs. A bodysuit cut high at the hip, velvet garters that would grip my thighs, stockings fine as whispers. And a ribbon collar meant to tie around my throat, the long tail designed to trail down between my breasts, drawing the eye to my cleavage, to my body, to everything I thought age had stolen from me.

I sat down hard in the chair, the lace pooled across my lap, my breath shallow. My nipples stiffened against the thin silk of my robe. I stroked the lace, and it felt indecent, as though even touching it was foreplay.

Something slipped free from the bag and landed at my feet. A card.

I picked it up with trembling fingers.

Welcome. Tonight at ten. Your guide will collect you. Wear what we've given you, and nothing else. Everything else will be taken care of. All you need to do is enjoy yourself.

Enjoy yourself.

Not orders. Not commands. An invitation.

I leaned back, pressing the lace against my bare stomach, imagining it stretched across my breasts, tight across my hips. My thighs parted without me even realising, the dampness spreading, unstoppable.

I let my robe fall open. The lace spilled down between my legs, delicate and soft, and I pressed it against my cunt, grinding until I moaned. My fingers slipped beneath, teasing my clit, already swollen from imagining what tonight might bring.

I thought of masked strangers. Of men restrained, waiting. Of women watching as I surrendered, as I touched, as I commanded. My hips bucked. I spread wider in the chair, shameless, the lace darkening with my wetness.

When my orgasm came, it was brutal. My back arched, my fingers slippery with my own arousal, my cunt clenching so hard it hurt. I cried out, the sound muffled against the lace I pressed to my lips, biting down as wave after wave tore through me.

Afterwards, I sat panting, flushed, dripping. The lace clung damp to my thighs, a black stain of desire.

Tonight, they had written. Tonight I would enjoy myself.

God help me — I already was.

Dubai
Chapter Three

The day dragged like treacle. I tried reading, walking the corridors, ordering more coffee, but my mind was elsewhere. Every thought circled back to the garment which I had now folded neatly on the bed. The lace. The collar. The stockings. The card.

By nine o'clock, I couldn't sit still.

I showered again, shaved, powdered, perfumed, fussing like a nervous bride. When I finally slipped into the lingerie, my breath caught.

The lace clung to me like liquid shadow, sheer across my breasts so that my nipples stood out hard and begging. The garters bit deliciously into my thighs, the stockings drawing a line that led straight to the ache between my legs. The ribbon tied snug around my throat, the tail curling downward, guiding the eye to cleavage that felt suddenly indecent.

I stared at myself in the mirror and for the first time in years, I didn't see age. I saw hunger. I saw a woman dressed to be devoured.

At exactly ten, a knock sounded at the door.

I froze, heart hammering, before padding across the carpet and pulling it open.

A woman stood there. Masked, of course. Her gown velvet black, her gloved hand extended toward me. "Are you ready?" she asked softly.

My throat was dry. "Yes."

She smiled as though she had expected nothing else. "Then follow me."

The corridor was hushed, the lights low, the air perfumed with spice and something else — musk, faint and unmistakable. My heels clicked softly on the carpet as she led me past door after door, each one draped in velvet. From behind one, I thought I heard a muffled cry. From another, laughter. My skin prickled.

At last we stopped before a heavy curtain. She turned to me, her eyes gleaming through the mask. "Your game is prepared. Inside, you are both guest and player. Do not be afraid. You will be guided."

I nodded, my knees weak.

She drew the curtain aside.

The room was low-lit, velvet walls glimmering in the shadows. In the centre stood three men, naked, blindfolded, their wrists bound loosely behind them. Their cocks were already hard, straining, glistening under the soft glow of a chandelier.

A low gasp escaped me.

Along the walls, masked women sat on cushioned benches, glasses of champagne in hand, watching silently. Their eyes turned to me, and I realised with a rush of heat that I was the centrepiece.

A voice, smooth and warm, drifted from the darkness: "Welcome. Tonight, you play the Hold-Out Game. Make them ache, make them beg. But remember — the first to spill loses."

The men shifted, their muscles tight, their cocks twitching.

And me?

I stepped forward, lace clinging to my breasts, my thighs trembling, wetness already soaking the thin strip of fabric between my legs.

Ten years of silence.

And now, three cocks waiting for my touch.

I licked my lips.

It was time to play.

The silence pressed in as I stepped closer. Three men, blindfolded, hands bound behind them, their cocks jutting forward like offerings.

The air was thick with the scent of arousal — theirs, mine, everyone watching.

My heels clicked softly on the floor. Each sound drew their attention, their bodies tensing, their chests rising as they scented me. They couldn't see me, but they could feel me, and that power lit something wild inside me.

I circled them slowly, my fingers trailing across shoulders, down spines, over the taut curve of arses. Their skin was hot beneath my hand. One of them shuddered when my nails grazed lightly down his thigh. His cock twitched.

The women along the walls leaned forward, masks glittering, champagne glasses forgotten.

Ten years without a lover, and here I was, centre stage.

I stopped before the tallest of the three. His chest rose and fell quickly, his cock already slick at the tip. I bent close, close enough to let my breath feather over the head. He groaned, low and desperate, his hips thrusting forward involuntarily.

"Not yet," I whispered, though he couldn't see me, couldn't know my lips were inches from him. My words were for me as much as him.

I let the tip brush my cheek, then my lips, then turned away suddenly. The sound he made — half-growl, half-plea — sent heat flooding between my thighs.

I moved to the second man. He smelt of salt and sweat. His cock was thick, heavy, twitching in time with his heartbeat. I wrapped my hand around the base, slowly, deliberately. Gasps echoed around the room

— not from him, but from the watchers. My palm slid upward, slow, until my thumb pressed against the swollen head.

He groaned so loud it made my clit throb.

"Hold," came the voice in the dark, reminding me of the rules. '*They must not cum.*'

I released him suddenly and laughed, low and throaty, wiping the slick across my thigh through the lace. My wetness answered it instantly.

The third man trembled before I even touched him. His cock pointed skyward, already glistening. I licked my finger and circled his tip, slow, teasing, then withdrew entirely. His whole body shook with the effort of holding back.

I stepped back, standing before all three, my own thighs trembling, my cunt soaked and pulsing.

I pressed two fingers against the lace covering my clit, rubbing in slow circles as they strained in silence, their cocks twitching, desperate. I wanted them to see, wanted them to smell how wet I was, even if their blindfolds hid me.

Gasps sounded again from the benches. I looked up to see masked women shifting in their seats, their hands slipping under skirts, fingers moving between their thighs. Watching me.

The power of it nearly undid me.

I moved back to the tallest, this time sliding my tongue across the head of his cock, one long lick from base to tip. His knees buckled. His head fell back. A guttural groan tore from his chest.

"Not yet," I murmured, before swallowing him halfway into my mouth.

The room erupted in sound — gasps, sighs, soft moans.

I sucked him slowly, letting my tongue swirl, pulling back before he could break. Then I turned to the second man, wrapping my fist around him, pumping, stroking, squeezing until his body convulsed. I stopped suddenly, laughing again, stroking his thigh instead.

The third man was already shaking. I flicked his tip with my tongue, again and again, watching his hips jerk, his cock desperate for more.

And then it happened.

He cried out, his cock throbbing violently in my mouth. Hot, thick cum erupted across my tongue before I could pull away. I swallowed instinctively, gagging slightly, then licking my lips as though savouring a feast.

The rules were broken. He had lost.

The room erupted in applause, muffled but unmistakable. The masked women clapped, laughed, some even moaned. The other two men groaned in frustration, their cocks still straining, still aching, desperate to spill.

I wiped my mouth with the back of my hand, smiling wickedly.

Ten years of silence.

Now, my jaw ached from cock, my pussy throbbed with wetness, my body alive in a way I thought I'd forgotten.

And this was only the first game.

Dubai
Chapter Four

The applause ebbed, replaced by a hush that seemed thicker, heavier, than before. The man I had undone sagged in his bindings, his body slick with sweat and release. But the other two… oh, the other two were still hard, straining, their cocks glistening in the low light, their chests rising fast as they fought to hold back.

The voice in the darkness returned, smooth and rich.

"Two held. One broke. They have earned you."

Earned me. The words made my cunt clench violently, a rush of wetness spilling against the lace that barely covered me.

Hands guided me from behind — not rough, not forceful, but sure, confident. They untied the two men, pulling away their blindfolds. Their eyes landed on me, blazing with hunger, as though they had been waiting not minutes but years for this.

I lay back on the velvet-covered dais in the centre of the room, the lace bodysuit already damp and clinging. My breasts spilled free as I tugged the fabric down, my nipples aching, begging for mouths.

The first man — broad, dark-eyed, with a cock thick enough to make my stomach tighten — moved between my legs. He pressed the head against me, just at my entrance, sliding it up and down my soaked folds. My hips lifted, desperate, my clit throbbing from the tease.

"Please," I gasped, my voice breaking.

With a groan, he pushed inside.

The stretch was brutal. Ten years of emptiness and suddenly I was full, split, stuffed with hot, hard flesh. I cried out, part pain, part ecstasy, as my body clamped around him like a vice.

"Fuck," he gritted, thrusting slow, then faster, his cock dragging along every nerve inside me.

The second, taller man knelt by my head, his cock already slick at the tip. He pressed it to my lips, and without thinking, I opened. His thickness filled my mouth, sliding down my throat, the salt of him mixing with the taste of the cum I had already swallowed.

I was taken at both ends, stretched, filled, my body trembling with the shock of it.

The first man pounded into me harder, his balls slapping against my ass, each thrust jolting me upward into the taller man's cock. My cries were muffled around the shaft in my throat, gagging, drooling, but I didn't care. I was being fucked, truly fucked, for the first time in a decade, and I wanted more, harder, deeper.

My fingers found my clit, frantic, circling, rubbing as they used me. My body lit up like fire.

I came with a scream torn raw from my throat, my cunt spasming around the cock inside me, milking him, my juices flooding down my thighs. The man groaned, thrust hard, and spilled hot cum deep inside me, filling me until it oozed out around his shaft.

I gagged harder around the cock in my mouth, and he growled, grabbing my hair as he shoved deeper. Hot spurts hit the back of my throat, thick and salty, sliding down as I swallowed greedily. Cum smeared my lips, my chin, dripping onto my breasts as he pulled free.

I lay sprawled on the velvet, wrecked, my body trembling, my pussy leaking cum, my face streaked with drool and seed.

Applause rose again, louder this time, as masked women clinked their glasses together, celebrating.

Ten years without touch. And now I was drenched in it — fucked open, filled, devoured.

And it was only the beginning.

✦✦✦

Dubai
Chapter Five

The curtain fell back into place behind me, and the silence of the corridor felt almost obscene after what had just happened. My legs wobbled, my thighs sticky, my throat still raw from swallowing every drop. I could still smell them on me, still taste them.

The masked guide said nothing, simply bowed her head as she led me back to my suite. No words were needed — my flushed cheeks, my swollen lips, the wetness still sliding down my inner thighs told the whole story.

Inside my room, I collapsed against the door, my chest heaving. I caught sight of myself in the mirror and barely recognised the woman staring back: hair mussed, lipstick smeared, breasts spilling from torn lace, ribbon collar untied and hanging loose. I looked ravished. And I was.

I peeled off the lace bodysuit, still damp with my arousal, with their seed. I brought the fabric to my face and inhaled deeply, my cunt clenching at the scent of sweat and sex soaked into it. A whimper escaped me, shameful and hungry all at once.

Ten years without a cock inside me. Ten years of silence, of denying what I was. And now? Now I was open, flooded, dripping, my body alive again.

I sank naked into the crimson sheets, spreading my thighs wide, fingers sliding instantly into the mess between them. The cum was still there, hot, thick, leaking, and I used it as lube, smearing it across my folds, circling my clit until I gasped. My cunt pulsed in time with the memory — the thrusts, the fullness, the taste of cock in my throat.

I rubbed harder, faster, hips rolling, breasts bouncing with the rhythm of my hand. I imagined tomorrow's game, imagined a new room, new men, new ways to be used and devoured. What would they give me to wear? Another lace bodysuit? A harness? Nothing at all?

The not knowing made me wild.

I came again, loud and messy, juices spilling over my hand, onto the sheets, my body convulsing until I thought I would faint.

When it passed, I lay spent, slick, trembling. My fingers traced lazy circles over my stomach as my chest rose and fell.

Somewhere in the room, the black garment bag waited again. I hadn't dared open it yet, but I knew it was there — waiting to reveal tomorrow's costume, tomorrow's test.

Sleep claimed me slowly, wrapped in the scent of sex and lace. My last thought before the darkness pulled me under was simple:

What would they ask of me next?

Dubai
Chapter Six

I woke late, the sun already hot against the gauzy curtains. My body felt heavy, deliciously wrecked. My cunt ached in a way I had almost forgotten was possible — deep, bruised, swollen, every nerve alive with soreness.

I spread my thighs experimentally beneath the crimson sheets, wincing at the tenderness. My pussy lips felt raw, stretched, still slick in places from the seed that had spilled out of me in the night. My clit throbbed faintly, a ghost-pulse of the orgasms that had torn through me hours earlier.

Ten years of drought, and now I had been split open, stuffed, filled until my body hardly knew how to close again. I smiled to myself, wry and filthy. This was no polite reawakening. It was a rebirth by fire.

I showered carefully, the water stinging as it hit the swollen folds between my thighs. My nipples were tender too, my throat scratched from the cock I had swallowed so greedily. And yet, even in the ache, I felt powerful. Alive. Wanted.

On the chair in the corner, another black garment bag waited.

I dried slowly, pulling the robe around me, heart beginning to thrum again. My fingers shook as I pulled down the zipper.

Inside lay a different kind of outfit. This wasn't lace — it was sheer silk, pale as smoke. A long gown, slit up both sides to the hip, with nothing underneath it but a matching thong of the thinnest satin. No bra. No garters. The design was clear: my body would be visible, veiled only by the whisper of silk.

Nestled on top of the gown was another card.

I lifted it, expecting orders, but again the tone was warm, conspiratorial, like a friend whispering a secret.

Tonight at eleven. The Chamber of Release. Wear what we've given you. You'll need nothing else. Enjoy!

My cunt clenched at the words. Release.

But there was something else in the bag. A small, black velvet pouch. I opened it and found a silver tube of gel, cool and sleek in my palm. Another note was tucked alongside it:

For the ache. Use it freely. Your pleasure matters as much as theirs.

For a moment, my throat tightened. This wasn't cruelty. This wasn't about breaking me. They wanted me at my best, my most open, my most alive.

I slipped a finger into the tube and spread the gel between my legs. It was cool, soothing, easing the swelling as I rubbed it gently into my folds. I gasped as the sensation spread, not just relief but a subtle tingle, a whisper of arousal blooming again under the balm. My clit hardened under my fingertip, my body betraying me even as it healed.

I closed my eyes, legs spread wide on the bed, silk robe falling open, massaging the gel into my cunt until it glistened, swollen but shining.

Tonight, the Chamber of Release.

I laughed softly to myself, breathless, my fingers sticky.

As if I had any left to give.

And yet — I already knew I'd come begging for more.

✦✦✦

Dubai
Chapter Seven

The masked guide's voice was low and conspiratorial as she tied the silk across my eyes.

"Tonight, you don't choose with your eyes. You choose with your body."

My heart hammered as the darkness closed in. Blindfolded, I felt the air differently — heavier, scented with musk, leather, sweat. My nipples stiffened under the silk gown, the thin thong already damp between my thighs.

I was led forward, barefoot across velvet. I could hear them before I touched them: three men breathing hard, their chests rising and falling, the shuffle of feet as they stood waiting.

"Three men," the voice explained, warm against my ear. *"All blindfolded. All bound. You will touch them, taste them, breathe them in. One cock you must take into your body. The other two, you must feed from your mouth. Do you understand?"*

"Yes," I whispered, though my voice shook.

A gentle hand guided me forward. My fingers brushed warm skin, the curve of a hip, the rigid heat of an erection jutting against my palm. I gasped at the suddenness of it. The man groaned in return, his cock twitching beneath my touch.

I slid my hand along his length, feeling the smoothness of the skin, the weight of it. Thick, heavy. I bent forward, inhaling — a scent of salt, raw and earthy. My tongue flicked against the head, tasting precum, salty-sweet. He moaned, his body straining toward me, but I stepped away.

Another guided me sideways. My hand found the second cock, slimmer but long, veined, throbbing in my grip. I wrapped my fingers around him, sliding slowly, hearing his breath hitch. I pressed the head to my lips and took him halfway into my mouth. His hips jerked, involuntary, a deep groan tearing out. He tasted sharper, muskier. My cunt clenched around nothing.

I pulled away, lips wet, and moved to the third.

The moment I touched him, I knew. Hot, thick, curved slightly upward, my hand barely wrapped around him. I bent close, inhaling deeply. His scent was darker, spicier, almost sweet. I licked, tasted, and the taste alone made my body quake.

Yes. Him.

"The third," I whispered.

Applause rustled softly from somewhere beyond the blindfold.

"Then the other two must spill for you," the voice said.

I sank to my knees, groping until I found the first cock again. I took him deep into my mouth, sucking hard, saliva dripping down my chin as I pumped the shaft with my hand. He groaned, his hips thrusting despite his bindings. My tongue swirled, my throat opened, and with a strangled cry he spilled into my mouth, hot jets hitting the back of my throat. I swallowed greedily, cum dripping down my lips, across my breasts.

Without pause, I turned to the second. He was already trembling, his cock slick with precum. I licked him from base to tip, then swallowed him too, pumping hard with my fist. He came almost instantly, spilling across my tongue, thick ropes painting my mouth, my chin, dripping onto my gown. I licked and sucked until he sagged against his bonds, spent.

A voice again, smooth, approving:

"Untie the chosen."

Hands freed him, rough fingers instantly pulling me against him. His cock pressed against my entrance, fat, hot, straining.

"Ohhh fuck—" I gasped as he pushed inside.

The stretch was brutal, splitting me wide, deeper than I had taken in years. My cunt clamped tight around him, my body trying to reject and devour him at once. He groaned, a guttural sound, and began to thrust.

Each stroke slammed into me, the head of his cock battering the deepest parts of me. My breasts bounced against my chest, the silk gown shoved open, my nipples raw from his mouth as he latched on, sucking, biting, tugging until I screamed.

His tongue dragged across my breast, lapping at the sweat, then down, down my stomach until he pulled free, leaving me trembling and empty.

"Please!" I cried, blindfold damp with sweat. "Don't stop—"

Instead, he spread my thighs wide, his breath hot against my swollen pussy.

And then his tongue.

"Ohhhh God!" I bucked up as he licked me, deep and filthy, tongue stabbing into my hole, then swirling against my clit. My legs shook uncontrollably, hands fisting the velvet beneath me. He pinned me down, his mouth devouring me, sucking at my clit until stars burst behind the blindfold.

I came with a scream, juices flooding his face, soaking the silk beneath me.

But he didn't stop.

He licked me through it, greedy, drinking every drop, tongue sliding over my cunt lips, into my folds, back to my clit. My body convulsed, pleasure turning to pain, then back to pleasure again. My voice cracked from crying out.

And then he was inside me again, cock pounding, faster this time, relentless.

My blindfold slipped with sweat, but I held it in place — I didn't want to see. I wanted only to feel.

He fucked me until I was babbling, my voice hoarse, my pussy gaping and leaking, my clit raw from his tongue. Another orgasm tore through me, violent and shaking, and still he drove on, groaning, his balls slapping against me.

When he came, it was with a roar, his cock pulsing deep inside me, spilling hot jets that filled me until I could feel it leaking out around him. He collapsed on top of me, his breath hot in my ear, both of us soaked, ruined, trembling.

I lay limp, the blindfold still covering my eyes, my thighs sticky, my body aching everywhere.

Exhausted. Fucked open. Licked raw.

And tomorrow, I knew, they would want me again.

✦✦✦

Dubai
Chapter Eight

I had barely managed to walk straight all day. My thighs ached, my cunt felt swollen, stretched, tender. Even sitting at breakfast, I could feel the slow ooze of the man's cum still seeping from me, a constant reminder of the night before. I'd been split, filled, licked, and pounded until I thought I would faint — and God, I loved it.

But tonight, the card in the bag told me something different. Part of me was grateful for the reprieve written on the invitation card:

Tonight you watch. No demands. Just eyes, ears, and heat.

By the time the guide led me into the chamber, I was almost trembling with anticipation.

This room was vast compared to the others, lit golden, with tiered seating like a decadent theatre. The scent hit me first: musk, sweat, perfume, lube. And the noise — low murmurs, nervous laughter, the wet sound of women already touching themselves in preparation.

At the centre, on two parallel rows of raised dais platforms, eight couples stood ready. Naked. Oiled. Glorious.

Four on one side. Four on the other. A relay race, but the baton was orgasms.

The announcer's voice rang out smooth and wicked:

"Two teams. Four couples. The rule is simple: a man may not fuck until the woman before her has squirted far enough to reach them. When the last man spills his cum across his partner's face, the team wins."

The audience roared approval.

I sat forward on the edge of my seat, silk robe falling open, thighs pressing together.

The first women were already on their backs, legs high in the air, fingers sliding furiously across clits. One used a toy, thrusting fast, juices spilling already. Their men crouched beside them, straining, cocks leaking, desperate to bury themselves but forbidden until their partner shot the starting arc.

"Begin!"

The first woman cried out almost instantly, spraying a hot gush over her belly, then again, harder, until it spattered her waiting teammate's thigh. We all cheered. The man beside her groaned and shoved his cock into her, pounding hard, his balls slapping as she writhed beneath him.

On the other dais, the rival woman arched her back, screaming as she squirted high into the air, droplets splashing onto her teammate's chest. Her man plunged into her the second it hit, fucking her with animal need, his partner beside them already trembling from watching.

It was carnage.

The second women — now "activated" — tore at their clits, fingering themselves while their men licked their breasts, sucked their nipples, kissed them hungrily. One man crouched down and licked his partner's pussy, slurping noisily, his tongue dragging across her folds until she convulsed, spraying a sudden violent gush that showered the third couple in line.

"YES!" her teammate screamed, leaping onto her man's cock, riding him wildly while squirting again mid-thrust. The floor glistened wet with female release, the air filled with cries and gasps and the slap of flesh.

I was shaking in my seat, hand sliding under my robe despite the ache, fingers circling my clit as I watched.

The second men couldn't hold back. They grabbed their women's hips, thrusting up into them, mouths latching onto bouncing tits, tongues licking sweat and cum. The women squirted and squirted again, wetting their teammates, passing the obscene baton down the line.

The third pairs erupted in chaos. One woman squirted so hard it hit the man beside her, drenching him before he even entered her. He howled with lust and shoved inside, fucking her so fast she sprayed again and again across the dais, her juices splattering the audience close enough to reach.

Then we all screamed approval, masked women fingering themselves, men jerking cocks in the shadows.

The final women in line were wild, bodies convulsing, clits raw from toys and tongues, their men licking, fingering, begging them to release.

Then one exploded.

She arched back, a fountain erupting from her cunt, splashing her man from chest to thighs. He roared, grabbed her by the hips, and drove his cock inside her with brutal force.

The rival team wasn't far behind. Their last woman screamed, her squirt hitting her partner in the face, dripping from his chin as he entered her hard, pounding, grunting, fucking like an animal.

Now it was down to the men.

Each thrust harder, faster, balls slapping, their women screaming as they were pounded open, tits bouncing. The audience counted aloud — "One, two, three…" — with every slap of flesh.

And then the first man broke.

He pulled out, face twisted, stroking furiously until jets of hot cum shot across his partner's face. White ropes splattered her cheeks, her lips, dripping down her chin. She licked her lips greedily, moaning as he painted her in thick seed.

The audience exploded into cheers.

But the rival team pushed on. Their last man pulled free, jerking desperately, his cock spurting across his woman's mouth, her tongue catching every drop before it rolled down her neck.

The announcer raised his arms.

"Winners — Team One!"

The room erupted. Masked women kissed each other, men groaned and came into their hands, the audience itself shaking with release.

And me?

I was shaking, soaked, my hand drenched between my thighs. I hadn't even been touched, but my cunt spasmed violently, climax ripping through me as I watched cum streak across women's faces, watched them lapping, licking, squirting until the room was soaked in filth.

I sagged back into my seat, robe clinging to my sweaty skin, my pussy throbbing.

Tonight I was an observer.

But tomorrow, I knew, they would make me play again.

✦✦✦

Dubai
Chapter Nine

I couldn't sleep.

Every time I closed my eyes, I saw it all again: the women tonight, their bodies convulsing, their cunts spraying like fountains, men's faces painted in squirts and cum. The audience moaning, fingering, cocks out in the shadows. The raw, obscene joy of it.

And more than that — the women.

Their thighs trembling, their breasts bouncing, their mouths open in screams of release. Women writhing, women begging, women squirting harder than I thought possible. My cunt clenched just remembering.

I realised, with a sudden heat in my stomach, that the women turned me on as much as the men. Maybe more.

Blindfolded, I had learned how much my body could feel when sight was stripped away. And now, lying in my bed, my hand slipping between my thighs, I wondered what it would be like to be blindfolded again… only this time with a woman's tongue on me.

The thought made me gasp.

I spread my thighs, my fingers sliding over the swollen lips of my cunt, still sore, still tender. The ache only made it hotter. I circled my clit slowly, moaning softly into the dark.

I pictured the squirting women on the dais — their legs wide, juices spraying across their men. I imagined crawling between their thighs, my mouth open, catching their spray, drinking it as they screamed.

My cunt spasmed at the image.

I rubbed harder, pressing two fingers into myself, groaning at the tightness, the ache. I imagined the woman's thighs gripping my face, her taste flooding my tongue, her hands yanking my hair as she squirted into my mouth.

“Ohhh fuck…” I whispered, shoving my fingers deeper.

My other hand pinched my nipple hard, twisting until pain flared sweetly. I imagined two women bent over me, licking my tits, sucking, while another licked my clit, while another straddled my face, her pussy dripping onto my tongue.

The room filled with the wet slap of my fingers plunging into my cunt, juices leaking down my thighs. I bucked against my hand, panting, eyes squeezed tight under the blindfold I wished I wore.

I came with a violent scream, my whole body shuddering, juices spraying messily across my sheets. My cunt gushed, pulsing, releasing in waves I hadn’t felt in decades.

I collapsed back against the pillows, soaked, trembling, my hand sticky with my own cum.

Women.

The thought scared me. But it also thrilled me.

Tonight I had only imagined it.

But tomorrow? Tomorrow, maybe, I would dare.

✦✦✦

Dubai
Chapter Ten

The silk blindfold went on again, and this time I didn't resist. I wanted the darkness now. I craved it.

The guide whispered against my ear, warm and deliberate:

"Tonight, you don't get to choose. Tonight, you surrender. Your body is theirs. And his."

His? I thought, confused. But when they led me forward and strapped me down — wrists bound loosely above my head, ankles spread wide apart — I understood.

The first thrust of the machine made me scream.

A thick, rigid cock, slick with lube, buried itself inside me, deeper and fuller than any man had. The machine withdrew, then slammed back in again. Slow. Precise. Then faster. Then slow again. The rhythm changed without warning, keeping me on edge, keeping my cunt stretched, dripping, hungry for more.

And then the hands came.

Everywhere.

Soft lips at my breasts, tugging, sucking. Fingers pinching my nipples until they ached, then soothing them with tongues. A wet mouth at my neck, licking, biting.

And then something hotter, wetter.

A woman climbed onto my chest, her thighs gripping my face. Her pussy pressed against my mouth, and before I could think, she ground down, her juices smearing across my lips. I opened for her, licking, tasting, drinking as she moaned above me.

"Oh fuck, yes—" she cried, grinding harder.

Another woman leaned over, licking her clit as she rode my face, their wetness spilling over me, soaking my cheeks, my chin.

The machine pounded harder, faster, my cunt spasming as I was stuffed, stretched, filled. My body jerked uncontrollably, my cries muffled under the woman's dripping cunt.

Hands tugged my hair. Fingers slid into my mouth when I tried to breathe, fucking my throat as the machine fucked my cunt. Another pair of lips latched onto my nipple, biting until I yelped.

Then — hot wetness.

A spray hit my stomach, then my breasts. A woman screamed above me, squirting violently, soaking my body. Another joined, gushing across my thighs, their juices mixing with the lube already flooding my pussy from the pounding machine.

I was drenched. My skin slick, sticky, slippery with cum — mine, theirs, all of it blending.

And then something else.

The woman riding my face shuddered, screamed, and exploded. A hot rush flooded my mouth, salty, musky, sharp — not just a squirt. Something thicker. Hotter.

I didn't care what it was. I swallowed greedily, lapping, licking, sucking her cunt until she collapsed against me, trembling.

The machine switched suddenly, slamming into me harder, brutal, relentless. My body convulsed, back arching, wrists straining against the binds. I screamed against the woman's cunt, my whole body shattering as orgasm ripped through me, violent, endless.

Juices sprayed from my pussy, soaking the machine, my thighs, the sheets. The women cheered, hands stroking me, mouths kissing me, fingers circling my clit even as I writhed in overstimulation.

I didn't know what was dripping from me anymore. Cum. Squirt. Something else entirely. My body had lost all distinction.

All I knew was that I loved it.

When the machine finally slowed, easing out of me, I sagged against the cushions. My body was wrecked — covered in cum, sweat, spit, squirt, everything. My cunt was swollen, lips puffy, clit raw. My face glistened with other women's release.

Blindfolded, bound, used, drenched…

And aching for more.

✦✦✦

Dubai
Chapter Eleven

I couldn't get clean.

I'd stood under the shower until the water ran cold, scrubbing myself with hotel soap, but I could still smell it — sex, sweat, squirt, cum, and something else.

Piss.

The thought made my stomach flip and my pussy ache at the same time.

Had it been squirt? Cum? Or had she pissed on me, laughing as I swallowed it in the dark, blindfolded and helpless?

I didn't know. But the thought that it might have been… God, that thought made my thighs slick all over again.

I lay in bed, naked under the sheets, staring at the ceiling, my cunt swollen, lips still bruised from the machine's assault. My clit throbbed as the image replayed: her grinding against my mouth, the gush flooding me, the taste, the heat.

I slid my hand down, spreading my folds with two fingers. Still sore, still wet. I circled my clit lightly, moaning.

What if it had been piss? What if I'd swallowed another woman's piss and loved it?

The thought shocked me. It should have disgusted me. But instead my cunt clenched around nothing, dripping onto the sheets.

I imagined it again, but differently this time. Not me drinking. Me giving.

On my back, legs spread, another woman between my thighs, her mouth open, waiting. My pussy twitching, my bladder aching, holding back until she begged for it.

And then — letting go.

Hot piss rushing out of me, spraying into her open mouth, splashing across her face, mixing with my cum as I came violently.

"Ohhh God," I moaned, shoving two fingers, then three fingers into myself, pumping hard despite the ache.

My other hand pinched my nipples, tugging them until pain flared sweet and sharp. My cunt gushed around my fingers, juices soaking the sheets.

I came once. Then again.

And still I rubbed, still I pumped, chasing the image. Her mouth wet with my piss, my thighs spraying, her swallowing everything as I screamed and squirted and came until my body gave out.

When the orgasm finally broke me, it was violent — my whole body convulsing, my cunt clenching so hard I thought I would tear. I sprayed across my own hand, unsure if it was squirt or piss or both.

I didn't care.

I collapsed, soaked, sticky, trembling. My sheets ruined. My body wrecked again.

For the first time in years, I didn't feel ashamed. I felt alive.

And I couldn't wait for them to push me further.

✦✦✦

Dubai
Chapter Twelve

By now I thought I had seen it all. The blindfolded games. The relays. The machine. The squirts. The women's faces painted in cum like trophies.

But tonight was different.

The card waiting for me was shorter than usual.

Tonight you observe again. Eight competitors. Anything goes. The first man and the first woman to release piss onto another are the winners.

I felt my cunt twitch the moment I read it.

Piss. The word sat in my mind like a forbidden fruit.

Until now, I hadn't known what had drenched me. Not for certain. But tonight would confirm it. Tonight I would see with my own eyes.

The chamber was bigger again, almost like a stage. Two groups of four couples, seated opposite each other on low couches, naked, oiled, and already touching. The rules were simple: do everything except cum. Hold back the orgasm. Hold back the cum. But whoever pissed first onto another body — man or woman — won.

The audience leaned forward in hushed silence, the kind that comes before an explosion. I sat near the front, my robe slipping off one shoulder, my nipples hardening as I drank it all in.

The signal came.

Instant chaos.

One woman dropped to her knees between a man's thighs, swallowing his cock, sucking hard enough that his hips bucked. He groaned, fists clenching, but he couldn't spill. Another woman climbed onto her man's lap, riding him hard, her tits bouncing as he fucked up into her, but every time he got close she stopped, pinching his cock cruelly until he groaned in frustration.

On the other couch, a man had bent his partner over the edge, tongue buried in her pussy, lapping furiously as his fingers spread her ass wide. She squirted, once, twice, soaking his face, but still it wasn't enough. The audience screamed, cheering for more.

Everywhere was flesh, wet and pumping. Tongues in pussies, fingers in asses, lips locked, tits sucked, nipples bitten. Men jacking themselves furiously then stopping just before climax. Women riding and grinding, moaning, begging, but holding back the final wave.

The scent of sex filled the room — musk, lube, sweat — and under it, something sharper, dirtier, waiting to break.

And then it came.

One of the women — blonde, slim, with her hair tied back — broke away from her man. She straddled another woman's stomach, squatting low, her pussy inches from her body. The audience held its breath.

She grinned wickedly, spread her lips with her fingers, and let go.

A hot stream burst from her, hissing as it sprayed across the woman's breasts, running down her stomach, pooling in her navel. The woman moaned, rubbing it into her skin, lifting her tits to catch more, sucking it off her own fingers.

The audience went wild.

"Yes! First woman!" the announcer cried.

The blonde pushed harder, piss flowing down, splashing the couch, soaking the woman beneath her. The audience clapped, some of them coming undone themselves in the shadows.

But the men weren't far behind.

One man, panting, pulled his cock from his partner's mouth, held it in his fist, and grinned at the other team. With a grunt, he let go, a stream of piss arcing across the room, splattering another man's thigh before running down to his cock.

The man groaned and rubbed it into himself, stroking, dripping, begging to come but denied.

"First man!" the announcer bellowed.

We all screamed again, stamping, clapping, cheering.

From there it collapsed into madness.

Men pissed across women's breasts, down their throats, into open mouths. Women straddled men's faces and let go, soaking them until their chins glistened. Couples rolled on the couches, bodies slick with sweat, cum they weren't allowed to release, and now hot piss mixing in, a filthy, musky perfume.

I was trembling, thighs clenched, hand pressed between my legs, unable to stop rubbing myself through the silk of my robe.

There was no doubt now.

What had drenched me the last night had been piss. And far from disgust, I felt my cunt spasm violently at the thought. The idea of releasing like that myself — hot, messy, uncontrollable — sent a flood of wetness through me.

When the final whistle blew and the winners were declared, I was already shaking, on the edge of an orgasm I wasn't supposed to have.

But when I stumbled back to my room, fell onto my bed, and spread my thighs wide, I knew there was no stopping it.

I wanted it.

I wanted to be pissed on again.

And I wanted to piss on someone else.

✦✦✦

Dubai
Chapter Thirteen

The invitation had been simple:

"Today you rest. Share. Listen. Connect."

Rest? I wasn't sure I remembered what that word meant anymore. My cunt still ached from the pounding machine, my thighs bruised, and my nipples tender. Every time I moved, I caught a faint scent on my skin — musk, sweat, and the sharp tang of piss. The thought of it made my stomach flip and my clit twitch in equal measure.

The lounge was different from the other nights. No velvet curtains, no dark chambers. Instead, the air buzzed with something lighter. Robes and champagne, low tables, soft music, easy laughter. It looked almost civilised, like a business retreat. If not for the marks on our bodies.

I took a glass of champagne and perched on the edge of a couch.

A woman with dark hair and an easy smile joined me. Her robe had slipped from one shoulder, exposing the faint trace of teeth marks across her breast.

"Relay night," she said, catching me looking. "He bit too hard, nearly lost us the round. But Christ, it was worth it." She sipped, eyes glinting.

We both laughed. But inside me, my cunt pulsed. The way she spoke of being bitten — as casually as someone might recall a good meal — made me ache.

The room slowly filled with conversations. Small clusters formed: men and women sprawled on cushions, comparing their nights. A tall, scarred man who had been blindfolded with me leaned back and described how he'd nearly come in the second round, his fists clenched so tight he'd left nail marks in his palms. The blonde woman — the first to piss in the orgy — told her story again, her eyes bright, her voice full of pride.

"I thought I'd be ashamed," she said, shrugging. "But the second I felt it gush, I didn't care. It was… freeing. Like giving up control of everything."

Glasses clinked in response.

I laughed with them. Nodded. Joined in. But I could feel the heat in my stomach, the slick between my thighs. I wasn't just listening — I was living it all over again.

And then I saw them.

Across the room, two women lay tangled together on a low couch, their robes discarded, their hands between each other's thighs. One lazily circled her partner's clit while sipping champagne with the other hand. The other moaned softly, head thrown back, her fingers buried inside the first woman, pumping slow, deep strokes.

No one looked shocked. No one interrupted.

It was as casual as sipping coffee.

I pressed my thighs together, biting my lip, watching them. Their bodies rocked slowly, hands slick, pussies glistening. I could see the damp spread under them on the cushion.

The blonde beside me leaned closer, whispering, "Normal here. You'll see it more. Soon you'll join in without thinking."

My cunt clenched so hard I nearly spilled my drink.

The conversations around me rolled on — women boasting about how far they could squirt, men talking about how long they could hold back. But my eyes stayed fixed on the two women across the room, moaning quietly as they fucked each other with lazy, knowing ease.

And my mind whispered the truth I hadn't dared to admit aloud:

I wanted it.

I wanted to be in the middle of that couch, fingers inside one woman while another licked my cunt until I flooded her mouth.

I shifted in my seat, pressing the glass to my lips to hide my breathless moan.

Rest day, they'd called it. But by the time I returned to my room, I was wetter than I'd been all week.

✦✦✦

Dubai
Chapter Fourteen

When the card slipped under my door that evening, my heart raced before I even opened it.

"Tonight is for women. No rules. No winners. No men. Just flesh, mouths, and desire. Spectators welcome."

I felt my cunt clench at once.

The lounge had been transformed into something softer, more decadent. Silken cushions scattered across the floor, low lighting, the scent of jasmine drifting through the air. The audience — masked men and women alike — took their seats in the shadows, already shifting in anticipation, some with hands casually stroking thighs, some already pulling robes open.

But in the centre: us.

Eight women. Naked. Glowing.

The atmosphere was different from the competitions. There was no edge of rules or timing. Just hunger. Curiosity. Lust.

We began slowly, circling each other, eyes roaming, hands brushing against skin. A brunette with wide hips and soft breasts stepped toward me first. She cupped my face, kissed me deep, her tongue sliding into my mouth with an urgency that made my knees buckle.

Her hands moved down my body, over my breasts, tugging my nipples, then lower, fingers sliding between my thighs. I gasped against her lips, already dripping.

And then another woman knelt behind me, her mouth hot against my shoulder, her hands pulling me open wider.

I was surrounded, consumed.

I gave in.

The brunette pushed me gently back onto the cushions. I spread my legs without thinking, her tongue diving into my cunt, lapping, swirling, fucking me with wet, hungry strokes. The woman behind me tugged my nipples, pinching hard, then bent forward and sucked one into her mouth, biting until I yelped.

The audience groaned. I could hear the slick sound of men stroking cocks, the soft cries of women fingering themselves as they watched us.

And then it was everywhere.

Hands and mouths, tongues and fingers. A blonde climbed onto my chest, straddling my face. Her pussy glistened, the musky scent of her arousal flooding me. She pressed down, grinding against my mouth until I opened. I licked her greedily, sucking her clit, tasting her juices as she rode my tongue.

Another woman slid between my legs, replacing the brunette, plunging her tongue inside me while fingers circled my clit. I screamed into the blonde's cunt, my hips bucking, juices gushing across the woman's face below.

The audience gasped, some crying out as they came just watching.

But I didn't stop.

I licked, sucked, fingered, let them use me and used them back. Two women tangled together beside me, fingering each other furiously until they squirted across the cushions. Another pressed her tits into my face, demanding I suck her nipples while she fingered herself beside me.

Everywhere was wetness. The cushions were soaked. Our mouths glistened with each other's cum. Our thighs were smeared with juices, our hands sticky and shining.

I came once. Twice. Then again. My cunt never stopped spasming, my body never stopped shaking. Each orgasm rolled into the next until I couldn't tell whose fingers or tongues were inside me, whose juices I was swallowing, whose thighs I was clinging to.

At one point, I was pinned beneath three of them — one grinding her pussy on my mouth, one riding my fingers, another licking my clit — and when I came again, squirting across them all, the audience erupted, men groaning, cum spurting across the floor, women crying out as they fingered themselves to climax.

The room was filled with the sounds of release. The spectators were as drenched as we were, cocks painted in cum, pussies dripping across seats.

When at last we collapsed together, tangled and soaked, our bodies heaving with exhaustion, I knew I had crossed another line.

There was no shame left.

Only hunger.

And one thought pulsed in my mind:

If tonight was women only, what on earth would tomorrow bring?

✦✦✦

Dubai
Chapter Fifteen

I woke up drenched.

My thighs were slick, the sheets beneath me soaked with sweat and cum, the faint tang of last night's women still clinging to my skin. I pressed a hand between my legs, wincing at the tenderness. My cunt ached like I'd been fucked by a dozen men, though it had been women — tongues, fingers, mouths, and the way they had wrung orgasm after orgasm from me until I was left a trembling wreck.

I smiled into the pillow. For the first time in years, I didn't feel alone. I felt used. I felt alive.

This was my last day. Tonight would be my last game. My last chance to surrender.

The garment bag waited on the chair. My heart thudded as I unzipped it.

Inside: a sheer golden gown. Almost invisible. Threads of silk and mesh that clung but revealed, the kind of dress that didn't hide a thing. With it came a card, written in the same warm script as always:

"Tonight, all doors open. All limits lifted. This is the final feast. Join us at midnight. Come empty, leave overflowing."

The words made my cunt twitch. My clit pulsed just reading them.

All day I tried to distract myself, wandering through the hotel, sipping coffee in the quiet garden, even trying to nap. But my body wouldn't settle. I felt stretched too thin, my nerves alive, like every inch of me had become a clit.

Other guests were the same. We passed each other in the halls with knowing smiles, eyes gleaming, robes clinging to damp bodies. Some couldn't even wait. I saw a couple pressed against a wall in a corridor, her robe bunched up, his cock inside her, pumping slow while she bit his shoulder to keep quiet.

By late afternoon, attendants arrived. I was drawn into a spa-like chamber where warm oils were poured over me, my body scrubbed, my hair brushed until it shone. I was pampered like a bride, though I knew tonight I was no bride. Tonight I was a vessel.

When they laid the golden gown over my skin, it shimmered in the light, catching on my nipples, barely concealing the soft swell of my mound. I looked at myself in the mirror and almost laughed. Fifty-eight years old, a lifetime of restraint behind me — and now I looked like a goddess whore, ready to be sacrificed on an altar of flesh.

As the sun set, the air in the hotel changed. The corridors hummed with something electric. The guests spoke softer, moved slower, saving themselves for the night.

And me?

I lay back on my bed, fingertips grazing my cunt through the gauzy fabric, and whispered to myself:

'Tonight, I give it all. Tonight, I take it all.'

When the knock came just before midnight, I was already wet, already trembling.

And ready.

✦✦✦

Dubai
Chapter Sixteen

The golden gown shimmered like liquid light as I was led through the corridor. The air was already thick — musk, wine, anticipation. I heard moans before I saw anything.

And then the doors opened.

It wasn't a room this time. It was a hall. Vast, velvet-lined, and filled with bodies. Dozens of them, men and women, naked, glistening, already in the grip of lust.

Mouths sucking. Cocks stroking. Fingers pumping. Tongues lapping. Everywhere I looked, flesh was sliding against flesh.

I felt my cunt gush instantly, wetting my thighs, soaking the golden silk.

Hands pulled me inside, stripping the gown away in a single tug. My nakedness was greeted with a cheer. Someone kissed me, deep, wet, hot. Another hand spread my thighs. A cock pressed between them, sliding up and down my wet folds, teasing.

And then I was down.

Flat on my back on a pile of cushions, bodies pressing in, mouths at my tits, a tongue at my cunt, another mouth kissing mine while I was fingered from behind.

I lost track of who was who.

A cock slipped into my mouth — hot, thick, pulsing. I gagged, sucked harder, drool spilling down my chin. Another cock slammed into my cunt, filling me, stretching me until my hips bucked.

I was being spit-roasted. My throat used. My pussy pounded. My tits mauled.

And then another mouth at my clit, licking around the cock inside me, sucking, slurping, pulling at me until I squirted across their face.

Hands flipped me. I was on all fours, one cock in my mouth, another ramming my pussy, another pushing at my ass. Lube, spit — I didn't know what slicked me, only that when he entered, my whole body screamed.

Two cocks now.

One in my cunt, one in my ass.

My mouth full of another.

I was split open, drenched, used like a toy.

Juices dripped down my thighs. My face was wet with spit and cum. My ass slapped with every thrust, my tits swinging, my clit begging for touch.

And then the spray.

Hot, sudden, sharp.

A woman straddled my back, squatting above me, and pissed down over me, streams running across my shoulders, dripping into my hair, my mouth. I swallowed greedily, moaning around the cock stuffed in my throat.

The dam broke.

Men pulled out, pissing across my tits, my stomach, my thighs. Women squatted, gushing on my face, soaking me until I dripped golden and clear and sticky all at once.

I was drenched. My body was a canvas of piss, cum, squirt, spit.

And still they used me.

My ass clenched around a cock, my cunt stretched by another, my mouth swallowing thick, salty loads that spilled down my chin. I tasted everything — bitter, sweet, musky, sharp — every flavour of filth.

I lost count of orgasms. Each time I screamed, squirted, shook, another hand pulled me open wider, another cock drove in deeper, another mouth sucked harder.

The hall became a frenzy. Couples, threesomes, piles of bodies writhing, licking, sucking, fucking, squirting, pissing, cumming. Moans echoed, cries overlapped, the scent of sex so thick it clung to every breath.

At one point, four women pinned me, licking every inch of my body, tongues at my clit, my nipples, my toes, until I drenched them with squirt. Then men replaced them, jerking over me, streams of hot cum splattering across my face, my tits, my belly.

And when I thought I had nothing left, they lifted me, carried me through the bodies like an offering. Women, men reaching out to touch, to lick, to fuck.

I didn't think I had anything left to give.

My cunt was raw, my ass stretched, my mouth aching from cock after cock. My body was glazed in sweat, piss, and cum.

And then she came to me.

A woman — small, dark-haired, with hunger in her eyes — crawled up my body, straddling my chest. She pressed her wet mouth to mine, kissing me deep, tasting the mess of men and women still dripping down my chin. When she pulled back, she whispered, "I want you to piss for me."

The words hit me like a lightning strike.

I had thought about it for nights, teased myself with the fantasy in the dark, but now… now it was here.

She slid down between my thighs, spreading me wide. Around us, the frenzy still churned — men moaning, women squirting, cum shooting across the room. But my world narrowed to her.

She pressed her mouth to my pussy and moaned. "Let go. Give it to me."

And I did.

The first stream was hesitant, hot and sharp, trickling against her lips. She opened wide, swallowing greedily, her tongue lapping at me as I released. The trickle became a gush, a flood pouring out of me, spraying into her mouth, across her face, running down her chin.

People cheered, clapping, moaning, some stroking themselves harder at the sight.

I arched my back, gasping, the relief and filth mixing into a wave of pure ecstasy. I pushed harder, letting go completely, pissing with force until her face was soaked, her mouth overflowing, her tits glistening with my spray.

My body convulsed. My clit throbbed. I came as I pissed, squirting and urinating all at once, screaming as my juices flooded her.

She swallowed, smiling, wiping her face with her hands and licking them clean. Then she climbed up, kissed me again, and I tasted myself on her tongue — salty, musky, shameful, divine.

In that moment, I was not a guest, not an observer, not a woman afraid of being too old, too prudish, too late.

I was a queen.

A queen who had given everything, and held nothing back.

✦✦✦

Dubai
Chapter Seventeen

The next morning, the silence was deafening.

No moans. No gasps. No cries of release echoing down the corridors. Just the soft rustle of sheets as I woke in an empty bed, my body aching in every possible way.

I lay there for a long time, staring at the ceiling. My thighs were still sticky, my breasts bruised, my cunt swollen. I had been used, filled, pissed on, squirted over, drenched in every fluid a body could give. And I had loved it. Every filthy, shameless second of it.

But now it was over.

The golden gown from last night lay crumpled in the corner, torn and ruined. My suitcase had been returned to my room, standing neatly by the door as if the entire week had been just another business trip.

There was no note. No card. No final instructions.

Only silence.

At reception, the staff greeted me warmly, as though I were checking out of any other luxury hotel. My bill had already been settled. The concierge smiled, wished me safe travels, and handed me a plain black envelope.

My heart lurched. The Crimson Key? Another invitation?

I opened it with trembling fingers.

Inside was a single slip of thick card, the same elegant handwriting as before:

"I hope all your wildest dreams came true. Bon Voyage."

That was it. No name. No signature. No hint of who had sent me the first key or who had orchestrated everything behind those velvet doors.

The car to the airport was waiting.

As I sank into the leather seat, Dubai's glittering skyline slipping away behind me, I pressed my thighs together, still sore, still tingling, still full of memory. My lips curled into a smile.

Whoever they were, whatever this had been — they were right.

My wildest dreams had come true.

Dubai
Epilogue

Home felt smaller.

The streets the same, my house the same, even my bed the same — yet I wasn't.

Every time I caught my reflection, I saw her. The woman who had been spread across cushions, drenched in cum, riding tongues and cocks with abandon. The woman who had squirted over strangers, swallowed piss, and let her own stream flood another's mouth.

At night, I still woke slick between my thighs, my hand reaching down before my eyes were even open. I couldn't stop reliving it — the blindfold, the machine, the women's orgy, the final night's chaos. It wasn't memory anymore; it was part of me.

And then, just as the ache became unbearable, it happened.

The post arrived one morning, ordinary bills stacked carelessly through the letterbox. But among them — another black velvet envelope. My heart stopped.

Inside was a single line, in the same elegant hand as before:

"The Key will turn again. Destination: Rome. Your suite awaits."

I sat down hard, breath catching in my throat.

This wasn't a one-off.

This was a series.

Six invitations in total, each to a different city, each to a different luxury surrounding, each unlocking new games, new bodies, new extremes. Dubai had been the first. Now Rome. And beyond that? Marrakech. Maui, Acapulco. Tokyo. Places I couldn't yet imagine — but already my cunt ached for them.

I held the crimson key in my hand, the weight of it pressing into my palm like a promise.

I smiled to myself, whispering into the empty room:

“Bon voyage indeed.”

The End

Rome
Prologue

It came the same way it always would: slipped under my hotel door, velvet black against pale marble tile, impossible to ignore.

The envelope.

I recognised the weight of it before I even bent down to pick it up. The texture was the same as the key that had unlocked my undoing in Dubai — that little piece of velvet that had pried open ten years of celibacy and turned me inside out with lust I hadn't felt since my youth.

My pulse quickened as my fingertips traced the soft fabric. I had promised myself, after Dubai, that I'd put it away, return to my safe, predictable life. But the sight of that crimson velvet brought the ache flooding back, low and insistent between my thighs.

I slid a finger beneath the flap and pulled out the card. Heavy stock, gilded lettering, a single line written in looping script:

"Your key still opens every door. In Rome, you will feast."

Beneath it lay a strip of cream silk, folded and perfumed faintly with something musky, exotic. A sketch of a laurel wreath crowned the corner of the card, as though daring me to imagine myself draped in white and gold, seated at some emperor's banquet table where flesh was the only meal worth serving.

I closed my eyes and, for a moment, I was already there — marble pillars towering above me, torchlight flickering, laughter echoing, men in togas sprawled like gods with women draped across their laps. The kind of decadence that would have scandalised my younger self and now, to my surprise, made my cunt throb with wet, restless need.

The crimson key still sat heavy in my travel bag, waiting. One key. One world. And now Rome was calling.

I knew then there was no turning back.

Rome
Chapter One

The plane dipped through golden clouds, and Rome unfolded beneath me — domes, ruins, terracotta rooftops glowing in the afternoon sun. I felt as though I were flying straight into history, or into some fantasy that had been waiting centuries just for me.

At the arrivals hall, a driver in a black suit held a sign with my name. No hotel logo. No corporate branding. Just 'Annabelle.' Clean. Private. Exactly as before.

He didn't speak beyond a polite nod, and I didn't ask. My heart beat too fast in my chest anyway, each thud a reminder that the crimson velvet key was in my handbag, heavy with promise.

The car slid through narrow streets, past fountains and piazzas where tourists clutched their guidebooks and cones of dripping gelato. None of them knew that hidden somewhere beyond their chatter, marble walls would echo with very different sounds tonight.

When we arrived, the hotel didn't look like a hotel at all. From the street it was an old palazzo, discreetly restored, its wooden doors tall enough for emperors. Inside, I was met with hushed grandeur — dark marble floors, high frescoed ceilings, candle sconces throwing pools of golden light.

A woman was waiting at reception, as though she'd been expecting me the moment I stepped out of the car. Not a receptionist in uniform — but someone elegant, wrapped in a toga-like gown of white silk, a thin band of gold resting across her forehead.

"Buona sera, Annabelle," she said, her accent soft but deliberate. "Your key, if you please."

I pulled it from my bag — that small crimson velvet smoothed from the touch of my fingers — and laid it in her open palm.

Her smile was knowing, almost wicked. She returned the key with both hands, as though giving back something sacred. Then she slid a new velvet envelope across the desk.

"Your chamber awaits. Tonight you will dine, and tomorrow… you will feast."

The card inside told me only the time and a single phrase:

"Togas and wreaths are provided. Indulgence is required."

My stomach fluttered, part nerves, part anticipation. I had thought Dubai had been a one-off descent into madness. But here I was, in Rome, standing on marble floors where centuries of power and lust had played out — and tomorrow night, I would be part of it.

I went to my suite — high ceilings, velvet drapes, a bed big enough for an orgy — and set the envelope down. My body already hummed with memory, with need.

For a while I simply stood at the tall window, staring out across the tiled roofs of the city, the fading light smouldering over the skyline. Ten years of celibacy had been obliterated in Dubai. I had gone from nothing to everything — blindfolds, cocks in my mouth, hands everywhere, strangers making me scream until my voice broke. I had thought I'd left it behind. But my cunt was wet just standing in a Roman palazzo.

I stripped slowly, as though someone were watching me. The white blouse slipped off my shoulders, my bra unclasped with a flick, my skirt falling in a heap at my feet. Naked, I stretched across the bed, letting the cool linen press against my nipples. My hand drifted to my thighs, spreading them until I could feel the humid heat of my own arousal rise.

I thought of Dubai — the taste of anonymous cocks on my tongue, the way my body had been used until my thighs ached, the laughter of women as they squirted across marble floors. The memory of it hit me like a drug.

I slid two fingers into my pussy, the wetness immediate, obscene. I teased my clit with the other hand, circling it the way that masked man had done until I bucked up against my own hand.

Then I imagined Rome.

Men in togas lounging like gods, women draped across them, laurel wreaths slipping down their hair as they licked, sucked, moaned. I pictured myself thrown onto a marble table, goblets toppling, a dozen hands parting my thighs, my cunt filled, my mouth gagged on cock while another woman's tongue worked my nipples.

The thought of it undid me. I thrust deeper, harder, wet sounds filling the room. My moans echoed against the frescoed ceiling. My body arched, toes curling, my clit pulsing beneath my desperate fingers until the orgasm ripped through me, hot and uncontrollable.

I came hard, gasping, grinding into the sheets as though I were already being taken. My thighs quivered, my cunt clenching on nothing, empty yet aching for the fullness I knew tomorrow would bring.

When it was over, I lay panting, slick between my legs, staring at the velvet envelope on the nightstand.

Dubai had been only the beginning.

Rome was going to devour me.

✦✦✦

Rome
Chapter Two

Dinner was laid out in a vaulted hall that looked as though it had been stolen straight from a history book. Marble columns, frescoed ceilings, long wooden tables with golden platters of food. Candles burned low in iron sconces, dripping wax that caught the shadows on the walls.

I wore nothing more than the robe left in my suite — toga-style, loose at the shoulders, belted with a rope of gold. When I walked in, the sight was almost surreal: men and women draped in similar garments, some eating, some drinking, some lounging like statues come to life.

The food was almost secondary. Grapes, figs, roasted meats, cheeses, poured wine in goblets that tasted dark and heady. But my eyes kept drifting from plate to bodies.

In one corner, a man leaned back against the stone, toga hitched up, his cock in his hand. A woman knelt in front of him, not touching, only watching, her own hand buried beneath her robe. He came quickly, silently, cum streaking across his belly as she moaned and licked her fingers clean.

Elsewhere, a pair of women sprawled on cushions, wine glasses discarded, kissing with tongues so deep it made me shift in my seat. One of them pulled her robe open to bare her breasts, the other sliding down to suck them with greedy abandon while a small group watched from a distance, sipping their wine.

I walked outside after eating, needing air, needing to stretch my legs — but the grounds were no less charged.

The garden glowed in torchlight, hedges trimmed in perfect lines, fountains burbling. At one of them, three men and two women were gathered, robes already discarded. One woman lay across the marble edge, her legs spread, while the other knelt between them, lapping at her cunt. The men circled, stroking themselves, one leaning in to press his cock into her mouth, another teasing her nipples with wet fingers.

She squirted suddenly, an arc of glistening liquid catching in the torchlight before splashing into the water of the fountain. The watching men groaned and came almost instantly, spilling into the pool, their moans echoing through the courtyard.

I couldn't look away. My wine glass trembled in my hand, my thighs slick beneath the robe.

Around the grounds, others wandered casually, some reading books under lantern light, some engaged in quiet conversations — as though the sight of bodies writhing and squirting metres away was no more unusual than a band playing in the background.

And maybe here, it wasn't unusual at all.

I sat on a stone bench, the night warm, the air thick with jasmine and sex. For the first time, I realised Rome wasn't going to rush me the way Dubai had. It was going to let me watch, let me wander, let me ache until I couldn't bear it anymore.

And then it would take me.

I left the fountain and wandered further, through corridors lined with statues, their marble eyes watching me as if they already knew the things I had come here for. My footsteps were muffled by thick carpets, the hush of the palazzo punctuated only by distant laughter and the occasional moan slipping under a door.

That was when I noticed it — a door, slightly ajar, a faint glow spilling into the hallway. I should have walked past, but curiosity has its own gravity, and mine pulled me closer.

I peered in.

Three women were inside. All in togas that had long since slipped from their shoulders, their bodies golden in the candlelight. They sat sprawled across a chaise and rugs on the floor, their eyes fixed not on me but on one another.

One had her legs splayed wide, fingers circling her clit with steady, ruthless precision. Another knelt opposite her, robe loose, breasts bare, two fingers buried deep in her own cunt as she watched. The third lay on her side, rubbing her slick folds with slow, lazy strokes, her tongue occasionally darting out to wet her lips as she moaned.

They weren't trying to shock anyone. They weren't putting on a performance. This was raw, honest, primal. Women pleasuring themselves while drawing energy from each other's arousal.

My breath caught. My pulse thundered.

I pressed my back against the wall just outside, careful to keep in shadow, but my hand was already sliding under my robe. The fabric clung to my damp thighs as I circled my clit, in time with the rhythm of their fingers.

The woman with her legs spread cried out, body jolting as she squirted across the rug, wetness splashing onto the candlelight. The other two gasped, and it drove them harder, faster, their moans layering into one relentless wave.

I couldn't hold back. My fingers slipped lower, thrusting into myself, my palm grinding my clit. My eyes stayed fixed on them, three women writhing in their own flood of lust, and I bit down hard on my lip to stifle my moans.

Heat roared through me, my body trembling, every nerve on fire. I came there in the corridor, hidden but shameless, wetness dripping onto my own thighs as my cunt clenched around my fingers.

I leaned against the wall, panting, the sounds of their orgasms still echoing in the room, their bodies collapsing in sweaty heaps against one another.

I pulled my hand out, my robe sticking to me, and staggered back toward my suite, my legs unsteady.

Rome hadn't even begun its games, and already I was undone.

Rome
Chapter Three

I woke to bells. Not an alarm, not a knock on the door — church bells spilling across the city, bright and unashamed in the Roman morning.

For a moment, I almost forgot where I was. The palazzo, the crimson key, the women in candlelit rooms moaning and squirting as I touched myself unseen. My thighs still stuck faintly with the memory of it. But when I pulled the curtains aside and saw the skyline — terracotta rooftops, domes glinting in sunlight, laundry strung across balconies — I realised I couldn't spend the day locked in a hotel suite waiting for nightfall.

I dressed simply, leaving the golden rope and robe folded on the bed. Outside, Rome was alive in a way the hushed palazzo never was.

The plaza I found was busy but not frantic. Cobbled stones warmed by sun, fountains bubbling, pigeons darting between café tables where locals sipped tiny cups of espresso. I took a seat beneath a striped awning, ordered a cappuccino I knew would be frowned upon at this hour, and let myself watch.

It was everything the night wasn't — chatter, clinking cups, the scent of fresh bread from a nearby bakery. A violinist played by the fountain, his bow worn but his music soft and insistent. Children chased one another, tourists studied maps, and for a while I felt… ordinary.

But under it all, I hummed with a secret.

The couple at the next table were bent close in conversation, their knees touching. I couldn't help wondering what they'd think if they knew what I'd seen last night. If they knew that in a few hours, I'd be back behind marble doors, watching women make themselves squirt while men knelt and begged to be allowed to cum.

The thought sent a sharp pulse straight through me. I shifted in my chair, sipping the thick coffee, trying to keep my face neutral. To anyone passing, I was just another woman enjoying the morning sun in Rome. They had no idea I was soaked beneath my dress, thighs clenching against a desire that was already building for tonight.

After coffee, I wandered narrow streets, trailing my fingers along warm stone walls. I bought figs from a market stall, their sweetness sticky on my lips. I ducked into a church, cooler inside, shafts of light cutting across the marble floor. My cunt ached at the memory of Dubai, of last night, of the card promising *In Rome, you will feast.*

I almost laughed at the audacity of it. By day, I was a tourist. By night, a worshipper of something far older and far filthier than any saint.

And tonight, Rome would welcome me again.

✦✦✦

Rome
Chapter Four

The summons came at dusk. Another velvet card slipped under my door, this one marked with a golden laurel.

"Tonight, clothed. Desire must find its way through restraint. Come to the hall when the torches are lit."

I wrapped myself in the toga that had been provided, the soft white linen falling loose but heavy against my skin, cinched at the waist with gold cord. No underwear — we had been instructed to come bare beneath. It made every brush of fabric against my body feel obscene.

The banquet hall had been transformed. Torches flickered along the walls, a long marble table set not with food but with cushions, goblets of wine, bowls of figs and olives. Guests drifted in, each wrapped in their togas, their bodies both hidden and tantalisingly accessible.

A man beside me leaned close, his toga brushing against mine as he whispered, "Tonight, we are Romans." His breath was wine-sweet, his thigh pressing to mine beneath the table.

The rules were clear: no one could fully undress. No cock could thrust bare into cunt. Every act of pleasure had to be forced through the toga — rubbing, grinding, teasing, licking what could be reached without disrobing. It was maddening. It was delicious.

The first cries came quickly. Across the table, a woman straddled her partner's lap, her robe still covering them both, but the frantic rocking of her hips made the fabric shiver and cling. His hands gripped her waist through the toga, grinding up against her, his face contorted as he came, seed spilling into his robe while she cried out, soaking herself against his cock, both of them collapsing together in a heap of wet linen.

Around me, the feast grew.

One man lay back on a cushion, his toga tented high. A woman slid down his body, pressing her mouth to him through the fabric. She sucked at him, hard enough that I could see the outline of his cock through the linen, wetness spreading where her tongue worked. He shuddered violently, spilling himself into the folds of cloth, her lips never once parting the fabric.

I felt hands at my sides. A man and a woman, each pressing close. His fingers brushed my nipples through the toga, rough and demanding, while hers slid along my thigh, up, up, until she cupped my cunt through the robe. I gasped, the fabric slick against me as she rubbed, circling my clit until I was bucking against her hand, moaning into the torchlight.

I turned to her, our faces inches apart, and kissed her hard. Our tongues met, wine and lust, her hand never leaving me, her fingers grinding through the toga until I screamed against her lips. I came hot and sudden, soaking the robe, the wetness spreading like a stain of proof.

The man pressed harder against me, his cock stiff under his toga, rubbing against my hip as he groaned. I reached for him, grabbed the bulge, and stroked him hard through the cloth until he spilled, cum soaking the white fabric in a dark, spreading patch.

The room filled with cries, moans, the slap of bodies clothed but frantic, the air thick with wine and sex. Everywhere, togas clung with sweat, dampened with seed, nipples and cunts teased through linen until everyone was spent, collapsed across marble and cushions in a haze of pleasure and frustration.

It was decadence, yes — but denial too. Rome was only giving us a taste. The true feast was still to come.

The hall finally dimmed, the torches guttering low, the air heavy with wine and sex. Guests lay tangled in robes, damp and exhausted, their bodies twitching with aftershocks even though no one had been truly bare. I staggered out, my thighs slick, my toga clinging with my wetness.

But the ache was unbearable.

My cunt pulsed, swollen, greedy, unsatisfied. It wanted to be filled. No amount of grinding or fabric-teased rubbing could make up for the emptiness inside me. Each step back to my suite was torture, the rough linen brushing against my clit, reminding me how close I'd come to losing myself in that hall — and how far I still was from the release I craved.

When the door to my suite closed behind me, I tore at the toga like it was shackles, yanking it over my head and kicking it aside. My skin was damp, my thighs glistening, my cunt aching so hard I could hardly stand.

And then I saw it.

On the bed, laid across the velvet sheets, was a phallus.

Marble, carved smooth, curved to perfection, cool to the touch when I picked it up. It was heavy, deliberate, a relic from some forgotten temple or a prop stolen straight from a Roman banquet — but unmistakably shaped to be inside me.

I almost wept.

I climbed onto the bed, spread my legs, and pressed the smooth head to my swollen cunt. The marble was shockingly cold at first, but my body swallowed it greedily, the tight ache easing as the length slid into me.

"Fuck," I gasped, arching, pushing it deeper until I was full, stretched, finally satisfied.

I rode it hard, hips grinding, my clit pressed against the cool base as I fucked myself like a woman possessed. The stone made obscene wet sounds as it thrust in and out of me, juices coating it, dripping down my thighs.

I thought of the feast — all those men and women cumming through their togas, spilling into fabric, denied the raw heat of penetration. And here I was, in my suite, taking what they couldn't.

The thought drove me over the edge. My orgasm ripped through me, violent and guttural, my body shaking, cunt clenching so hard around the marble I nearly dropped it. I screamed into the pillows, my voice hoarse, my body slick with sweat.

But I wasn't done.

I fucked myself again, harder, faster, slamming the phallus into me until another orgasm tore through, then another, until I collapsed, trembling, drenched, the marble slippery with my cum.

When I finally lay back, panting, the phallus slipped from me and landed on the sheets with a wet thud.

Rome had given me a taste. And tomorrow, it would take everything.

✦✦✦

Rome
Chapter Five

The summons came as twilight painted the city gold. Another velevt envelope waited on my bed, the card inside bearing just two words in Latin and English beneath:

"Feminae liberae. Women free."

The rules for the night were clear before I even entered the hall: women were to bare themselves fully, every curve, every secret revealed. Men, still draped in their togas, were forbidden to strip. They could press, grind, even attempt penetration through the cloth — but their skin could never meet ours fully.

It was our night.

I loosened the gold cord at my waist and let the toga fall, stepping into the torchlit hall naked. My nipples tightened instantly in the cool air, my cunt already wet from the thought of being seen. Dozens of eyes turned to me, men groaning softly in their robes, women smiling knowingly as they shed their coverings too.

The hall became a sea of bare female flesh — breasts bouncing, thighs slick, mouths parting. The men, still wrapped, looked like desperate gods denied, their erections obvious beneath the folds of linen as they shifted, groaned, and pressed themselves against us.

A woman approached me first. Tall, dark-haired, her nipples hard, her cunt already glistening. She took my hand, pulled me onto a low couch, and straddled me. Her breasts brushed my face as she leaned down and kissed me, deep and hungry, her tongue stroking mine.

I moaned into her mouth as her fingers slid down, spreading my thighs, circling my clit with practiced skill. My hands gripped her hips, pulling her closer, until I could taste her cunt as she lowered herself onto my mouth.

She was divine. Musky, wet, the taste of pure arousal dripping onto my tongue. I licked her furiously, drinking her moans as she rocked against my face. Her juices slicked my chin, my cheeks, until she screamed and gushed, squirting across my mouth and chest.

Men crowded around us, their cocks straining beneath their togas, rubbing themselves frantically against thighs, against couches, against each other. But none could enter. Not bare. Not tonight.

I was pulled away by another woman, smaller, fair-haired, who pushed me onto my back and sank her mouth onto my cunt. Her tongue was relentless, her fingers plunging into me, curling until I sobbed with pleasure. I grabbed her hair, grinding against her face, my body arching as orgasm ripped through me, hot and endless, squirting across her hand.

The hall was filled with cries — women licking each other, fucking with fingers, clits grinding against thighs, tits bouncing as mouths sucked and bit. Everywhere I looked, women writhed together in pleasure, while men knelt uselessly, rutting through their robes, spilling into their linen in desperate frustration.

At one point, a man pressed against me from behind, his cock stiff beneath his toga as he tried to grind between my cheeks. I laughed, reaching back to grab the fabric-wrapped bulge, stroking him through it until he came with a muffled groan, spilling hot cum into his robe, dripping down his thigh.

But my attention stayed on the women. Their wet mouths, their hungry fingers, their bodies free and untamed. I licked, I sucked, I came until my thighs trembled and my voice was hoarse.

I was slick with the taste of women, my thighs trembling, my body exhausted and yet aching for more. Everywhere around me, women writhed and came, their cries echoing against the frescoed walls, while the men looked on like starving animals, grinding their erections against any willing thigh or palm that would allow it.

One of them caught my eye. Tall, broad, his toga tented obscenely at the front, the outline of his cock pressed hard against the linen. He stood still, chest heaving, watching me lick the last of another woman's cum from my fingers.

I beckoned him closer.

He came without hesitation, his cock straining, twitching beneath the fabric. I reached for it, running my hand slowly along the length, feeling every ridge and pulse through the cloth. It was hot, desperate, and so hard I gasped.

"Fuck… I need to feel you," I whispered, though I knew the rules. I pressed my face to him, licking and sucking the fabric, the taste of his pre-cum seeping through, warm and musky against my tongue. He groaned, head thrown back, hands gripping the folds of his toga as though to keep himself from tearing it off.

But I wanted more.

I turned, bent forward onto a couch, and reached behind me to grab the thick shape through his toga. "Push," I urged, grinding my wet cunt back against him.

He positioned himself, cock stiff and slick through the soaked fabric, and thrust forward. The linen pressed into me first, rough, frustrating, but then the head of his cock bulged through the cloth and found my opening.

I moaned as he forced himself against me, the fabric dragging between us, but the heat of him unmistakable, stretching me. Each thrust made the wet cloth slap against my folds, my clit catching on the texture, sending shocks through me.

"Harder," I begged. "Deeper. Even through the robe… fuck me."

He obeyed, driving into me, cock straining against the toga, until my body shuddered and released. I squirted over the fabric, soaking it, drenching his cock beneath the linen. He groaned, thrust again, and came violently, his seed spilling into the robe, soaking through until I could feel the heat of it drip against my thighs.

When he pulled back, the toga was clinging to him, stained dark with sweat, cum, and my wetness. He collapsed onto the couch beside me, panting, still half-hard beneath the sodden folds.

I licked my lips, tasting the musky salt that lingered on the fabric, and smiled.

The rules had been kept. His cock had never touched me bare.

And yet I had been fucked.

✦✦✦

Rome
Chapter Six

The sunlight was merciless when I finally woke. My body ached from the night before — breasts tender from mouths that had sucked them raw, cunt swollen from fingers, tongues, and the maddening thrust of a cock wrapped in linen.

I lay sprawled on the cool sheets, replaying it all.

The taste of women had lingered in my mouth long after I returned to my suite. Slick sweetness, musky and heady, the way one had ground her cunt against my face until I was drenched in her squirting release. I had always wondered, in some quiet, buried place, if I could long for a woman — and Rome had answered without hesitation.

But it wasn't just the women.

That man, thrusting against me through his toga, hot cock straining, desperate. The feel of him pressing into me even with the barrier of cloth, the heat of his cum soaking through, dripping onto my thighs. It had been frustrating and yet… almost more arousing. The denial sharpened everything.

I touched myself lightly, tracing circles across my clit, wondering what Rome would bring me next.

Later that morning, I ventured out into the city again. Rome in daylight was a different world — noisy plazas, fountains throwing silver arcs into the sky, children chasing pigeons. I sat at a café in the square, a small glass of wine sweating in my hand, listening to the sing-song chatter of locals.

They had no idea.

They had no idea that only hours ago, I had been on my knees, licking another woman's juices while men came into their robes watching me. They had no idea I'd been bent over, begging to be fucked through linen, cumming so hard I soaked a stranger's cock and thighs.

The thought made me grin into my glass. My secret was delicious.

By evening, another velvet card waited on my bed.

This time it read:

"The men revealed. The women concealed. Tonight, you will take what is offered."

I dressed in the robe laid out for me — deep burgundy this time, soft and heavy, covering me from collarbone to ankle. My skin itched beneath it, desperate to be bare again.

But when I entered the hall, my breath caught.

The men were naked.

Everywhere I looked: cocks hard, balls heavy, bodies bared in torchlight. They stood tall and proud, their arousal shameless, their eyes already hungry. Some stroked themselves idly, others waited, stiff and dripping.

The women, in their robes, became the hunters.

It was our turn to stay clothed while they stripped. Our turn to feel the heat of skin against fabric, to grind our covered thighs against their bare cocks, to decide if and when they were allowed to spill.

Rome had flipped the game.

And I was ready.

The hall had transformed into something primal.

Men stood bare, their cocks hard and swaying in torchlight, while women in burgundy and ivory robes circled them like predators at a banquet.

I sat back at first, watching.

One woman pressed her robed body against a man, grinding her covered cunt against his cock until he moaned. His hands clutched at the folds of fabric, desperate to lift it, but she slapped them away. He had to rut against the cloth, spilling onto it while she laughed, her robe marked with his seed.

Another knelt between two men, stroking them both with covered arms, their cocks glistening as they dripped onto her robe. She licked her lips but never bared her skin. They came across the burgundy folds, thick white streaks painting her chest as she moaned at their release.

It was intoxicating to watch — women wrapped, men exposed, the power shifted completely.

But I couldn't sit still for long.

The hunger in me was unbearable. Watching those cocks bob and swell, the way their heads shone with slickness, the way men groaned when women ground clothed thighs against them… I wanted it. I needed the taste.

I rose, my robe heavy around me, and approached a man standing against a column. His cock was thick, flushed, dripping already, his eyes locked on me.

I sank to my knees.

The rules never said I couldn't use my mouth.

I wrapped my lips around the head, tasting salt and musk, sliding him deep into my throat until he groaned and slammed his hand against the marble behind him. His cock pulsed on my tongue, hot and heavy, and I sucked hard, dragging my nails down my clothed thighs to ease my own ache.

More men gathered, their cocks hanging close, heavy and ready. One brushed against my cheek, smearing pre-cum across my skin. I moaned around the one in my mouth, sucking greedily, my hand reaching to stroke another, pumping him until he shuddered.

The man against the column lost control first, his cock jerking as he spilled hot cum down my throat. I swallowed every drop, licking my lips, moaning as another cock pressed into my mouth, filling me again before I could breathe.

The room blurred into cries, moans, seed dripping onto robes, onto covered breasts, onto the floor. Women remained clothed, but men were undone, spilling over and over, their nakedness their weakness, their cum our reward.

I swallowed and licked, one cock after another, my robe soaked with the spray of their release, my cunt throbbing, aching to be filled but content, for now, to be their mouth, their hunger, their release.

When I finally pulled back, my lips swollen, my robe sticky with cum, I laughed breathlessly.

Rome had stripped the men bare.

And I had devoured them.

The taste of cock lingered thick on my tongue. My robe clung, streaked with wet seed, the fabric heavy where men had spilled across me.

But still I wanted more.

A man approached, cock stiff, balls hanging heavy. I reached for him, stroking with my robe-covered hand, then pulled him into my mouth. My lips stretched wide, my throat aching as I swallowed him deeper.

His hips bucked helplessly, his cock slamming against the back of my throat until he erupted, hot cum gushing straight down. I gagged, swallowed, and moaned — my cunt dripping with every pulse of his release.

Behind me, a woman pressed close. I felt her robed thigh slide between mine, grinding against my soaked cunt through the fabric. Her breath was hot on my neck, her hand cupping my breast beneath the folds.

"Come for him," she whispered, her voice a dare.

I bent forward, cock still in my mouth, while she pushed her thigh harder against my clit. My hips rocked, soaking the robe, smearing wetness across her leg.

Another cock brushed my lips, then another. I let them in turns slide against my tongue, smearing slick across my face, painting me. My cunt throbbed, hungry, frantic, the grinding friction unbearable.

I cried out, muffled around the cock in my mouth, as my orgasm tore free.

But it wasn't enough. I wanted to flood, to drench, to give.

I pulled back, gasping, and shoved my robe up just enough to bare my cunt. The rules blurred in my desperation — but no one stopped me.

A man knelt instantly, mouth open, eyes blazing. "Feed me," he begged.

The words broke me. I ground against his mouth, his tongue lashing my clit, and I squirted hard, hot gushes flooding into him. He swallowed greedily, moaning as I drenched his tongue, his chin, his chest. My thighs trembled, my body collapsing forward into another man's arms as he stroked his cock, spilling across my breasts in thick white lines.

The room erupted around me — women grinding, men kneeling, cum and sweat and squirt soaking the marble floor. My body shook, emptied and alive, my robe clinging in wet folds.

I looked down at the man still kneeling, lips glistening with my release, his eyes glazed with worship.

Rome had stripped him bare.

And I had baptised him.

✦✦✦

Rome
Chapter Seven

The morning light felt almost too pure after what had happened in the torchlit hall. I woke to the scent of the city drifting through my window — warm bread from a bakery below, the distant clang of church bells, the hum of scooters already filling the cobbled streets.

My body still ached from the night before, thighs tender, breasts marked with dried streaks of seed, my cunt still swollen from grinding, squirting, and moaning until I could barely stand. I had half a mind to stay in bed and let my fingers wander down again. But Rome was out there, calling.

I dressed in something simple — loose linen trousers, a cotton blouse — and slipped out of the hotel into the streets.

The city felt alive in a way Dubai hadn't. There, the heat had pressed like a weight, sending me scuttling from air-conditioned lobby to shaded courtyard. But Rome… Rome was meant for wandering. I let the cobbled streets lead me, past little cafés with wicker chairs spilling onto pavements, flower boxes tumbling down balconies, the smell of espresso and pastries everywhere.

I stopped in Piazza Navona, watching an artist paint tourists in quick sketches, couples kissed against statues that had seen centuries of lust and love. It was almost laughable to think — none of them had any idea what I had been doing each night, none of them knew the secrets that were playing out in candlelit chambers only a few streets away.

The thought made me smile as I sipped my espresso.

Later, I ducked into a small shop near the Pantheon, full of trinkets and souvenirs. I picked up a few — a set of delicate olive wood rosary beads for a friend who pretended to be devout, a silk scarf embroidered with Roman ruins for another who loved her little luxuries, and a bottle of red wine with a label I couldn't read but looked expensive enough to impress.

They would never know.

To them, I was on a "quiet Roman holiday," enjoying retirement, sightseeing, indulging in art and food. If only they knew the truth — that my nights were soaked in wine, cum, and sweat, that I had sucked cock after cock until my lips were raw, that I had squirted into the mouth of a stranger while others came all over me.

I laughed softly to myself as I paid the shopkeeper, tucking the souvenirs into a bag. My friends would never believe me anyway.

And perhaps that was part of the thrill.

By late afternoon, the sun was dipping low, painting the terracotta rooftops in shades of gold and bronze. I walked slowly back toward the hotel, my bag of souvenirs swinging at my side, the clatter of my sandals echoing on the cobblestones.

It almost felt like I was leading two lives.

One was here in the daylight: a woman in her late fifties enjoying a Roman holiday, buying trinkets, sipping coffee, admiring art and ruins. The other came alive only after dusk, in hidden halls scented with oil and wine, where my cunt was soaked nightly and my body treated like it had been waiting decades to be worshipped, used, and filled.

The thought made my thighs press together as I entered the marble foyer of the hotel.

When I reached my suite, the now-familiar sight awaited me. A velvet pouch rested on the bed. I set my bag of souvenirs aside and untied the cord, my pulse quickening. Inside was a card, the edges gilded, the letters in bold golden script:

"Tonight: all walls fall.
Nothing covered. Nothing denied."

Beneath it, a single item lay folded — not a robe this time, not a hint of concealment, but a delicate golden laurel wreath.

A crown.

For a moment, I just stared at it, my breath shallow. A crown to be worn, naked, among the others. No fabric between cock and cunt, no barrier between mouth and flesh. Tonight, for the first time, there would be nothing hidden.

I traced the wreath with trembling fingers, a grin spreading across my face as heat pooled low in my belly.

Rome had teased me, clothed me, denied me, drenched me.

Tonight, Rome would strip me bare.

And I was ready.

When dusk fell, the air itself seemed to thicken with anticipation. I bathed slowly, perfuming my skin with the oils left in crystal bottles by the bath, then stood before the mirror. For the first time in Rome, there was nothing to cover me. No robe, no toga, no veil. Only the laurel crown, gleaming gold against my dark hair.

I had never felt more naked.

I walked barefoot to the hall, the cool marble beneath my soles, every step echoing like a drumbeat of inevitability. The doors stood open, torchlight blazing, laughter and groans already spilling out.

And then I saw it.

A sea of flesh.

Men and women both, completely bare, their bodies shining with sweat and wine, cocks already stiff, cunts already slick, mouths open in moans. No restraint, no cloth, no rules but one: everything was allowed.

A man took my hand the moment I entered. His cock was hard, hot against my thigh as he pressed me back against a pillar, kissing me hungrily, his tongue plunging deep into my mouth. Another woman knelt, spreading my thighs, her tongue lapping at my cunt before I could even cry out.

I gasped, my laurel crown slipping as I clutched at the man's shoulders, while the woman's mouth worked furiously below. My juices dripped down her chin as I came in violent spurts, my thighs trembling, my scream lost in the din of the orgy.

I was pulled away, spun into another embrace — this time a woman's. She pressed her breasts against mine, kissing me fiercely, grinding her cunt against my thigh until her slickness coated my skin. Behind me, a man pressed his cock against my arse, thrusting until he slid inside, bare at last, filling me with every inch.

The shock of it stole my breath. Hot cock, skin to skin, nothing between us. My body clenched around him as I moaned into the woman's mouth, my cunt stretched, finally bare, finally fucked as it had been begging to be.

All around me, the hall was chaos: women riding men's faces, men fucking women from behind, women locked together in chains of mouths and fingers. The air reeked of sweat and sex, wet sounds echoing from every corner, cries and groans bouncing off the marble walls.

I was pulled down onto a couch where two men lay waiting. One guided his cock to my lips, pushing deep into my throat until I gagged and moaned; the other slid between my thighs, his cock pounding into me until my whole body shook. I sucked and fucked at once, my crown tilting as sweat dripped into my eyes, my mouth overflowing with cum as my cunt spasmed and squirted around the man inside me.

I didn't stop. I couldn't stop.

By the time I collapsed back against the cushions, seed streaked my chest, my belly, my face. My cunt was raw, stretched, dripping cum that wasn't mine, my body trembling from orgasm after orgasm.

But I looked around and knew — the night was far from over.

Rome had finally stripped us bare.

And we were drowning in each other.

Hands were everywhere. I had no idea whose. Some grabbed my breasts, pinching my nipples until I gasped. Others spread my thighs wide, opening me to whoever wanted to plunge inside.

A cock filled me again before I could breathe — thick, raw, sliding into my soaking cunt with an obscene squelch. I cried out, only to have another cock pushed between my lips. My mouth stretched wide, throat working as I gagged, then relaxed, swallowing him down.

I was being fucked at both ends, my body used, and I moaned into it, clinging to the man in my mouth as the one beneath pounded me harder, harder, until my juices gushed over his thighs.

When they pulled away, I was spun, turned, bent over. A woman crouched before me, spreading my folds with her fingers, licking my clit while another cock slid into me from behind. The pleasure was blinding. My cries echoed across the marble as the woman sucked and flicked, the man fucked and rammed, and my cunt exploded in a gush that drenched her mouth.

She drank greedily, moaning, while the man groaned and came inside me, hot seed flooding me, dripping down my thighs.

Before I could even collapse, two more replaced them.

One lifted my legs onto his shoulders, slamming into me hard. Another pressed his cock to my lips, then deeper, until my throat bulged with him. I gagged, drooled, choked, but I didn't stop. I wanted them all.

When the one inside my cunt pulled out, another slid in instantly, slick and hot, his balls slapping against me as he drove me into the cushions. My body was a vessel now, a hole to be filled, emptied, and filled again.

Women took their turn too — climbing onto my face, grinding their wet cunts against my mouth until I drank them, licking their clits, their pussies, their arseholes. They screamed above me, squirting into my mouth, over my chest, while men stroked themselves, shooting across us both.

I lost count of how many cocks I sucked, how many times I came, how much cum dripped from my cunt and down my thighs. My skin was coated in it, my hair matted, my crown glinting as though mocking the filth beneath it.

By the time dawn broke, I was limp, my body trembling, my cunt stretched raw, my mouth swollen, my skin sticky with seed and squirt.

And still, even then, when one last cock pressed to my lips, I opened my mouth for him.

Rome had turned me into their feast.

And I had devoured every moment.

✦✦✦

Rome
Chapter Eight

I woke at noon.

My body was wrecked — thighs trembling, cunt sore, lips raw from sucking cock after cock until I lost count. My hair was matted stiff with cum, my skin streaked with drying seed and the scent of women still clinging to me. The laurel crown had slipped to the pillow beside me, as though mocking the ruin it crowned.

I bathed for almost an hour, scrubbing, soaking, sighing as the water turned cloudy with sweat and sex. Even clean, though, I still felt marked. My pussy ached with every step, the ache so deep it was almost sweet.

This was meant to be a day of rest. No velvet pouch awaited me, no summons to a chamber. Just a chance to mingle with the others, to wander the hotel grounds, to let my body recover.

But Rome never truly rested.

I walked into the garden courtyard and saw a couple stretched across a stone bench, the woman's robe hiked up, the man kneeling between her legs, his tongue buried in her cunt as she writhed and moaned.

By the fountain, another woman leaned back against the marble rim, two men crouched before her, one tonguing her clit while the other slid fingers deep inside, their faces slick with her juices as she cried out.

Even on the shaded terrace, where a few guests sipped wine and chatted, one woman had her hand beneath another's robe, stroking lazily, the table shaking with the movement. No one blinked. No one interrupted. It was as normal as breathing.

I sipped my wine and strolled among them, my own thighs rubbing as the memories of last night came flooding back. My cunt still throbbed, swollen, but the sight of cocks hardening in the garden, women squirting on marble, men groaning against thighs — it was enough to make me wet again despite myself.

I sat beneath an olive tree, pretending to read, when a shadow fell over me. A man stood there, cock half-hard, eyes locked on me. Without a word, he sat beside me, pulled my book from my hands, and guided them to his cock.

I stroked him lazily, in the open air, while the courtyard went on around us. He groaned softly, gripping my thigh under the linen, his cock swelling thick in my palm.

Even in rest, Rome was relentless.

This wasn't a hotel. It was a world where sex had become air, food, water — necessary, constant, inescapable.

And God help me, I didn't want to escape.

✦✦✦

Rome
Chapter Nine

By nightfall, the promise of a quieter day had dissolved completely.

The dining hall was heavy with candlelight and the scent of roasted meats, garlic, and wine. Long tables stretched beneath gilded ceilings, their surfaces laid with silver platters, decanters of deep red, bowls of olives and figs. It felt, at first glance, almost civilised. Almost.

But in Rome, nothing remained untouched for long.

I took my seat midway down the table, the velvet cushion soft beneath my sore thighs. I sipped at my wine, listening to the low murmur of conversation, the clatter of forks and knives. And then I felt it — a touch against my ankle.

I froze, glass halfway to my lips.

The touch became a stroke, sliding up my calf beneath the tablecloth. Then another hand joined it, this one softer, smaller. Fingers slipped higher, teasing the inside of my thigh, brushing the edge of my cunt.

I glanced around. No one flinched. No one even pretended not to notice. All along the table, men and women sat with flushed cheeks and strained voices, their plates shifting slightly, their wine spilling as hands worked beneath the linen.

I gasped as a mouth found me, hot breath between my thighs. A tongue flicked against my swollen clit, sending a shiver through me so sharp I nearly dropped my glass. The woman — I could tell by the softness, by the angle — licked me eagerly, her tongue sliding up and down my folds, dipping inside, sucking hard until I bit down on a fig to keep from screaming.

Around me, it was everywhere. A man opposite me groaned mid-bite, his eyes rolling back as someone clearly sucked him beneath the table. Another woman leaned back, her fork clattering to the floor as her robe shifted, her breasts spilling free while unseen hands made her moan.

It was a banquet of flesh, food, and fucking.

I spread my thighs wider, shameless now, gripping the edge of the table as the woman's tongue worked me harder, faster, until I came in wet bursts, my juices soaking her mouth. She didn't stop — if anything, she drank greedily, sucking every drop from me as I shuddered, face flushed, wine spilling down my chin.

Beside me, a man groaned and jerked, his cum shooting across his plate, mingling with the sauce of roasted lamb. The woman next to him laughed and dipped her finger in it, licking it off like honey.

The hall was madness — eating, drinking, and being eaten all at once. My second orgasm tore from me while I chewed a slice of bread, my body shaking as I fed myself with one hand and gripped the table with the other.

Rome had turned dinner into debauchery.

By the time dessert was served — figs soaked in honey and almonds — the room reeked of sex. Plates glistened not just with oil and sauce, but with cum spilled freely across silver and porcelain.

I licked honey from my fingers, cunt still throbbing from the tongue beneath the table, and thought:

I would never look at a meal the same way again.

✦✦✦

Rome
Chapter Ten

The organisers starved us on purpose.

After breakfast, the hotel offered nothing — no trays of fruit, no bread baskets, no wine. By midday, stomachs growled audibly, guests wandered the corridors restless, and the smell of the kitchens tormented us. Hunger gnawed at me, making my body weak, my cunt still tender from endless nights but restless again.

By the time night fell, desire and hunger blurred into one.

The dining hall had been transformed. Long tables groaned under mountains of food: roasted pheasants glistening with fat, wheels of cheese, baskets of warm bread, platters of figs and grapes, bowls of olives, cakes dripping with honey, even whole roasted pigs with apples in their mouths. But none of it was for eating — not yet.

Not until it had been fucked.

A bell rang.

At once, the room surged into chaos.

Women climbed onto tables, stripping, spreading themselves over platters of food. Grapes were crushed beneath arses as cocks slid into them. Honey drizzled over breasts as tongues lapped it away. Bread rolls were shoved into cunts, fucked out again, torn and devoured dripping with juices.

I was pulled onto a table myself, laid across a silver platter surrounded by figs. A man spread honey thick over my nipples, then sucked and bit until I screamed. Another pushed olives into my cunt, then licked and tongued them out before swallowing them whole.

I squirted over a roasted chicken, soaking its golden skin until men tore it apart with greasy fingers, licking my juices mixed with the fat.

The smell was overwhelming — meat, wine, sweat, sex. Cum and cream mixed with olive oil, honey, butter. Plates and bellies glistened, food smeared over cocks, cunts, faces.

A woman knelt between my thighs, licking honey and salt from my pussy as a man fed me figs soaked in wine. Another man stroked his cock over a loaf of bread until he came thick across it — the woman bit into it immediately, moaning as his seed smeared across her lips.

Every delicacy had to be baptised in lust before being eaten.

Cheese wedges pushed between tits, then licked clean. Cakes smashed into cunts, icing dripping down thighs, sucked and devoured from skin. Bottles of wine uncorked, poured over asses, tongues lapping it up before mouths drank deep.

I fucked until I ached, ate until I gagged, came until I couldn't move. Food and flesh, hunger and lust, it was all the same by the end. I didn't know if I was swallowing honey or cum, licking butter or cream from a cunt, biting bread or biting flesh.

By midnight, the tables were wrecked, the food ruined, the guests collapsed in heaps of sticky, fucked-out bliss. Plates were smeared with seed, floor slick with wine and juices, air thick with groans and the reek of sex.

I lay on my back, cunt leaking, belly full, lips swollen, my crown askew.

Rome had not just fed me.

It had consumed me whole.

✦✦✦

Rome
Chapter Eleven

The morning after the Feast felt almost unreal.

The dining hall, once a battlefield of food and flesh, now smelled faintly of polish and soap. Servants had scrubbed away every trace of what we had done — the honey, the wine, the cum, the sweat. Even the air seemed innocent again, as though the night before had been nothing but a fever dream.

But my body knew better.

My cunt ached when I shifted in bed, raw from the endless parade of cocks and tongues. My belly was heavy, filled from both food and seed. My thighs were still sticky in places I hadn't managed to wash. I stretched, wincing, and smiled to myself., but then knew my body needed bathing a waking up.

It was time to leave.

I packed slowly, folding each garment I had barely worn, tucking my souvenirs into a corner of my case. My laurel crown lay on the dressing table, gleaming softly in the morning light. I touched it once, twice, then placed it in the velvet pouch with the others.

There was no card waiting this time.

No note of invitation, no instructions, no hint of what came next. Only silence.

I checked the bedside drawer. Empty. The wardrobe. Empty. The marble bathroom. Empty.

Only the crimson key remained.

I held it in my hand for a long time, tracing its shape, its weight. That was all I had needed in Dubai. That was all I had needed here. Wherever the next city waited, whatever debauchery and delirium it held, the key would open it.

At reception, I wheeled my case across the marble floor. The clerk smiled politely, bowed his head, and asked only for the key. I placed it on the counter. He slid it back across to me, untouched.

“Safe travels, Signora,” he murmured.

I slipped the key into my bag, my lips curving into a secret smile.

No goodbye. No explanation. No closure.

Rome was over.

But the crimson key still burned hot against my palm.

And I wondered — was this only the beginning.

Rome
Epilogue

The plane hummed softly beneath me, a cradle of clouds outside the window. A glass of red wine sat untouched on my tray table, the swirl of it reminding me too much of last night's feast — red lips, red fruit, red cunts glistening under torchlight.

Dubai had been precision. Controlled. The games were structured like contests, each rule laid bare before it began. Blindfolds. Bound hands. Cock machines pounding with mechanical rhythm and even water sports. It was decadent, yes, but orderly. A secret society running on ritual.

Rome… Rome was something else entirely.

Rome was chaos. Food, flesh, sweat, and seed spilling into one another until you couldn't tell hunger from lust. Where Dubai had tested me, Rome has teased and devoured me. Dubai had eased me back into touch after ten years of silence; Rome had torn me wide open and reminded me that I could be feasted upon until I barely remembered my own name.

In Dubai, I had been chosen, guided, measured.
In Rome, I had been surrendered, consumed, crowned and fucked like a banquet offering.

And yet, both cities left me the same gift: the crimson key.

I smiled to myself, watching the clouds roll away.

I reached into my bag to touch the key — and my fingers brushed against something else.

Another pouch. One I hadn't noticed before.

Black velvet, like the first, but smaller. My heart jolted as I drew it out, my breath caught in my throat. Inside was a card, the script looping, elegant, and unmistakable:

"Your journey is not over.
The key will open your next door.
Marrakesh awaits."

I pressed the card back into the pouch, my cunt tightening with a rush of heat I hadn't expected. Dubai had been ritual. Rome had been feast. What in God's name would Marrakesh be?

I sat back in my seat, the hum of the engines steady, the wine rich on my tongue, and let the thought make me wet all over again.

The End

Marrakesh
Prologue

The key had not cooled since Rome.

I carried it with me everywhere — in the pocket of my coat, in the clasp of my handbag, even tucked beneath my pillow at night. It burned faintly against my skin as though reminding me that another door waited, though I had no idea where.

Until Marrakesh.

The letter had been waiting at my flat when I returned from Rome. Creamy parchment sealed in burgundy wax. Inside, no instructions, only a date, a flight, and a single line:

"Your crimson key will be enough."

And so I went.

The air of Marrakesh hit me like a furnace. Dry, spiced, laced with orange blossom and dust. Calls to prayer echoed from minarets as I wound through crowded markets, the cries of merchants blending with the scent of saffron, cumin, and mint. Men in kaftans brushed past, women glided in flowing abayas, the city pulsed with devotion — and I, clutching the crimson key, felt like a heretic.

The car that collected me turned from the clamour into silence. Walls rose high, gates opened, and suddenly the world outside disappeared. The palace loomed, hidden behind carved stone, its courtyards glistening with mosaics, its gardens humming with fountains.

A woman veiled in crimson silk greeted me at the steps. Her eyes were kohl-dark, her hands cool as she pressed them to mine.

"Welcome," she whispered. "Here, nothing is forbidden."

Inside, the palace glowed. Lanterns swung low, casting gold across tiled walls. Silken cushions spilled across the floors, brass trays gleamed with figs and candied almonds, though no food was offered

— not yet. Ramadan reigned beyond these walls, and restraint itself was part of the theatre.

They gave me a chamber draped in red and gold, a bed wide enough for ten. On the table rested a pouch of black velvet. Inside, not a card this time, but a folded square of silk — pale, sheer, a veil meant to cover my mouth and eyes.

The message was clear: my games would begin in secrecy.

I undressed slowly, my fingers trembling as they brushed the silk. My cunt throbbed and clit twitched with memory — of Dubai's blindfolds, Rome's feasts — and now this new place of shadows and veils.

I slipped the key beneath my pillow, as I always did, and lay back on the bed. Outside, I could hear the distant call to prayer mingling with the trickle of fountains. Devotion, restraint, purity.

But inside the palace, something else was stirring.

And the crimson key had brought me here to claim it.

✦✦✦

Marrakesh
Chapter One

The first morning in Marrakesh rose golden and merciless. Sunlight poured through the lattice windows of my chamber, cutting the air into sharp angles of heat and shadow. I dressed simply — a loose kaftan the colour of sand, my hair tied back, sandals laced. The palace's courtyards were quiet, the fountains whispering, but beyond the walls the city called to me.

I wanted to see Marrakesh before it devoured me.

The gates opened onto chaos. Narrow streets pulsed with life, vendors calling out in Arabic and French, the scent of spice and roasting meat thick in the air. I drifted through the medina like a stranger in a dream.

There were pyramids of saffron, turmeric, and cinnamon, their colours so bright they looked painted. Lanterns hung from stalls like captured stars, brass polished to a shine so deep I saw my reflection flicker back at me. Leather bags swung from hooks, carpets sprawled in great woven cascades, kaftans and silks whispered against my hands as I touched them.

And then there was the sound — the haunting rise of the muezzin calling the faithful to prayer. The entire market seemed to pause for a moment, a stillness in the heat, before life carried on as though it had never stopped. I felt the weight of it, the restraint, the devotion.

And I felt like a thief.

Because hidden in my bag, wrapped in velvet, was the key. And I knew that when night fell, behind the walls of that palace, restraint would give way to indulgence. The contrast made my nipples tighten beneath the kaftan, my cunt clench with a warmth I hadn't expected.

I wandered into a quieter square, where a fountain trickled beneath an orange tree heavy with fruit. Two women sat on a bench, their heads bent together, giggling over something I couldn't hear. One of them licked her finger slowly, almost absentmindedly, and the other's cheeks flushed. I looked away quickly, embarrassed at the way my body reacted to the simple gesture.

I bought a pouch of dates from a stall, the vendor smiling with gold teeth as he pressed the bag into my hands. "For sweetness," he said.

Sweetness.

I carried them with me as I walked back to the palace, the sun heavy on my shoulders, the crimson key heavy in my bag.

Tonight, the games would begin.

And Marrakesh, I sensed, would test me differently than Dubai or Rome. Here, the city itself seemed to conspire in whispers and shadows, in veils and glances, in the dangerous thrill of what is forbidden.

I pressed a date to my lips, tasted its sticky sweetness on my tongue, and swallowed. My body ached already, and night had not yet fallen.

I lingered in the cool shade of the archway before stepping back into the palace. Servants passed silently, their eyes lowered, their movements precise. Yet I could feel it in the air — the knowledge of what would come. The crimson key was no secret, not really. In this place, secrets were currency, traded with glances and silences, with the brush of a hand too close to the wrist.

My chamber felt smaller now, almost suffocating after the expanse of the souk. I loosened my kaftan and let it fall open, air moving against the thin cotton of my slip. My skin was slick with heat, damp at the hollow of my back, between my thighs. I thought of the women by the fountain, of the way one finger slid across her lips, and shivered.

I lay back on the bed, dates still in their pouch beside me. I took one, bit into it, the syrup coating my tongue. My fingers were sticky as I licked them clean, tasting sugar and sun, and for a moment I let myself imagine another mouth there, feeding me, watching me.

The city hummed beyond the walls. Drums somewhere in the distance, low and steady, like a heartbeat carried through the streets. Marrakesh had no patience for innocence. It pulled at me, coaxing, testing how far I would go.

When I finally rose, the sky was already bleeding into evening. The muezzin's call echoed again, softer this time, but my body answered differently. The crimson key burned in its wrapping, demanding its use.

Night would not be gentle.

And neither, I suspected, would I.

✦✦✦

Marrakesh
Chapter Two

They came for me at midnight.

A soft knock, no words, only the sound of the door opening and the faintest swish of silk. My pulse quickened before the cloth slid over my eyes. Darkness wrapped me, velvet and absolute. Hands guided me through the corridors — silent, sure. The scent of incense grew thicker, spiced and smoky, until I no longer knew where in the palace I was.

When the doors opened, the air was different. Cooler, heavy with musk and something sharper — the smell of skin. Fingers at my elbow steered me forward.

I heard them before I touched them: the soft shift of bodies, the catch of breath, a low moan cut short. Eight of them, I realised, close, waiting.

My hands trembled as they were released.

I reached.

Skin met skin — warm, slick, alive. A shoulder. A throat. The curve of a breast. My fingers learned strangers without sight, without permission, without names. A woman's breath shuddered as I brushed her lips with mine, tasting salt and sweetness. A man's chest pressed against my palm, his scent darker, sweat and spice, filling me until I felt drunk.

The game was cruel in its simplicity: touch, scent, taste. Choose.

I let my body answer. I lingered on the heat of one woman, the swell of her hip beneath my hand, the way she leaned into me as though she already belonged. Then the man — broad, his jaw rough against my fingers, his mouth seeking mine in the dark.

I chose them.

Hands returned, firm, guiding me away. Back through silence, back through corridors.

When the blindfold slipped away, I was alone again. My chamber glowed with candlelight. The bed was no longer bare — it was covered in toys. Glass, leather, steel. Shapes designed for every hunger. I touched them one by one, a flush rising through me. My nipples ached, my cunt already wet, the crimson key lying forgotten on the bedside table.

A knock.

The door opened.

They were brought in — naked, blindfolded, their skin gleaming in the light. My choices. My prizes.

And at last, the game began.

They stood before me, blindfolded, stripped, waiting. The woman's breasts rose and fell with shallow breaths; the man's cock already stirred with a faint pulse. Candlelight painted them gold.

I let them feel the weight of my gaze, though they could not see it. The silence bound us tighter than rope.

On the bed, the toys gleamed like jewels in the firelight. Some were familiar — glass, leather, steel — others strange, twisted shapes designed to stretch, to press, to open. I let my fingers wander across them as though selecting instruments for music, savouring the anticipation.

The first toy I lifted was glass, cool and heavy. I pressed it to the woman's lips, tracing the line of her mouth. She gasped softly, parting for me, her tongue brushing the smoothness. I slid it down the length of her throat, across her nipples until they hardened, and lower still, between her thighs. The coldness made her body jolt, hips rising instinctively, offering herself without sight.

The man groaned, shifting as if the sound alone aroused him. I turned to him, holding the toy slick from her wetness, and pressed it against the head of his cock. He shivered, his breath breaking into a low moan.

Next came leather — thin straps, pliant. I wound them around their wrists, not to bind fully, but to remind them of my control. My hands lingered, stroking the lines of tension the straps created, watching their muscles tighten then surrender.

Steel followed. A narrow wand, curved at the end. I let them hear the faint ring of it against glass before touching it to the man's chest, cold enough to draw a gasp. I trailed it lower, over his stomach, circling his cock without relief. His body strained toward me, helpless in the dark.

The woman I teased with a different shape — a ridged device, almost grotesque in its design, yet made to pleasure. I pressed it slowly inside her cunt , feeling the resistance give way to heat. Her cry was muffled by her own bitten lip, her hips trembling as I worked it deeper, twisting, pulling at her clit, sliding.

Their blindfolds turned them into creatures of sensation, every touch magnified. I used my mouth freely — licking the syrup of her cunt from the strange toy, tracing my tongue up his long, hard shaft, biting gently until he groaned.

Then I took them both.

I placed the man behind me, guided his cock against me, slow, filling, thick. My cunt clenched around him, hungry, my moan breaking the stillness. At the same time, I bent to the woman, sucking her nipples, sliding my fingers inside her still-stretched heat. She writhed against me, her blindfolded face pressed to my shoulder, her cries hot against my skin.

Toy after toy joined us — clamps on nipples, beads that swelled as I drew them free, a curved device that forced my cunt open wider around his cock until I thought I would shatter. Every shape was used, every edge explored. We became slick with sweat, cum and spit and the shining gloss of arousal.

The rhythm built until it was no longer a game but a storm. He fucked me harder, the slap of his balls against me, filling the chamber; she clung to me, grinding her soaked cunt against my thigh, desperate and wild. I guided her hand to the final toy — a humming wand, strange and relentless. She pressed it to her wet cunt and screamed, her body convulsing as she came, squirting, thighs trembling.

The sound broke him. With a growl, he emptied his cum inside me, hot, sudden, unstoppable. His release sent me over the edge too, my orgasm gushing, tearing through me, my body clenching, shuddering, surrendering.

When it was done, we collapsed in a tangle, blindfolds still in place, bodies spent and gleaming with sweat and arousal.

The key lay untouched on the table, silent, patient.

And I realised this was only the beginning.

They were led away as silently as they had arrived. The door closed with a whisper, and I was left alone, trembling in the sheets that still smelled of sex. My breath was uneven, my skin damp with sweat, my thighs slick.

When I reached for the toys, I found the bed stripped bare. Every glass, steel, leather shape had been taken, as though they had never existed. The chamber looked innocent again — too innocent.

But my body knew better.

I rolled onto my back, my cunt aching, my nipples still tight and swollen. The release I'd been given was not enough. My hunger only sharpened, gnawing, impatient.

I searched the room, restless. My eyes caught on a tall brass lantern by the bed, its frame cool beneath my fingertips. I lifted it, ran the smooth metal edge along my thigh, higher, until it brushed against the damp heat between my legs. The sensation made me gasp.

I spread myself open, daring, pressing the hard edge against my clit, sliding it slowly, teasing, the ridges catching just enough to make me shudder. My free hand found my breast, pinching until pain and pleasure blurred.

The lantern was strange, heavy, unyielding — and all the more intoxicating for it. I rubbed against it harder, grinding, desperate, until sparks lit behind my eyelids.

When my climax came, it ripped through me raw, cum gushing over my hand, over the brass lantern, fierce, unstoppable. My cry echoed in the chamber, a sound no blindfold could silence.

I collapsed against the pillows, the lantern still clutched between my thighs, its brass warm now from my heat.

Somewhere deep in the palace, I thought I heard footsteps. Perhaps they had heard me. Perhaps that was the point.

The game was not only about choice. It was about hunger.

And mine, I realised, had only just begun to show itself.

Marrakesh
Chapter Three

I thought it was over.

My body was still trembling from the climax I'd stolen with the brass lantern, the taste of metal still sharp on my tongue. I had sunk into the pillows, exhausted, slick, ready for the relief of sleep.

But the knock came before my breath had even slowed. Three sharp raps — urgent, insistent.

The door opened before I could answer.

Two figures stepped in, veiled in shadow, their movements silent but commanding. My pulse surged. Hands lifted me, guided me, before I could think to resist. A cloth was tied once more across my eyes. Darkness again.

I was not finished, they seemed to say. Neither was the game.

The corridors felt longer this time, my bare feet cool against the tiles, the silence pressing close. When the door opened, the air was thick with heat, musk, quiet but with the unmistakable sound of bodies moving, gasping, moaning.

The blindfold stayed in place.

Hands guided me forward, into the storm. I felt skin against me from every side — lips at my neck, teeth grazing my shoulder, fingers stroking, spreading, probing. My breath broke into ragged gasps.

One mouth claimed my breast, sucking until I cried out. Another tongue traced the inside of my thigh. A hand gripped my hair, pulling me into a kiss so fierce it stole what breath I had left. My body was no longer my own; it was taken, opened, filled from every angle.

The sensation was relentless — bodies pressing, cocks sliding, mouths devouring, toys replaced by living hunger. Every nerve was claimed, every inch of me used, stretched, made raw with pleasure.

My cries melted into theirs, the sound of many throats, many bodies, colliding in the dark.

I no longer counted how many. I no longer cared.

The game was no longer about choice. It was about surrender.

And I surrendered, shattering again and again until I no longer knew where my body ended and theirs began.

When it was done — if it was ever truly done — I collapsed into waiting arms, blindfold still in place, the world spinning.

The crimson key burned somewhere close, silent, patient, reminding me: this was only the beginning.

I barely had time to catch my breath before the knock came.
Three sharp raps, a command more than a request.

The door opened, and hands guided me up, blindfold still over my eyes., my body still wet, still aching from the nights games so far but there was more.

I was led quickly through another corridor. This time there was no silence: I heard it before the door even opened — the sounds of sex. Low moans, the slap of flesh, the gasps of release. The air inside the chamber was thick with musk, sweat, incense.

And then I was among them.

Hands everywhere. A mouth at my throat, sucking hard enough to leave a mark. Fingers spreading me, dipping inside before I could take a breath. Teeth at my shoulder. A cock brushing against my lips, another pressed against the curve of my arse. I moaned into the dark, blind and helpless, but my body opened to it, desperate, greedy.

One tongue circled my nipple, wet and relentless. Another licked the seam of my cunt, teasing, then plunging in with shocking force. I cried out, clenching around it, while a thick cock was guided between my lips. The taste filled me, musky, salty, alive.

The rhythm built quickly. I was turned, bent, lifted, spread. My mouth full, my cunt full, my arse teased until I thought I'd shatter.

Their voices surrounded me, groans and cries, every sound pulling me deeper.

I was fucked until I lost count of them. Fucked until my body convulsed, orgasms tearing through me one after another, leaving me shaking but never finished. They came inside me, over me, against me, and still others took their place.

Every hole, every inch, claimed.

And through it all, I surrendered. Blind, used, consumed, I surrendered to the endless hunger of the game.

When at last the storm began to ebb, I collapsed against the cushions, slick with sweat and seed, the blindfold still in place. Hands lifted me gently, almost tender now, laying me back in my own chamber.

The crimson key lay beside me on the pillow.
Silent. Waiting.

I understood then: this was not one game, but many.
And Marrakesh would demand more of me than any city before.

✦✦✦

Marrakesh
Chapter Four

Morning came too soon.

I woke sore, my thighs bruised with pleasure, my body overwhelmed from the night. The blindfold lay crumpled on the floor, its scent of sweat and incense clinging to the air. For a moment I wondered if I had dreamt it, if the storm of bodies had been some delirium.

But then the door opened.

A servant entered silently, carrying a silver tray. Breakfast: oranges peeled in perfect spirals, a bowl of honey, flatbread still warm. And beside them — another object.

but the moment I looked at what had been placed on the tray, I knew there would be no peace.

The dildo waited, thick and gleaming with oil.

I ate fruit first — oranges, dates, honey — letting sweetness coat my tongue while I stared at the toy. My cunt throbbed in answer, sore but alive, as though the night had only been a beginning.

When I lifted it, the weight surprised me. Solid, unforgiving. I pressed the tip against my lips, dragging the oil across my breasts, down my stomach, until my skin glistened. Then I spread my thighs and pushed it inside.

The stretch was obscene. My breath caught, my belly straining to take its girth. Inch by inch, I fed it into me, until I was full, aching, helpless. My cunt clenched around it, and the first orgasm came too quickly, tearing through me like a flash of fire.

But I didn't stop.

I pulled it out slowly, feeling every ridge, then thrust it back in harder, my cries filling the empty chamber. I rolled onto my knees, riding it, bracing myself against the bed, my cunt dripping onto the sheets.

Another climax ripped through me, harder this time, leaving me shaking, gasping.

Still I wanted more.

I used the honey next, dipping my fingers, smearing it over the toy, licking it from my skin as I worked the thick length inside me again. The sweetness mixed with my own wetness, sticky, filthy. I fucked myself until I collapsed forward, trembling, my orgasm almost painful in its intensity.

I lay on my back, sweat running down my skin, the toy lying across my stomach. But the ache remained — that gnawing hunger that no number of orgasms seemed to soften.

So I began again.

The entire morning disappeared in waves of pleasure. On my back, on my knees, pressed against the wall, sprawled across the floor. The dildo never left my body for long, pushing me wider, deeper, making me scream until my throat was raw. Each climax blurred into the next, some short and sharp, others long and rolling, leaving me sobbing with pleasure.

By the time the sun was high, I had lost count. My cunt was swollen, my thighs slick, my body spent — and yet I knew I would do it again the moment I could breathe.

I licked the last of the honey from my fingers and smiled through exhaustion.

The palace wanted me broken.
Instead, it was teaching me how endless my hunger could be.

A knock startled me from the haze of sweat and honey. I pulled a sheet around my body, though my thighs were still slick, my cunt still swollen from the morning's endless games.The door opened. A servant stepped in, his eyes lowered, carrying a folded garment of deep crimson silk. He set it down on the chair without looking at me.

But I saw the way his hands trembled.

I saw the rise and fall of his chest.

And when his gaze flickered — just once — to my bare leg beneath the sheet, I knew.

Desire. Hidden, forbidden.

"It is for tonight," he murmured, his voice tight.

I rose slowly, letting the sheet slip from my shoulders. His eyes widened, though he tried to turn away.

I crossed the floor barefoot, the scent of sex still clinging to me. I pressed the silk back into his hands, leaning close enough that my breath stirred against his cheek.

"I don't want it for tonight," I whispered. "I want you. Now."

His jaw clenched. His knuckles whitened on the fabric.

"You know…" he began, his voice unsteady, "…this cannot be allowed."

But his cock betrayed him. I saw the bulge hardening beneath his robe, straining, urgent. My hand slid down, brazen, cupping him through the cloth. He shuddered, torn between duty and hunger.

"It is forbidden," he whispered again — yet his hips pressed into my palm.

I pulled the garment from his grip, let it fall to the floor, and guided his hand to my cunt, still slick and aching. His fingers grazed me, hesitant, then bolder, pressing inside. The sheet fell away completely.

"I've spent the morning with toys," I moaned into his ear. "But nothing will satisfy me until I feel your cock inside me."

His breath broke into a ragged sound — half prayer, half surrender.

And then he gave in.

His hesitation broke in an instant. One moment he was trembling, whispering of restraint, the next he had me pressed against the wall, his mouth hot and desperate against my throat.

The robe parted under my hands. His cock sprang free — thick, pulsing, slick from pre cum already at the tip. I gasped, grinding my cunt against it, smearing myself on him, shameless in my hunger.

He groaned as though the sound were being dragged from the deepest part of him. "We mustn't…" he tried, but the words dissolved when I guided him into me.

The stretch was sharp, sudden, glorious. My cunt clenched tight around his hard throbbing cock, aching from the morning's games yet greedy for more. I cried out, nails raking down his back as he thrust, hard, deeper, filling me.

There was no rhythm at first, only a frantic need. His cock slammed into me, every stroke wet and loud, our bodies colliding with the violence of desire denied too long. I wrapped my legs around him, forcing him deeper, my head tipping back against the wall as the forbidden pleasure consumed us both.

The thought of being discovered — of rules shattered, of sacred law broken — made the heat unbearable. My cunt pulsed around his cock, sucking, desperate, and he growled into my ear, fucking me harder, faster, until a decorative sheet slipped from the wall and crumpled to the floor beneath us.

I came first, spasms ripping through me, my cry muffled by his mouth as he kissed me fiercely. My climax dragged him over the edge with me — his cock jerking, spilling hot cum deep inside, thick pulses flooding me until it ran down my thighs.

He sagged against me, breathless, his body trembling. The weight of what we had done hung heavy in the silence.

And yet, as he slipped from me, his cock dripping from our juices still hard, I knew we were not finished.

The crimson garment still lay on the floor, untouched.

The day was far from over.

Marrakesh
Chapter Five

The crimson garment was no more than a whisper against my skin. Sheer, clinging, it betrayed me with every breath. When the servant bound my wrists and led me into the chamber, I already knew I would be undone.

The sight stopped me cold.

Eight figures stood tied to poles around the room — men and women, each wrapped in gauze so thin it was an insult to modesty. Their nipples, their cocks, their wetness, all visible, glistening in the lantern light. I was tied among them, rope burning into my wrists, ankles spread wide.

The rules were simple.
No touch.
No movement.
Only words.

The air was thick, waiting.

A man's voice began, rough and deep, describing how he would spread me open and lick the honey from my cunt until my thighs shook. Another followed — a woman — her tone low, promising to suck my nipples until I begged her not to stop.

The words circled me, coiling tight around my body. Every phrase was a hand I could not feel, a tongue I could not taste, a cock sliding into me without ever entering.

By the time it was my turn, I was shaking. My voice broke at first, then grew stronger as the need poured out of me. I told them how I had fucked myself that morning until my cunt was raw, how the servant had broken his restraint to fill me, how I still ached for more. My words painted every dirty detail, and the room groaned in answer.

The game stretched on, heat building, bodies straining against their ropes. Hard nipples and wanting erected cocks stretching from the sheer cloth. The sound of need was everywhere — ragged breath, whispered filth, moans swallowed back.

And then it happened.

My orgasm ripped through me, gushing cum down my thighs, sudden and violent, my cry echoing against the stone walls. My legs buckled, the ropes burning against my wrists as my cunt clenched and pulsed helplessly.

The servant stepped forward and untied me. My body was free, trembling, desperate.

And with freedom came power.

I turned first to the man who had spoken of honey, dropped to my knees, with one hand wrapped around his thighs caressing his hard shapely buttocks and the other I took his cock into my mouth, vigorously wanking him fast then slow then faster still until he cried out, his hips jerking against me, his words dissolving into broken sounds.

When he came, it was violent, spurting into my mouth, spilling hot cum across my tongue, he too was released. The ropes fell, and now his hands were on me, pulling me close, pressing my slick cunt against his thigh.

One by one, the others followed. The next orgasm freed another body, and another, until the chamber was no longer bound but writhing.

An orgy erupted — silk tearing, ropes falling, fingers on clits, mouths in cunts, devouring cocks sliding into cum filled holes. Women kissed women, men fucked men, bodies twisted and joined in every shape of hunger. The rules dissolved into chaos, only pleasure remained.

I was everywhere at once — riding one cock, sucking another, wanking another, my nipples clamped between wet mouths, my cunt spread and filled until I screamed. Every release freed another, every cry dragged the room deeper into madness.

By the end, no one was clothed, no one untouched. We collapsed together in a tangle of limbs, sweat and cum, the crimson garment discarded, forgotten.

The second game was over.

And yet I knew — Marrakesh was only beginning to show me what it had in store.

Morning light should have brought calm. Instead, my body burned with a new boldness. The night's game had unshackled something in me. And the forbidden taste of the servant's cock that morning — hot, desperate, forbidden — lingered on my tongue.

The souk burned with colour and noise. Lanterns glimmered, spices spilled their perfume into the air, and sellers called out with honeyed voices. I moved through it all still humming from the night before, the crimson silk hidden beneath my robe brushing against my skin like a secret.

One stall drew me — a cave of polished wood, silver charms, and carved boxes scented with cedar. The owner looked up from his counter, and his eyes caught mine. Dark, steady, too steady.

I let my robe slip back from one shoulder. Just a little. Enough for the faintest shimmer of crimson silk to show. His gaze flickered down, then quickly away. He smiled politely, but his hands stilled on the items he was arranging.

I picked up a silver trinket — a small box, engraved with vines. "It's beautiful," I said softly. "But what would you hide inside it?"

His lips parted, but no answer came. His throat worked as he swallowed.

I leaned closer, inhaling the cedar scent that clung to his robe. "Perhaps something precious," I murmured. "Something forbidden."

His jaw tightened. He stepped back. "Madame," he said carefully, "it is… not the time."

I smiled, trailing my fingers along the edge of the counter. "Not the time… or not allowed?"

His eyes flicked to mine, sharp with warning, and yet his breath betrayed him — shallow, quick.

I let my robe slip a little further, the outline of my breast clear through the sheer silk beneath. His knuckles whitened on the wooden box he held.

"You know what month this is," he said, his voice rougher now. "What is forbidden cannot be touched until the night."

I circled slowly through the shop, brushing fabrics with my fingertips, swaying my hips just enough to catch his eye. "And yet," I whispered, "your eyes are already touching me. Your cock is already hard. The night is too far away."

He turned, pretending to busy himself with a shelf, but I followed, close enough that my robe brushed his arm. My perfume wrapped around us both.

I leaned near his ear. "Do you have a room here… away from watching eyes?"

His hands stilled. He did not turn, but I saw his body stiffen, caught between restraint and hunger.

"You tempt me into sin," he said hoarsely.

I smiled, sliding a finger along the inside of his wrist. "Then sin with me. Just once. I promise no one will ever know."

At last he looked at me, and I saw it — the moment his resolve fractured.

He turned back to his counter, trying to steady his breath, but I saw the truth. The outline beneath his robe — his thick, straining cock—betrayed him.

I let my robe slip further, the silk clinging to my breasts, the peaks of my nipples hard against the sheer fabric. His eyes flicked there once before he dragged them away, but the damage was done. His cock twitched, visible even through the folds of cloth.

"You are strong," I murmured, stepping closer. "But not stronger than this."

I leaned against the wooden counter, arching my back so my breasts pressed forward, the crimson silk whispering with the movement. My fingers brushed idly over the curve of one nipple, a feather's touch, enough to make my breath catch audibly.

His jaw clenched. His knuckles rapped the counter in frustration.

"Stop," he said. The word was sharp — but his voice trembled.

I smiled and turned, slowly bending as if to admire a carved box on the lower shelf. My robe fell open. The silk stretched tight over my arse, my thighs bare. I shifted deliberately, rubbing myself against the corner of the counter, pressing the fabric between my legs. A low moan slipped from my lips, quiet but clear.

His breath broke. I heard it — a sharp intake, strangled, as though the sound alone was enough to torture him.

"You see?" I whispered, still grinding slowly, "my cunt is already wet. It doesn't care what month it is. It only knows what it wants."

He took a step toward me, then stopped himself, fists clenched at his sides. His cock was obscene now, bulging against the robe, the tip outlined clearly.

I turned, leaned back against the counter, and let my robe slide completely off one shoulder. My breast slipped free, bare, flushed, the nipple hard and aching. I cupped it, squeezing gently, circling my thumb until I gasped again.

His eyes locked on it. He bit down on his lip, shaking his head as though trying to pray the sight away — but his body betrayed him, hips thrusting slightly forward, straining for relief.

"You are already inside me," I whispered. "In my mind. In my body. Can you feel it?"

He groaned, low and guttural, like a man being torn apart.

"Show me the room," I breathed. "Before your cock tears that robe apart."

A bell tinkled at the door.

The shop owner flinched, tugging his robe across himself, hands folded low to hide the rigid swell between his thighs. He forced a polite smile as an older man wandered in, stooping to examine the silver trinkets laid out on a shelf.

I should have stepped back, hidden my hunger. Instead, I leaned against the counter, robe slipping looser still. My breast was bare now, the nipple stiff in the lantern glow. Slowly, deliberately, I licked my fingers — one, then two — sucking the sweetness of honey I had smeared there earlier. Then, with eyes fixed on the shopkeeper, I circled my wet fingertips over my nipple.

His throat bobbed as he swallowed. His knuckles whitened on the wood he gripped to keep from reaching for me.

The customer muttered to himself, shuffling through charms. I let out a low sigh — quiet, but sharp enough to cut through the air. The shopkeeper shot me a warning glare, but the bulge under his robe betrayed him again, even harder than before, pressing against the fabric so tightly the outline of his cock was obscene.

I slid my hand lower, under the hem of the crimson silk, tracing the dampness already spreading between my thighs. My breath caught as I rubbed myself softly, circling my clit, rocking my hips against my own touch.

The old man glanced up briefly, frowning at nothing, then bent back to his inspection. The shopkeeper turned rigid, his face a mask of forced calm, but his eyes burned into me — desperate, furious, undone.

I moaned again, this time muffled, biting my lip as my fingers worked faster beneath the silk. My thighs trembled with pleasure, spread slightly wider, the crimson fabric clinging to every outline of my cunt.

The customer straightened at last, choosing a small trinket and shuffling to the front. The shopkeeper hurried to wrap it, his hands shaking so violently the paper tore.

I licked my wet fingers clean as he fumbled, my gaze never leaving his.

The customer paid and left, the bell jingling as the door shut. Silence fell again — heavy, blistering.

And then I whispered, just loud enough to break him:

"Lock the door. Now."

The bell had barely stopped ringing when the last customer left. The shopkeeper stood frozen, chest heaving, his face tight with a war he had already lost.

Then, without a word, he wrenched his robe open.

His cock sprang free — thick, flushed, slick with pre cum at the tip, so hard it looked painful. He gripped himself in both hands, as if the act of hiding it any longer would break him, and began to wank furiously, his breath tearing from his throat in ragged bursts.

I watched, spellbound. My cunt clenched, wetness flooding as each stroke dragged faster, rougher, his hips jerking helplessly. The silence of the shop filled with the obscene sound of his hand working over his cock, wet and urgent.

"Look at me," I whispered.

His eyes locked on mine, wild and burning. That look — desperate, forbidden, undone — made me moan aloud. I lifted the silk hem of my garment, baring myself completely, spreading my thighs so he could see how wet I was.

He groaned at the sight, pumping harder, faster, until his whole body shook.

"Cum for me," I said softly, my fingers deep inside my cunt and thumb circling my clit as I watched him unravel.

And he did. With a cry half-choked in his throat, his cock erupted, thick hot streams of cum spilling across the floorboards, his hand milking every pulse until he sagged against the counter, gasping.

The sight of him cumming— forbidden, undone, spilling himself for me in daylight — tipped me over the edge. My orgasm ripped through me as I furiously rubbed myself, crying out, my silk clinging to my warm soaked cunt.

The room smelled of cedar and sex, of sweat and broken restraint.

When the silence returned, he stood trembling, ashamed and aroused all at once. I pulled my dress back into place, smiling.

"I'll come back tomorrow," I whispered.

And I left him there, still shaking, his cock softening in his cum filled hand, while my body still overflowed with triumph.

✦✦✦

Marrakesh
Chapter Six

The palace was quiet when I returned, the corridors dim against the brightness outside.

The note waited for me on my pillow, its wax seal pressed deep. Another game tonight. Another night of silk ropes and whispered rules.

But the palace no longer felt like enough.

I wanted more. I wanted the heat of daylight, the thrill of men undone where they should have been strongest, the raw obscenity of desire spilling out into the ordinary. The shopkeeper had shown me the taste of it, and now I craved it again.

So I slipped back into the souk, the crimson silk beneath my robe clinging like a secret no one else knew.

The first stall was piled high with brass lamps, their polished sides catching the sun. The keeper was older, dignified, his beard streaked with grey. I leaned close to one lantern, letting the robe gape open just enough that the swell of my breast brushed the cool metal. His gaze darted there, sharp, then away. I licked my lip, slow, deliberate. He cleared his throat, muttered a price, and would not look at me again.

The second was younger, selling carved boxes of sandalwood. I bent low, pretending to inspect the joints of the wood, while the silk stretched tight over my arse. I shifted, rubbed myself subtly against the counter's edge, let a small sigh escape my throat. His hands froze mid-gesture, the blood rising in his cheeks — but still, he would not break.

The third was stronger, bolder. He sold knives, their hilts inlaid with bone. I let my robe slip, baring the line of my thigh as I trailed a fingertip along the blade's edge. His eyes followed the movement, darkening, his knuckles flexing on the counter. For a moment I thought he might give in — but he clenched his jaw, turned his back, and busied himself with arranging stock.

I smiled to myself. The tension thrilled me. Each glance, each caught breath, each bulge beneath a robe was a victory, even when they fought me. Especially when they fought me.

By the fourth stall, I knew. The keeper was tall, his shoulders broad beneath simple cloth. He sold silks, but his eyes lingered not on his wares, but on me the moment I stopped. He looked, then looked again, as though unable to stop himself.

I let the robe fall from my shoulders, the crimson garment beneath sheer as water, showing everything it claimed to cover. My nipples hard beneath the silk, the damp outline of my cunt already spreading the fabric darker.

His breath caught, audible.

I leaned forward, close enough that only he could hear.

"Do you want to see more?" I whispered.

And I saw it in his face — the crack of restraint, the hunger ready to devour him.

His eyes clung to me, no longer darting away. Hunger made them heavy, desperate.

I slid my robe fully off, letting it pool at my elbows. The crimson silk beneath clung like wet skin, leaving nothing to the imagination. My nipples pressed hard against the fabric; the outline of my cunt was a dark, damp patch spreading wider with every breath.

I picked up a roll of silk from his stall, held it against my chest, and moaned softly as though it were caressing me. Then I let it drop, slowly, deliberately, so that his eyes fell with it — down to where my thighs parted just enough for him to glimpse the glistening wetness through the sheer fabric.

His lips parted. His hand twitched at his side.

"You're hard already, aren't you?" I whispered, my voice low, taunting.

He swallowed, but the bulge under his robe betrayed him, thick and impossible to hide. His breath came quicker now, chest rising and falling, and I knew his restraint was at its limit.

I slipped my hand under the silk, brushing my clit, my face twisting with pleasure as I moaned aloud. I licked the wetness from my fingers, staring into his eyes.

That broke him.

With a guttural sound, he yanked open his robe. His cock sprang free — thick, dark, glistening at the tip. He gripped himself hard, wanking furiously, his breath ragged, eyes locked on my breasts, my thighs, my shameless touch.

The sight made my cunt throb. I spread my legs wider, circling my clit faster, gasping as I watched him unravel. The wet slap of his hand on his cock grew frantic, obscene, echoing in the small stall.

"Cum for me," I moaned, voice trembling with my own rising climax. "Let me see it."

He groaned, head tipping back, hips jerking forward. His cock pulsed, thick ropes of cum erupting across the floor, spattering the wood, his hand milking every drop until he shook with release.

The sight dragged me over the edge — my orgasm tearing through me, squirting across the dark wood floor, silk clinging soaked to my cunt as I cried out, shameless, shuddering.

When the silence returned, he stood panting, robe hanging open, his cock softening, wet and glistening from his own hand.

I gathered my robe, covering myself with a smile.

"I'll remember you," I whispered.

And I left him there trembling, the air heavy with the smell of silk, sweat, and spilled desire.

Marrakesh
Chapter Seven

Night fell heavy and slow, the city quieting under the muezzin's call. I returned to my chamber still buzzing from the souk, the taste of daylight arousal clinging to my skin. The memory of the shopkeeper spilling himself before me had left me wetter than any velvet-clad ritual.

But the Palace did not wait for memories.

On my bed lay another garment — black this time, sheer as smoke, with thin golden chains that jingled when I lifted it. A note lay beside it, written in the same precise hand as before:

Tonight you will be tested in silence. No cries. No words. Break, and you forfeit.

I shivered. My body betrayed me instantly — nipples hard, cunt aching.

The garment slid over me like a shadow. When they came for me, I was ready.

The chamber they led me to was darker than the last. Lanterns burned low, scenting the air with amber and musk. Figures surrounded me — masked, silent, their eyes glinting. I was guided to a platform in the centre, laid down, wrists and ankles bound with silk cords.

The rules echoed in my head. *No cries. No words.*

The first touch was soft — a feather trailing over my breast. I arched, but kept my mouth closed. The second was sharper — a tongue flicking my nipple, teeth grazing. I bit down on my lip, stifling the sound rising in my throat.

Then fingers spread my thighs, warm breath brushing my cunt. The lick was sudden, deep, relentless. I gasped, nearly moaned, but swallowed the sound.

They worked me in silence — mouths, hands, cocks pressing against my skin, entering me one after another, building me higher and higher. I writhed, straining against the cords, my body convulsing with the effort of holding back.

Every thrust, every lick, every bite became torture. My orgasm built like a storm, desperate to break free, and still I bit down, holding the cry in my throat.

The game was merciless.

The cords held me wide, the black silk biting into my wrists and ankles. Every nerve of my body screamed to be touched — and they gave me everything, all at once, everywhere.

A mouth at my breast, sucking, teeth grazing until fire lanced through me. Another mouth at my other nipple, tongue circling, pulling it taut, harder, harder, until I thought I would scream.

A hand slid between my thighs, fingers spreading my cunt wide, slick already. The first stroke of a tongue over my clit nearly broke me — a cry caught in my throat, bitten down into silence.

Then more. Fingers thrusting inside me, curling, stretching, finding every angle that made my body jerk. A cock pressed to my lips — I opened, gagging on the thickness, my throat aching as it slid deep. I moaned around it, the sound trapped, strangled, forbidden.

Another cock nudged at my cunt, sliding inside, full, hard, pounding deep. My body spasmed, wanting to cry out, needing to scream, but I clenched my teeth, nails digging into my palms as the cords pulled me tighter.

My body was fire. Mouths devoured me — sucking my nipples, biting my thighs, licking the sweat from my skin. Hands slapped my arse, pinched my clit, twisted my nipples until tears pricked my eyes. The pain was unbearable, exquisite, laced with pleasure so sharp it hurt.

I came once, twice — my cunt convulsing, wetness pouring — but still I held the cries inside, my lips bitten bloody to keep them down.

The torment grew crueler. A mouth sucking hard at my clit, fingers stretching me wider, another cock filling my arse slowly, mercilessly. The pressure made me shake, made me sob soundlessly, my chest heaving, my eyes wild beneath the mask of silence.

Every thrust was a demand. Every lick, every bite, every slap of flesh was a test of my will. My body wanted to scream, to moan, to plead — but I forced it all back, swallowed it, let the agony and ecstasy writhe inside me unspoken.

It was pain now, holding back. Pain sharper than any hand could give me. My body twisted against the cords, straining, trembling, soaked in sweat, my jaw aching from the silence.

Still I endured.

Still I did not break.

I had no sense of time — only of touch, of fire, of restraint.

It was too much. Too many. Too deep. My body convulsed, orgasms shattering through me again and again, each one sharper, tearing me apart — but still I swallowed the cries, choked them down until I thought I would die from the effort.

Pain. Pleasure. Silence.

A mouth locked on my clit, sucking so hard my hips bucked helplessly. The cocks inside my arse and cunt thrust in perfect rhythm, pounding me open, raw, stretched. My breasts ached from the bite of teeth, my throat burned from the silence I could not keep.

I was breaking.

The scream clawed its way up, strangled, then tore free.

It ripped out of me, raw, feral, unstoppable. The sound filled the chamber, echoing off stone, my body convulsing as I screamed my orgasm into the air.

And in that moment — they all released.

Hot, thick streams of cum spilled over me — across my breasts, my stomach, my thighs, my face. Cocks pulsed against my skin, spraying their cum, marking me. I was drenched in their climax, covered, claimed, my body heaving, sobbing, broken open by my own voice at last.

The cords loosened. My arms fell limp, my body trembling, soaked with sweat, cum, and tears.

The game was over.

I had failed the silence.
But in failing, I had freed them all.

And I lay there, bathed in release, knowing Marrakesh had only begun to teach me the cost of surrender.

They carried me back to my chamber when it was over. My body was too weak to walk, my thighs trembling, my wrists raw where the cords had bitten deep. The black silk was gone, torn away, replaced by nothing but the cooling mess of sweat and seed drying on my skin.

I collapsed onto the bed, the sheets soft but cruel against my bruises. Every muscle screamed when I moved, every nerve still alight. My nipples ached, swollen from relentless mouths, my cunt throbbed, stretched and sore. My arse burned with the memory of fullness.

And yet it was not only my body that felt punished.

The silence I had broken — the scream I could not hold — still echoed in my ears. And beneath it, another memory pulsed: the shopkeeper spilling his seed for me in daylight, the thrill of watching him stroke himself to ruin under my gaze.

It was as if the game tonight had been crafted for me alone — a punishment, not for what I did in the chamber, but for what I had dared in the streets.

I turned on my side, wincing. The soreness between my thighs was a brand, a reminder. Every ache was an accusation.

I licked the salt of sweat and cum from my lips, tasting shame and triumph mingled together.

Had they known? Could the Palace somehow feel what I had done beyond its walls?

The note had warned me of silence. I had failed.
But perhaps failure had been inevitable.

I closed my eyes, body wracked, cunt still pulsing, and thought of tomorrow.

Would the games punish me again for what I sought in daylight? Or would Marrakesh simply demand more — more daring, more hunger, more sin?

I trembled, sore and aching, but sleep would not come.

The Palace punished.
The city tempted.
And I was caught, burning, between the two.

✦✦✦

Marrakesh
Chapter Eight

The morning came without summons.

No note. No garment.

Only silence.

Breakfast was waiting — figs, honey, olives, warm bread, mint tea — but the servants would not meet my eyes. Their smiles were polite, their gestures practised, yet something in the air had shifted.

When I asked about the city, they told me the gates were closed. Guests could not leave the Palace today. A matter of safety, they said. Unrest in the souk, a passing disturbance. Nothing for me to worry about.

But their words slid too easily from their tongues. Rehearsed. Prepared.

And I wondered.

Because the unrest was in me.
And it had begun the moment I had stepped into that shop and lured a man to sin in daylight.

The thought sank heavy into my chest as I ate, the figs too sweet, the honey cloying. My body ached in every place the game had punished me, but my mind was darker than my flesh.

Ramadan. The holy month.
I had made a man, then another break fast with their seed, spill their desire when they should have been unshakable. I had seduced them in daylight, when even lovers bound by marriage would abstain.

It hadn't felt like crime then — only hunger, only power. But now, with the gates barred and whispers in the corridors, I felt the weight of it press against me.

Not just breaking a rule.
Not just failing a game.
But breaking something larger. Something sacred.

The baths did little to soothe me. I lay in warm, perfumed water, my skin stinging where the ropes had bitten, my cunt still tender, swollen, used. Every shift of my thighs reminded me of last night's silence, the scream I could not hold, the release I could not deny. But beneath that ache was another: suspicion.

Had someone seen me?
Had a customer whispered of the woman in crimson silk who licked her fingers in the marketplace?
Did the Palace already know that I had gone beyond the games, into sin?

I thought of the locked gates. Were they closed for all… or for me?

Back in my chamber, the silence thickened. The note on my pillow had always told me what came next. Tonight there was nothing.

It felt less like reprieve than sentence.

By nightfall, I lay awake, staring at the ceiling lattice, listening to the fountains beyond the courtyard. My body was healing. But my mind circled darker truths.

The Palace could punish me with games.
The city could punish me with law.
And I had placed myself in the middle — a woman dripping with silk and seed, one scream away from ruin.

Night crept slowly across the Palace. Still no summons, still no note.

A servant brought me wine — ruby-dark, sharp with spice — and left me alone. I curled in the corner of my bed, a book open but unread, the words blurring as the silence pressed in around me. My body was calmer, bathed, oiled, fed. But my mind was restless.

It was then I heard it.

At first, I thought it was the wind through the lattice windows — a sigh, a shift of air in the courtyard. But then it grew clearer, cutting the stillness. A sound carried from somewhere deep within the Palace.

A scream.

Not sharp with terror, but long, shuddering, guttural. The kind that comes from release.

I froze, wine glass in hand, listening harder. And then more followed — low groans, moans, the unmistakable rhythm of bodies in pleasure.

Sex games. Somewhere nearby.

But why not me?

Had they chosen others tonight, leaving me to my solitude? Or was the sound not what I thought at all — the corridors playing tricks, my own guilt painting shadows into moans?

I rose, crept to the window. The courtyards were dark, only the fountains whispering. Yet still the sounds came, distant but steady. Flesh on flesh. Voices breaking. Someone coming apart in the night.

I pressed my palm to the stone wall, my cunt tightening at the echo of it, even as suspicion gnawed deeper.

Were they punishing me by excluding me?
Or was it my own imagination feeding me what I longed for most?

I returned to my bed, restless, the sounds still bleeding through the stone. The book lay forgotten, the wine unfinished.

I lay in silence, listening.
Moans, groans, cries.
The Palace alive while I was locked away.

Whether real or imagined, the effect was the same.

By the time I fell into uneasy sleep, my thighs were wet with longing.

I dreamed of ropes and cries and the locked gates — and woke with my body wet, my sheets tangled, and no certainty at all.

✦✦✦

Marrakesh
Chapter Nine

By morning, the gates were open again.

Servants moved easily through the courtyards, trays of fruit and bread carried in the sun, voices calm, laughter even. It was as though nothing had happened. As though yesterday's confinement had been a dream.

But whispers carried through the Palace walls. I caught them in passing — fragments exchanged between women pouring wine, guards speaking low at the gates.

Unrest in the city, they said. A blasphemous event. A disturbance that had unsettled the souk, made it unsafe for guests.

Blasphemous.

The word struck me like cold water. My heart lurched in my chest.

Had they seen me?
Had word spread of the woman who lured shopkeepers into breaking their fast with their own seed? Was I the reason the gates had locked, the Palace retreating inward while the city seethed?

I told myself it was impossible. That there must have been something else, something I had no part in. But the thought burrowed into me, sharp, inescapable.

It felt like mine.
As though the whole city had turned against me without ever knowing my name.

I ate in silence, the figs heavy in my mouth. The thought of the souk no longer thrilled me. The taste of daylight sin soured into fear.

No more.

I decided then: the shopkeepers, the teasing, the power of watching men undone — it had been too dangerous, too close to something I could not control. The Palace games were one thing — they expected my body, demanded my screams. But the streets… the streets could consume me.

Until I left Marrakesh, I would remain within these walls.

Better to be punished by silk and rope than by law and faith.

The day passed in uneasy quiet. I stayed within the courtyards, reading a book I still hadn't passed the first chapter of, watching the fountains rise and fall, listening to the rustle of palms in the dry heat. The thought of the city pressed at me like a bruise — the noise of the souk, the stolen glances of men, the obscene moment when restraint broke. Once it had thrilled me. Now it felt sharp with danger.

The Palace was safer.
Or at least, safer in its own way.

When I returned to my chamber later that afternoon, I saw it at once.

A card, folded on my pillow. The wax seal pressed firm.

My heart leapt, relief flooding through me as I broke it open.

Tonight, the game begins at midnight.
Garment provided.
Your silence is ended. You may scream as you wish.

Beside the card lay the garment — deep green this time, sheer as smoke, with golden thread at the seams. I lifted it, and the fabric slid through my fingers like water. The scent of jasmine clung to it faintly, calming, intoxicating.

The Palace had not abandoned me. The games had not ended.

My punishment, if there had been one, was over.

I pressed the garment to my skin, feeling its cool promise. The knot in my chest loosened. My clit twinged as in a reminder to why I was actually in Marrakesh. Whatever had happened in the city, whatever whispers of blasphemy haunted me, it would remain outside the walls.

Tonight, I belonged again to the Palace.

And I would scream.

Marrakesh
Chapter Ten

The hour of midnight came with silence so thick I could hear my own heart.

The chamber was alive with candlelight. Dozens of flames shimmered in tall holders, dripping wax that perfumed the air with honey and smoke. At the centre, gleaming under the glow, was the silver bowl — wide as a basin, already heaped with fruit. Figs split and swollen, dates sticky and dark, peaches soft to the point of collapse, pomegranates cracked open to show their red jewelled seeds. The scent was intoxicating, sweet and overripe, mingled with the musk of naked flesh.

We gathered in a circle, men and women, all bare save for thin veils of green silk draped across our shoulders. They fell uselessly against our backs, translucent, hiding nothing. My nipples stood taut in the cool air, my cunt already wet with anticipation, clenching at the thought of what I would soon be forced to carry.

A voice spoke — low, deliberate, echoing against the stone.

"Each woman will take a fruit into her body. Each man will drive it deeper until his seed joins it. When all have been filled, the fruit will be returned to the bowl. Only then may the feast begin."

My thighs trembled.

When the basket was brought to me, I reached with a shaking hand and chose a fig, round and purple, its skin splitting under my touch. I held it low, pressed it between my thighs, gasped as the sticky flesh began to slide inside. The stretch was slow, obscene, filling me in a way no cock ever had. The juice ran down my inner thighs. My cunt clenched instinctively, holding it in, my muscles straining with the effort.

I glanced up — saw the other women doing the same, sliding fruit into their glistening cunts, biting their lips, shuddering as they closed themselves around the forbidden sweetness.

Then the men came forward.

A man approached me from behind, his cock already hard, thick and glistening in the candlelight. He placed his hands on my hips, steadying me, and thrust inside with one sharp stroke. The sensation was unbearable — his cock crushing the fig deeper, the juice spilling over his length, filling me with a sweetness turned filthy.

He fucked me steadily, each thrust grinding the fruit deeper, bruising it inside me, his balls slapping against the sticky wetness already dripping down my thighs. My breasts swung with each impact, nipples grazing the silk veil, my breath ragged as I fought to hold the moans in my chest.

When he came, it was sudden, forceful. His seed spilled deep, soaking the fruit, mingling with its juices until I felt full, swollen, obscenely stuffed.

He pulled free, leaving me trembling, the fig inside me heavy and slick, soaked in both our fluids.

Around me, the same was happening everywhere. Women bent forward, men thrusting, the air filled with wet sounds and guttural cries. Fruit was being driven deep into slick cunts, crushed and soaked with lust. The chamber smelled of sex and sweetness, cloying, overpowering.

When all the men had spent themselves, the command came.

The large bowl was placed in the centre of the circle. One by one, we women were made to kneel, spread wide, and release what we had carried.

The first woman shuddered, her face twisted as she pushed. A peach slid from her cunt, wet and glistening, falling into the silver bowl with a soft, obscene splash. The sound made my cunt clench around my own fruit, desperate and aching.

Another woman released a date, slick with seed, followed by another and another. Each splash into the bowl echoed like a drumbeat. The fruit gleamed wetly, shining in the candlelight, a collection of obscene offerings.

When my turn came, I knelt, thighs parting. My muscles strained, pushing, and at last the fig slid out, heavy, soaked, dripping thick streams of fluid into the bowl before it dropped with a wet thud. My body clenched with relief, leaving me trembling and hollow, yet burning still.

When the last woman had released, the bowl was full. Glimmering, glistening, heaped with fruit now transformed by what we had done.

The voice spoke again: *"Now, we eat."*

The bowl was lifted high, passed among us. Fingers reached in, taking figs, peaches, dates, feeding them to one another. A hand pressed a dripping peach to my lips. I opened, tasted the sticky sweetness mingled with the sharp salt of seed, swallowed, my stomach tightening at the filth of it. Another pressed a pomegranate jewel between my teeth, the juice bursting on my tongue like blood, metallic and sweet at once.

Around me, moans rose again as mouths fed mouths, fingers slid fruit across lips, seeds and pulp smeared across breasts and thighs. The feast was not just eaten — it was played with, worshipped, smeared into our bodies as though our flesh was the table.

By the time the bowl was empty, we were glistening, dripping with juice and sex, our mouths stained, our thighs sticky. My skin smelled of figs and musk, my lips sweet with dates, my body trembling from the obscenity of what I had swallowed.

A sacred feast.
A blasphemy.
And I had never felt so devout.

The silver bowl was empty, the fruit gone, our mouths and bodies glistening with its juices. Candles guttered low, the chamber heavy with the smell of musk and sweetness. My lips were sticky, my thighs raw, and yet the hunger in the room was far from sated.

We were herded down a corridor, our green veils trailing, laughter and panting filling the silence where words were not needed. At the end, great double doors opened onto the baths.

Steam rose from pools lined in marble, lanterns glowing faintly through the mist. The water shimmered with oil, floating petals of jasmine and rose scattered across the surface.

We slipped in together, the heat closing over our sore, used bodies. At first there was only sighing, groans of relief, hands sliding water over bruised skin, mouths kissing sweat and juice away.

But the cleansing quickly became something else.

Hands slipped lower, spreading thighs under the water. Cocks grew hard again, sliding between slick legs. Mouths found nipples, teeth nipped, fingers plunged deep. The bath became a tangle of limbs, of thrusts muffled by the splash of water.

I was pulled against one man's chest, his cock pushing into my cunt under the surface, the water bubbling around our bodies. Another knelt before me, mouth on my breast, sucking until I cried out, my sound swallowed by steam. Behind me, hands spread my arse, a tongue pressing in, water lapping as I bucked against them both.

The pool was alive — women riding hard steamy cocks, men licking cunts under the water, mouths full of juice and cum once more. The scents of jasmine and sex mingled until the air was thick enough to choke.

I lost myself in it. One cock in my cunt, another pressing at my lips, opening my mouth filling my throat until I gagged and swallowed. Fingers pinched my nipples, rubbed my clit, slapped the water against my skin until it echoed like drums. I came again and again, each orgasm gushed violently, ripped from me, my body shuddering, my screams muffled by mouths and steam.

The bath was no longer for cleansing. It was a baptism in filth, a fuck feast in water and light.

By the time dawn hinted at the lattice windows, we were spent — floating, panting, tangled together in the pool like survivors of a storm. My skin reeked of rose, musk, and bodily juices.

And yet, even in exhaustion, I knew this:
Marrakesh had taken me deeper than any city before.
And I did not want to leave.

✦✦✦

Marrakesh
Chapter Eleven

I woke in my chamber with sunlight spilling across the floor, the lattice window cutting it into golden stripes. My body ached in new ways — thighs tender, lips swollen, skin sticky still with rose and musk despite the oils in the bath. Every breath seemed to carry the taste of last night.

I lay still, letting the memories wash through me.

The fruit sliding inside my wet, warm cunt, soft and obscene, the fig bursting as his cock drove it deeper. The juice trickling down my thighs, sticky, sweet, sinful. The weight of it inside me until at last it spilled into the silver bowl, wet and heavy, as though I had given birth to blasphemy itself.

The taste of it between my lips — figs soaked in seed, pomegranates bursting with both blood and lust. My mouth full of sin, my tongue coated with sweetness and salt, my stomach turning with pleasure and shame all at once.

And then the baths.

Hands everywhere, mouths everywhere, bodies colliding in water that steamed and churned with our filth. Fingers plunging into me, cocks filling me, tongues spreading me wide until I screamed against the mist. My cunt was sore even now, as though it had not yet released me from the night.

I touched my breast lightly and gasped; the memory was sharp. Teeth had bitten me there, tongues had pulled until I was raw. I slid my hand down, over the curve of my stomach, to the heat between my thighs. Even tender, even aching, I was wet again, my body betraying me to memory.

My cunt pulsed as I thought of their faces, their groans, the sound of fruit splashing into the bowl, the smell of juice and seed mingling in the steam.

I came slowly, deliberately, this time with only my own hand. My orgasm rippled through me like a ghost of last night, quieter, softer, but no less deep. I moaned into the sheets, hips lifting, circling my clit. cunt clenching tight, remembering them all.

When it was over, I lay in silence, trembling. The Palace had left no note yet. No summons. Only the memory of what had been done to me, what I had eaten, what I had become part of.

I licked my fingers clean, tasting myself mingled with the faint sweetness of fruit still on my skin.

Last night had not just been a game.
It had been a ritual.
And my body would remember it forever.

The sheets clung damply to my skin, my body still overwhelmed from the climax I had given myself. I stared at the ceiling lattice, sunlight dancing in golden shards, and the weight of it pressed down on me.

Last night was no ordinary indulgence.

It had been a crime. A sin dressed in silk and smoke.

I thought of the fruit again — figs swelling inside cunts, crushed by cocks, dripping with seed. Women groaning, men spending, the silver bowl filling piece by piece with obscene offerings. Each splash had been both sacred and foul.

And we had not hesitated. Not one of us.

The shame burned me hotter than the sun, yet even as I tried to banish the images, my cunt clenched, wetness seeping anew.

Because it wasn't just me.

Every woman there had spread her thighs, straining, moaning, releasing her fruit into the bowl. Every man had fucked, spilled, pressed his lust into something meant to be eaten. And then we had fed it to one another, laughing, moaning, devouring.

We had taken what should have been holy — figs, dates, pomegranates, fruits of the Prophet's table — and turned them into vessels of filth. And then we had swallowed them down as though it were communion.

I rolled onto my side, clutching the pillow, my thighs trembling at the thought.

The taste was still in my mouth — thick, sweet, salty, cloying. When I closed my eyes, I saw their lips stained with juice, their chins dripping, their tongues slick with both fruit and seed.

And my guilt sharpened into something darker: pleasure.

The more I thought of how forbidden it had been, how utterly blasphemous, the hotter my body burned. The shame only made me wetter.

I pressed my face into the pillow and whispered into the linen: 'It wasn't just me. We all sinned.'

And somehow, knowing I was not alone made the memory sweeter still.

I lay curled in the sheets, the sun high now, my skin sticky with sweat and memory. My thighs still ached, my breasts tender, my cunt swollen from too much use. Yet it was not the soreness that consumed me.

It was the knowing.

That I had taken part in something beyond obscenity. That I had swallowed what should never be swallowed. That figs and dates — fruits of prayer and blessing — had been turned into vessels of lust and seed, and I had moaned with delight as they slid down my throat.

The guilt was heavy, pressing into my chest. But beneath it was something darker still: the undeniable throb of pleasure. The more I tried to push it away, the more my body betrayed me, aching with the memory of it.

I whispered to myself, to the silence of the chamber: 'It wasn't just me. We all did it. We all sinned.'

And perhaps that made it worse.

The Palace was quiet today. No summons yet. But I knew my time in Marrakesh was drawing short. One final night remained.

My heart beat faster as I thought of it. If the last game had demanded such blasphemy, what would the final one unfold?

I pulled the sheet tighter around me, shivering though the air was warm. My body wanted it, my soul feared it. And between the two, I lay waiting, trembling, listening for the sound of footsteps outside my door.

The final night was coming.
And I could not tell if I prayed for it to be merciful — or merciless.

By late afternoon the walls of the Palace pressed too tightly around me. My body still overflowed with guilt and pleasure from the night before, but another thought troubled me — the small souvenirs I had meant to take home, tokens of Marrakesh that were mine alone, outside of these games.

So I braved it.

The gates were open again, the guards watchful but silent as I passed. I walked quickly through the souk, keeping my robe close, my eyes lowered. The stalls were just as bright, the air just as thick with spice and noise, but today no glances lingered, no teasing, no games.

I bought two small trinkets — a silver pendant shaped like a star, a pouch of saffron wrapped in paper. Simple, ordinary things. When the vendor pressed them into my hands, I felt almost human again, as though last night's rituals belonged to some other woman.

And it calmed me.

By the time I returned through the gates, the Palace seemed softer, less like a cage. My souvenirs rested in a velvet pouch by my bed, proof that the city had not turned against me, that the whispers of blasphemy had not reached here.

But when night fell, a new note was waiting.

Tonight: the final game in Marrakesh.
Midnight.
Garment provided.

Beside it lay a hooded robe of white silk, cut low, barely modest. And beside the robe — a large golden cross, a small leather-bound bible, a string of wooden rosary beads.

I froze. My throat tightened.

The fruit had been one thing. Sacred, yes — but this? These objects did not belong here, not in candlelit chambers, not in games of lust.

Could I do it? Could I take what I had been taught was holy and let it be used as a toy, a prop, a tool of indulgence?

My cunt throbbed with betrayal at the very thought. Guilt pooled in my chest, heavy and choking.

The note's words glared back at me.
The final game.

I sat with the robe in my lap, the cross cold in my hand, and wondered:

Would I refuse?
Or would I step into the chamber and surrender, as I always had, no matter the cost?

The night held its breath.
And so did I.

Marrakesh
Chapter Twelve

I dressed slowly, the white silk robe laid out for me untouched. My fingers brushed its smoothness, but my chest ached with resistance. The cross, the rosary beads, the small Bible — they sat beside it on the bed like accusations, daring me to surrender.

But I could not.
Not tonight.

The fruit feast had been blasphemy enough. My body had trembled with guilt even as I came, even as I swallowed cum, fruit, cocks and cunts. But this… this was something else.

I pressed the bell-pull, and when the servant came, I met his eyes.

"Tell them," I said, my voice low but steady. "I will not play tonight."

For the first time since my arrival, I felt something like power — the act of refusal, the right to say 'no.' He bowed, silent, but I thought I caught a flicker of something in his face. Disappointment? Pity? Warning?

When the door closed, I sat on the bed in silence, my pulse hammering. I picked up the small velvet bag where I kept my souvenirs. And there, tucked at the bottom, was the Crimson Key.

The same key that had been given to me in silence and secret at my retirement party. The key that had opened everything.

I turned it over in my fingers, tracing its weight, its ornate design. And that was when I saw it — not engraved into the surface, but printed faintly, almost invisible, so small I had never noticed before.

I held it to the light.
Words.

Once invitation has been accepted, all guests are obligated to play without question.

My throat went dry.

Obligated.
Without question.

The hooded robe of white silk seemed to glow brighter in the corner of my vision, an accusation, a demand. The cross lay cold against the sheets, the rosary beads silent as bones.

I gripped the key so hard it cut into my palm. My heart raced, the uneasy calm I had felt in the market gone in an instant.

I had said no.
But perhaps no was not mine to give.

The night stretched long ahead, heavy with silence. And I no longer felt in control of what would unfold.

I lay on the bed, the Crimson Key clenched tight in my hand, the tiny words still burning into my mind. *Obligated. Without question.*

The book I tried to read lay heavy in my lap, its words swimming, meaningless. I sipped the wine left on the table, but it soured in my mouth. I wanted distraction, but unease wrapped itself around me like a veil.

Then I heard it.

Distant, faint, carried through the stone: the moans and groans of the games.

At first a single cry, low and guttural. Then more — voices rising, gasps, a woman's scream as she came, a man's groan of release. The rhythm of flesh on flesh echoed faintly down the halls.

The others were playing.
Without me.

I pressed the book to my chest, eyes closing, my body betraying me, my cunt wet even as fear prickled along my skin. Excluded, yes — but punished too, in a different way. To be left outside, hearing it all, was torment of its own.

Then, silence.

The sounds ebbed away, leaving the Palace heavy with stillness once more. My heart slowed, unease settling like ash. Perhaps it was over. Perhaps my refusal had been accepted, even if reluctantly.

And then, the soft scrape of paper against stone. The faint hiss of something being pushed beneath my door.

I froze.

Slowly, I slid from the bed, my bare feet cool on the tiles. A single card lay on the floor, its edges catching the light.

I picked it up, hands trembling. The wax seal was darker this time, almost black.

I turned it over, broke the seal, unfolded it.

One line, written in the same precise hand as always:

Punishment for disobedience will be delivered.

No time. No instructions. No garment.

Just the promise.

The card slipped from my fingers, falling soundlessly to the floor. My heart hammered, my body shivered, torn between fear and a pulse of unwanted arousal.

I climbed back onto the bed, pulling the sheets around me, staring at the door as though it might open at any moment.

Sleep would not come.
The night had only just begun.

✦✦✦

Marrakesh
Chapter Thirteen

I did not sleep.

All through the night I lay rigid beneath the sheets, staring at the door, waiting for the sound of footsteps, the turn of the key, the moment of punishment promised on the card. My body remained tense, my mind circling, my heart thudding. But dawn came, and the door stayed closed.

For a brief, foolish moment, I believed it had been a bluff. That perhaps the Palace meant only to frighten me, to remind me of the Crimson Key's fine print, but not to act upon it.

By midday my cases were packed. I was told I would be driven to the airport. Relief softened me. I even smiled faintly as I followed the servant down the steps into the hot sun.

But then, on route to the airport the car turned.

Off the main road, down a track of dust and stone. To a warehouse at the edge of a barren yard. Its doors stood half-open, shadows yawning wide.

My relief dissolved into ice.

Inside, they waited.

Twelve men. Not masked, not veiled. Faces I almost recognised. The stallholder who had sold me dates. The man with the brass lanterns. The leatherworker with gold teeth. And others. Shopkeepers. Men of the souk.

The men I had teased.
The men, whose cocks I had made hard in the daylight, lured with glances, breasts bared, fingers deep inside my cunt then licked.
The men whose cocks had strained against their robes, whose cum had spayed across the shop floor because of me.

Now they stood together, summoned as one. Their eyes hard, their silence heavier than any words.

I knew. This was no game. This was my punishment.

I dropped to my knees before they spoke a word. Shame was a collar around my throat, tightening with each breath. I opened my mouth, a thick warm hard cock slid down my throat. spread my thighs, let them take me in every way, in every hole. My cunt stretched, clit pinched and twisted, my lips bruised, my skin coated with their cum until it dripped from me. One after another, they used me, spilling cum across my breasts, my belly, my face, into my hair, over my back. My body became nothing but a canvas for their release, painted in filth.

And still I did not resist.

For this was not punishment by pain — it was punishment by exposure.

When the final cock had spilled his cum over my face, I was ruined. My clothes clung in wet patches, stretched and torn at the seams. My hair was matted with dried seed, my thighs streaked, my breasts sticky. I smelled of cum, I smelled of sex, I smelled of all of them. I could not hide it.

They gave me no time to wash, no cloth to clean myself, no chance to gather my dignity. I was led back to the car, my body trembling, the taste of salt and shame still in my mouth.

And then — the airport.

The bright, ordinary world where travellers queued with cases, children cried, voices chattered in a dozen languages. And me — stepping out of the car into the hard glare of daylight.

People stared.

My clothes clung crookedly, straps torn, breasts almost spilling free. My hair stuck to my cheeks, stiff with dried seed. My lips were swollen, my cunt was swollen, my face streaked, my walk unsteady from being fucked in the arse, cunt and mouth too many times.

The security guards at the door looked away quickly, but not before their eyes widened. A woman passing with her child pulled the girl closer, whispering something sharp in Arabic. A group of men in suits followed me with their eyes until I disappeared into the terminal.

I wanted to vanish. To melt into the floor. But every step made me more visible, my disgrace louder without a word being spoken.

And this — this was the punishment.

Not the warehouse. Not the cocks, not the seed. I had taken those willingly, even hungrily.

But this.
To be paraded through the airport like this.
To feel eyes on me, whispers following me, strangers knowing without knowing.

By the time I boarded the plane, my body stank. My clothes clung to me like damp shame, my hair still heavy with the smell of cum and men.

Passengers looked at me in disgust, Cabin Crew looked in disbelief as I sank into my seat, trembling, staring at the window as Marrakesh fell away into cloud. The Crimson Key lay heavy in my bag, its hidden words now carved into me: *all guests are obligated to play without question.*

And I knew this:
The punishment was complete.
But the game itself was not over.

✦✦✦

Marrakesh
Epilogue

Home.

I stripped the moment I walked through the door. My clothes, my underthings, everything from Marrakesh was thrown into a refuse bag and thrown away, tainted beyond saving. I ran the bath as hot as I could stand, sank into the water, and stayed there until my skin was pink, my hair heavy, my body clean.

I scrubbed again and again, as if the humiliation clung deeper than flesh. The smell of them, the taste of them, the eyes at the airport — they had travelled home with me like ghosts. Only when the water cooled did I climb out, wrap myself in fresh linen, and crawl into my bed.

But sleep never came.

The punishment had been exact. Not the sex — I had taken cock after cock in my ass, my cunt, my mouth willingly, hungrily, even as my shame burned. No, the punishment had been the exposure. Being led into the bright ordinary world, cum stained and ruined, where strangers saw what I was. Where my secrets were no longer mine.

I thought of the men. The shopkeepers. Proof that Marrakesh had watched me, judged me, reported me. I thought I had been playing a private game of power, but the city itself had carried my lust back to the Palace. I had been caught.

And yet — I could not deny what else had happened.

I had loved it.
Every game, every surrender, every cock, every cunt, every clit, every breast, every secret ritual. Dubai, Rome, Marrakesh. Each had

stripped me bare in different ways, awakened hungers I had never known. I had cum until I thought I would break. And still I had wanted more.

Until Marrakesh scarred me.

The scrape of the post against the letter box made me shudder the next morning.

I froze where I sat, heart pounding, unable to move. The ordinary sound of envelopes falling had become something else, something heavy with dread.

When I finally stood and gathered them, I saw it at once. The envelope was thick, cream, sealed in wax. My stomach twisted before I even touched it.

My fingers trembled as I broke the seal.

Your invitation awaits.
Maui.
The games continue.

I sank onto the chair, the card shaking in my hand.

Part of me wanted to burn it, to throw it away, to pretend Marrakesh had ended everything. I did not want to go. Not again. Not after this.

Yet the Crimson Key glinted on the dresser, a silent reminder. Once accepted, all guests were obligated to play without question.

Then I realised the truth: Marrakesh had not broken me. My own lust had. I had stepped beyond the rules, taunted shopkeepers in daylight, sought pleasure where it was forbidden. The humiliation had been mine to earn.

If I stayed within the lines, if I submitted only as the games demanded, I would be safe. I would be fine.

I clutched the card to my chest, my body already aching at the thought of Maui — Paradise, the ocean, the fire, the unknown games waiting.

Fear and desire pulled me in equal measure.

But whatever else I knew:

I knew I would go.

The End

Maui
Prologue

The air in Maui was soft, salted, alive with the rhythm of the ocean. As I stepped from the plane, the scent of hibiscus and sea clung to me like a veil.

For the first time since Marrakesh, I breathed freely.

The island shimmered in colour — flowers spilling down hillsides, waves rolling in endless blue, mountains rising sharp against the sky. It should have been paradise. It should have been safe.

And yet, the Crimson Key weighed heavy in my bag.

I could still feel Marrakesh on my skin. The baths, the fruit, the punishment and humiliation at the airport — a shame I had scrubbed away in hot water but not erased from my bones. I had told myself I would resist, that I would not play again. And yet, here I was.

At the villa overlooking the sea, I found it waiting. Another velvet card. Another command.

Welcome. Today rest. Tomorrow midnight.
Garment provided.

A robe of deep red lay folded on the bed, silken, thin as water. Beside it, a garland of fresh flowers, fragrant and damp.

I pressed the card to my lips, shivering.

Marrakesh had scarred me, but Maui promised something different. Here, the games would not be bound by stone walls or guarded gates. Here, the ocean itself would swallow me.

I should have turned back.
But paradise was already under my skin.

And this was only just the beginning.

Maui
Chapter One

I woke to the sound of the ocean, waves breaking against black volcanic stone. The curtains lifted with the breeze, carrying salt and the faint perfume of flowers from the surrounding gardens.

My body stirred before my mind. Even in sleep, it remembered Marrakesh — the bruises still on my thighs, the soreness between my lips, the taste of seed and fruit I had swallowed in shame. The punishment had marked me.

I slid from the bed naked, my robe fallen in a careless heap. The floor was cool beneath my feet, the morning warm against my skin. On the balcony, I leaned into the air and let it touch me everywhere at once. The ocean's rhythm sounded like breath, like a slow thrust that never ended.

I touched myself without thinking. A finger circling the tender clit between my thighs, still swollen from all that had been done to me. My nipples tightened in the breeze, hard enough to ache. I thought of Marrakesh's baths, of being surrounded, fucked in all holes from all angles, drowned in heat and seed, and my cunt pulsed with wetness.

I should have stopped. But my hand slid deeper, fingers sliding deep inside my cunt. My thighs parting wide, dipping into slickness that had nothing to do with the sea. I moaned into the wind, low and broken, as though Maui itself could hear me.

When I came, it was soft — not the tearing orgasms of Marrakesh, but a slow wave that rolled through me like the tide, shuddering my body in gentle tremors. I sagged against the balcony wall, breathless, thighs trembling, clit still throbbing under my touch.

And then I saw it.

On the table inside, the velvet card I had left unopened the night before. Its edges seemed to glow in the morning sun. I already knew what it would say.

Tonight. Midnight.

I licked my cum soaked fingers clean and smiled, guilty and eager in the same breath. Maui was already inside me.

And I was ready.

I stepped from my balcony into the garden naked and barefoot, the grass still damp from dawn, and the lei of orchids brushed against my breasts with each movement. The petals were soft and damp, the perfume so heady it made me dizzy.

The Pacific spread before me, endless blue shimmering under the sun, the sound of it rolling into me like a pulse. Each crash against the rocks seemed to echo through my chest, down into my belly, deep between my thighs. My cunt throbbing again.

I felt alive in a way Marrakesh had not allowed. No stone walls, no locked gates, no watchful eyes. Here, everything was open, exposed, wild. The air clung to my skin as though it wanted to taste me.

I closed my eyes, letting the breeze slip between my naked thighs, brushing coolness against the clit. My nipples already stiff, aching. The lei's petals stroked me as I moved, brushing across bare skin as though reminding me of what awaited.

The island was teasing me. The flowers, the sea, the sun — everything caressed me, lured me, aroused me.

And my mind could not help but wander to the night ahead.

Would they take me to the ocean? Would I be bound beneath the moon, waves breaking over my body as I was spread, opened, filled? Would fire and torches mark my skin, the heat scorching me even as the water cooled?

My cunt clenched at the thought, a sudden rush of wetness slipping down my thighs. If anyone had been watching, they would have seen it all — my nipples hard, my lips swollen and slick, my body begging before a single hand had touched me.

I bit down on the lei and moaned softly, the taste of flowers sharp on my tongue, the perfume in my lungs, the ocean roaring inside me.

I was already half-undone, and the day had only just begun.

Tonight, Maui would take me.
And I would not resist.

✦✦✦

Maui
Chapter Two

Later that day I wondered the resort. The gardens seemed endless, but it was the sea that drew me down.
The sand was pale, soft as flour beneath my feet, the water foaming at the shore. And there — carved into the cliffside — the dark mouths of caves, wet with spray, waiting.

I stepped inside.

The air was cooler, thicker, alive with the scent of tide and stone. Droplets fell from the ceiling in slow rhythm, each strike echoing like a heartbeat. Shadows flickered against the rock as the sun shifted outside.

I pressed my palm to the wall. It was damp and ridged, the stone rising in thick folds beneath my hand. The ridges were hard, curved, jutting — almost obscene in their shape. Like a cock straining beneath skin.

My throat tightened. My body ached.

I traced the stone with both hands, letting my fingers follow every swell and ridge, stroking it as though it might swell further under my touch. My breasts brushed the cold surface, nipples stiffening against it, the chill only making the heat between my thighs sharper.

I spread my robe, letting it fall open until the air licked at my cunt. Wetness slid down the inside of my thigh.

The cave was alive around me — dripping, throbbing, echoing with every sound I made. I leaned against the stone, grinding against it, the hardness pressing back into me. My hips moved of their own accord, slow at first, then faster, as though I were riding it, as though the ridges were cocks, too many to count, all around me.

My moans bounced back from the walls, multiplied, surrounding me in sound. It was as though the cave itself was answering, groaning with me, taking me deeper.

My fingers found my clit, slick and swollen. I circled it until my knees trembled, then slid two fingers inside, my cunt clutching, greedy, desperate. My other hand pressed against the wall, stroking the ridge like a shaft, smearing my wetness onto the rock.

I edged myself cruelly, pulling back when the wave crested, forcing my body to ache, to beg, to need. Again and again, I denied it, until I was shaking, my breath ragged, my cunt dripping so heavily the stone beneath me was slick with it.

Finally, I let go.

The orgasm broke over me like the ocean itself, fierce, unstoppable. My body convulsed, my cunt spasmed around my fingers, juice spilling down my thighs. I cried out, the sound echoing in endless waves, until it seemed the whole cave was filled with my climax.

I sank to my knees on the damp stone, robe tangled, breasts heaving, thighs trembling. My hand slid free, wet and shining, my body still quaking with aftershocks.

The cave was silent now, save for the drip-drip of water. But I could feel it — the press of stone still against my skin, the phantom hardness inside me, the echo of my moans still alive in the rock.

Maui had already taken me.
And the night had not even begun.

✦✦✦

Maui
Chapter Three

The villa had been silent all day. Too silent.

I had wandered the gardens, the beach, the caves, but had seen no one but the resort staff — silent, efficient, expressionless. No other guests, no glimpses of the Key's other initiates. By sunset, I began to wonder if I was alone in this place, if Maui was only for me.

But when the card's instructions summoned me at midnight, I knew otherwise.

The path down to the beach was lit with torches, their flames bending in the breeze. The sound of the sea was joined now by the low thrum of drums, steady and primal, pulsing through the sand.

And then I saw them.

Twenty figures gathered in a circle by the water's edge. Men and women, their skin gleaming in the firelight, bodies adorned only with garlands of flowers and wide green leaves covering their genitals. The flowers glowed against bare flesh, the leaves swayed with each breath, hiding yet not hiding.

I stepped into the circle, the red robe slipping from my shoulders, my own body laid bare except for a green leaf and lei wound tight around my neck. The firelight licked across my skin, the sea behind me a black mirror.

One of the staff — masked in flowers, faceless — raised a bowl high. Seeds, glistening with oil, spilled from it into the fire, crackling, sending a sharp scent into the night. *"The game,"* the voice announced, *"is fire and water. Flowers and seed. The leaves will be lost, one by one. And the first to stand naked, touched by the sea, will know the blessing."*

My stomach clenched.

I watched as the staff stepped back, leaving the circle to the creatures of the tide. Small, dark shapes moved at the edge of the waves, sliding forward. At first, I thought crabs. Then no — something stranger. Rounded shells, quick limbs, claws delicate but insistent. They moved together, scuttling into the circle.

The rules had been spoken: *no hands allowed.* Wherever the creatures went, we must stay. And they were hungry.

The first man hissed, his body jerking as one of the creatures scuttled up his thigh. Its claws found the edge of his leaf, pulling, tugging. The leaf shifted, and his cock sprang free, hard in the torchlight. Gasps, laughter, moans followed.

Another woman arched as a creature climbed her calf, moving between her thighs. She spread her legs wider, trembling as it tugged at her leaf. When it fell away, her cunt gleamed in the firelight, wet and glistening, her moan carrying over the drums.

Then one came for me.

Its shell was slick, its legs quick on my skin. It climbed my shin, over my knee, onto my thigh. I froze, hands raised, body trembling as it reached the leaf that shielded my sex. Its claws teased, tugged, scraped — and I gasped, the sharpness sending jolts of arousal through me.

The leaf shifted, loosened, began to fall.

I felt the night watching me — twenty bodies, fire and sea, the creatures themselves. I wanted the leaf to go. I wanted to be stripped, shown, taken by more than hands.

When it dropped, my cunt was bare to the firelight, wetness shining as the drums quickened. I moaned, and the circle moaned with me.

Leaves fell one by one, creatures scuttling from body to body, stripping us all until the firelight revealed nothing hidden. Cocks stiff, cunts glistening, breasts swaying with each gasp. Naked, garlanded, trembling.

The fire spat and roared, seeds bursting as they burned, their sharp scent clinging to the air. Around us, twenty naked bodies gleamed with sweat and sea spray, our garlands shifting as we breathed.

The staff reappeared, carrying bowls carved from coconut shells, filled with petals and seeds slicked with oil. They passed them around the circle, each of us receiving one. The petals were damp, soft, fragrant — hibiscus, frangipani, orchids. The seeds clung to them like dew.

"The second trial," the voice declared, muffled by flowers. *"The flowers must drink. The seeds must grow. The gift is come."*

My breath caught.

We understood.

Men began stroking themselves, hands sliding quick and hungry over cocks still swollen from the stripping game. Women parted their thighs, fingers circling, dipping, coaxing their bodies into wetness. Moans rose, mingling with the drums.

I pressed petals to my breasts, scattering seeds across my skin. My nipples stiffened as I stroked them, my cunt aching for touch. I slipped my fingers inside myself, then dragged them slick over the petals, soaking them with my wetness.

Beside me, a man groaned as he spilled his warm cum into his bowl, thick white streaks falling over the seeds. Another knelt, pressing petals to his throbbing, bouncing cock, pumping until he came, coating them with his thick white cum.. The smell of sex mixed with the perfume of flowers and the sharp scent of burning seed — heady, overwhelming.

When it was my turn, I took a fistful of petals and held them against my aching cunt, grinding until the soft blooms were soaked through. My climax tore through me, wetness flooding over my hands, the petals glistening as they slid down my thighs. I gathered them back into the bowl, sticky with juice, mixed with cum, ready for the offering.

One by one, we cast the bowls into the fire. Petals sizzled, seeds popped, cum hissed as it met flame. Smoke rose thick and sweet, curling into the night, carrying our mingled sex into the air.

The staff chanted low, words I could not understand. The fire answered, sparks flying. The sea surged closer, waves licking at our feet as though the ocean itself hungered for us.

We were marked now. Stripped, opened, mixed with flowers and seed. Nothing left but flesh.

And that was when the orgy began.

The fire hissed as the last bowl was thrown in. Petals, seeds, and cum vanished into flame, smoke rising thick and perfumed.

And then the circle broke.

Hands were on me before I could think. A man's cock pressed against my thigh, wet with oil and seed. A woman's mouth closed over my nipple, tongue circling, teeth grazing until I gasped. Someone's fingers slid between my ass cheeks, slick and insistent, spreading me for whatever would come.

Everywhere I turned, there was flesh. Hard cocks jutting in firelight, cunts gleaming with wetness, mouths open, hungry.

I was pushed to my knees, a cock filling my mouth as another slid into my cunt, thick and hard, driving me into the sand. My throat opened, my cunt clenched, my moans smothered by the cock I sucked.

Hands pulled my ass wider, and then I was filled again, a third cock forcing its way into me, stretching me until I screamed into the night. My body was nothing but holes to be used, filled, consumed.

I came with each thrust, each invasion — helpless, ruined, trembling — and still they took more. My cunt dripped down my thighs, my mouth ran with spit and cum, my ass stretched and aching.

Around me, the same frenzy unfolded. Women straddled faces, their cries sharp and sweet. Men fucked into mouths and cunts and hands, spilling and hardening again. Flower garlands tangled with hair, with limbs, with seed. The sand was soaked with our sweat, the sea rushing in to lick at us, cooling overheated flesh only for the fire to burn hotter still.

At one point I lay spread in the surf, waves crashing over me as three mouths found me at once — one on each nipple, one on my clit — while fingers pushed into my cunt and ass until I thought I would break apart. I came so hard I nearly drowned, the ocean stealing my breath, the night stealing my body.

When finally the frenzy slowed, I was coated — breasts, belly, thighs, hair — every part of me marked by them. I licked my lips and tasted salt, cum, smoke, flowers.

The fire burned low. The sea pulled back. Twenty bodies lay tangled in the sand, spent and gasping.

And I knew: Maui had claimed me.

This was only the first night.

✦✦✦

Maui
Chapter Four

I woke with the taste of smoke still in my throat and the scent of sex clinging to my skin. My body ached everywhere — cunt sore, ass raw, throat tender. The garland had tangled into my hair, sticky with salt and seed.

I rose slowly, every muscle protesting, and slipped into the bath that had been drawn for me. Steam rose from the surface, carrying the scent of hibiscus oil. I sank into it with a moan, the water stinging where I was bruised, soothing where I was raw.

That was when I saw them.

Small red marks scattered over my thighs, around my hips, even close to my cunt. Little crescent bites, left by the creatures from the stripping game. Their claws had nipped, their mouths had tasted, and the proof remained on my skin.

The sight should have unsettled me. Instead, I felt a shiver of something darker — arousal mixed with unease. Maui was marking me in its own way.

I closed my eyes, trying to let the water wash it away, but another image rose unbidden. A face.

Among the frenzy of bodies the night before, one man had stood out. Firelight only his cheekbones, saltwater dripping from his hair, the shape of his jawline as he watched me writhe beneath three others. His eyes had caught mine for a moment — only a moment — before I was pulled under again.

But it had been enough.

For the first time since Dubai, since Rome, since Marrakesh — I wanted someone. Not just the game, not just the rule, not just the surrender. Him.

I touched the bites on my thigh, imagining it was his teeth. My cunt clenched, a fresh pulse of wetness between my legs. I spread myself in the bath and slid one finger, then two fingers into my cunt, curling them deep inside, moaning, I slid my wet fingers out, away, then stroked the wetness over the tender marks, then lower, circling my clit until I trembled.

I came quickly, gushing, the water rocking with my shudders, his eyes still bright in my mind.

This was new.

Maui was not only stripping me, not only punishing me. It was tempting me. Drawing me toward something I hadn't yet dared — desire that was mine, not just theirs.

I wanted him.
And somehow, I would have him.

I dressed lightly after the bath, slipping into a pale wrap that clung in the right places. My body still buzzing from release, but my mind was restless.

Time for breakfast.

The restaurant was quiet, the resort staff as discreet as ever. I chose it out of curiosity, scanning the tables, wondering if he would be there. My heart jumped at shadows, at every glimpse of broad shoulders or greying hair — but he wasn't there. Just the rustle of cutlery, the soft pad of servants' feet, the sound of the ocean through open shutters.

I lingered over fruit and coffee, pretending to savour, though all I tasted was disappointment. His image wouldn't leave my thoughts.

After breakfast, I wandered the grounds again. The gardens seemed brighter, flowers heavy with scent, bees humming lazily between them. The sea glittered, endless, its rhythm steady and cruel. And then I felt the pull.

The caves.

My feet found the sand, carrying me to the dark mouths in the cliff. I stepped softly, drawn deeper by a sound that wasn't the sea.

Moans. Low, broken, unmistakable.

I pressed my back to the stone, creeping closer, heart hammering. The sounds grew clearer — a woman's gasp, a man's growl, the wet slap of bodies colliding.

When I peered inside, I froze.

It was him. The man from the night, the one whose eyes had caught mine. His back was slick with sweat, muscles straining as he drove into the woman beneath him. Her legs wrapped tight around his waist, her nails clawing at his shoulders. She arched and cried out, her cunt swallowing him greedily as his thrusts grew harder, faster.

Her mouth found his chest, sucking, biting. His hand tangled in her hair, pulling her head back, his tongue sliding into her mouth as he pounded her. Their bodies were desperate, beautiful, locked in rhythm.

I pressed my thighs together, heat flooding me. My cunt ached, wetness seeping, as I watched him withdraw and sink his cock into her mouth. She sucked him hard and hungry, endless seed spilling across her lips, her tongue chasing every drop. He pulled her back onto his cock immediately, fucking her until she screamed and shuddered, her juices spilling down her thighs.

I bit my hand to stifle my own moan. My hips rocked against the stone, my clit throbbing as though I were being fucked too.

When they collapsed together, panting, slick and tangled, I pulled back into the shadows, breathless, trembling, soaked with want.

I had seen enough to know.

I wanted him more than ever.

And I would find a way.

Back in my villa, I could not still myself.

I paced the balcony, the gardens and sea spread before me, yet all I saw was him — the way his muscles strained, the way he held her, the way she cried his name into the stone. I had wanted him, imagined him, and now another woman had taken what I desired.

Who was she?

One of the twenty from the night before, I was sure. But which one? Had they come here together — lovers hidden behind leis and leaves? Or had he chosen her freely, drawn to her cunt and mouth, while I was nothing but another body in the circle?

The thought made my stomach twist.

In Rome, in Marrakesh, even in Dubai, I had never cared who touched who. Bodies were bodies, mouths were mouths. It was the game, nothing more.

But now I cared.

Why her? Why in the cave, away from the circle, away from the firelight? Was it secrecy, or passion, or both?

I tried to remember her face — the curve of her breasts, the fall of her hair — but all I could see was his, sharp with pleasure, lips parted as he emptied his huge load into her mouth.

The image made me wet again. My fingers slid between my thighs. I buried three, hard, deep into my cunt, then out, in then out, splashing wetness over my hand and thighs. I stood at the balcony wall , pounding myself, trying to turn jealousy into release. But even as I came, even as my cum gushed violently from me, biting down on my knuckles, the question remained.

Who was she?

And how could I make him choose me instead?

✦✦✦

Maui
Chapter Five

By evening the air was alive with scent — roasted fish, spiced fruit, wine heavy as syrup. The restaurant had been transformed. Torches lined the terrace, shadows flickered across tables, and every guest was already bare but for their garlands, laughter spilling like wine from their mouths.

Tonight was no ritual.
No rules, no cards, no instructions.

The card on my bed had said only: *Mingle Night. Do as you please. Anywhere you please.*

The freedom unsettled me.

I dressed only in the red lei, its flowers brushing my breasts, my cunt bare, still sore from the night before. When I entered the restaurant, eyes turned, lingering. But my eyes sought only one face.

Him.

He sat at a long table, a goblet in his hand, a smile at his mouth. Beside him, her. The woman from the cave. Her head tilted against his shoulder as though it belonged there, her laugh bright as though he had whispered it into her ear.

My stomach tightened, a rush of heat not unlike arousal but sharper, darker. Was she his? Were they a couple, bound together before Maui had ever stripped us all bare? Or was she simply the one he had chosen, her cunt the one he wanted, her mouth the one he spilled into?

I lingered at the edge of the room, wine pressed into my hand by a servant. Around me, bodies already touched, mouths already open, hands sliding over cocks and breasts as easily as lifting food to lips.

But all I wanted was to know.

Why her?

Why not me?

The drums began again, softer this time, playful, urging. Guests began to peel away from the tables, slipping into corners, out onto the beach, into the shadows of the gardens. Moans already rose, blending with laughter. The whole resort was opening, every inch a stage for sex.

I drained my goblet, my eyes never leaving him.

If tonight was mine to choose, then I would choose him.

The wine had warmed me, but it was not the drink that made my body burn. It was the sight of him slipping away from the restaurant with her — the woman from the cave.

I followed at a distance, my bare feet silent on the sand, heart drumming louder than the faint beat of the music behind me.

The caves again. Of course.

When I reached the mouth of one, I heard it — moans, low and urgent, wet sounds echoing off the stone. I edged closer, pressing myself to the cool wall, peering into the shadows.

They weren't alone.

She was there, spread on her back, thighs wide, cunt glistening. He knelt between them, tongue buried deep, his shoulders tense as he licked her until she writhed. And beside them, another woman — younger, darker — straddling his face as he feasted on them both at once.

The sight stole my breath.

The woman from the cave cried out, hips grinding against his mouth. The other clawed at his hair, riding his face, smearing herself over him. And when he pulled free, large hard cock glistening, he drove it into the first with a groan that shook me to my core.

I pressed my thighs together, slickness already spilling down them. My hands trembled as I clutched the stone, every thrust he gave her echoing inside me as though it were my cunt taking him.

I wanted him.
I wanted his tongue, his beautiful cock, his sweat, his ton of seed.

But when?

Should I walk into the cave now, strip off the lei, drop to my knees and take him in my mouth while he fucked her? Should I wait until they finished, until he was spent, then claim him as mine? Or should I keep watching — silent, aching — until the night gave me my chance?

My nipples ached, hard as stones. My clit throbbed so violently I thought I might climax just from watching.

I bit my lip until it bled, torn between hunger and fear, desire and shame.

For the first time since the Key had been given to me, I wasn't sure if I wanted to be chosen — or if I wanted to choose.

And still, I watched.

I pressed myself deeper into the shadows, watching them writhe together on the cave floor. His cock slid wetly into her, the sound obscene, her cries echoing against the stone. The second woman sucked at his balls, licked the long, thick shaft as he pulled back, then swallowed him into her mouth before he drove himself into the first again.

I was trembling. My cunt was so wet it dripped down my thighs, slick and aching, begging to be touched.

I couldn't hold back.

My fingers slipped between my lips, spreading myself open. I rubbed hard, circling my clit, pressing, sliding, desperate to match the rhythm of his thrusts. I moaned before I could stop myself — low, breathless, but loud enough.

His head turned. His eyes caught me.

For a moment I thought the women might notice, but they were too lost in him, their mouths and cunts full of his cock, their nails digging into his skin. He kept moving, fucking, sucking, groaning — but his gaze didn't leave mine.

I moaned again, louder, rubbing myself furiously as I watched. My cunt clenched, juice slicking my fingers, my nipples straining as though his mouth were on them.

He slowed his thrusts, then drove harder, deeper, eyes still locked on me. I saw the sweat bead on his chest, the strain of his muscles, the way his cock glistened with their wetness.

I rubbed faster, biting my lip, my breath ragged. He never looked away — not when the first woman screamed and shuddered on his cock, not when the second swallowed him down to her limit, not even when he spilled his huge load into her mouth, thick streams glistening as she licked him clean.

His eyes stayed on me.

I came hard, hips jerking, my body collapsing against the stone, my cunt pulsing around my fingers. My moan echoed through the cave, a raw cry that mingled with theirs.

And still, he watched me.

I pulled my fingers free, trembling, soaked, cum dripping down my thighs. I licked my juices from my fingers, eyes locked on his, I wanted to step forward, to take him, to lick the cum from his cock and taste the women from his skin.

But I didn't.

Not yet.

I slipped away into the shadows, my body still quaking, my mind burning with one thought only:

He knew.
And he wanted me to know he knew.

✦✦✦

Maui
Chapter Six

I didn't sleep.

Not because of the sounds of Maui — the ocean crashing, the wind through the palms, the rustle of creatures on the sand. No. I didn't sleep because his eyes wouldn't leave me.

He had fucked her, and the other one, too. He had spilled himself into their mouths, into their cunts, and still his eyes had been on me.

That was power.

And for the first time since the Key had been touched by my hand, I felt something shift. I had always been the one stripped, the one bound, the one surrendered. But now, I could hold something back. I could make him ache.

The thought made my cunt tighten in the sheets.

When morning came, I bathed slowly, lingering, oiling my skin until it glowed. I chose a sheer wrap, pale enough to show the curve of my breasts, dark enough to hint but not reveal. I draped the lei low across my hips, where its petals brushed the lips of my cunt when I walked.

I wanted him to see me.
I wanted him to want me.
But I would not make it easy.

At breakfast, I saw him across the room. He looked tired, satisfied, sated from the night — and yet his gaze sharpened when it landed on me. He watched me lift fruit to my lips, slow and deliberate. He watched me lick juice from my fingers.

I looked back once, just once, and then turned away as though he were nothing.

The game had begun.

Later, I wandered the gardens. I knew he was there — somewhere in the grounds, somewhere watching. I let the robe fall from one shoulder, exposing the swell of my breast, then pulled it back into place as though it had been an accident.

I bent to smell a blossom, the lei shifting, showing the wet shine between my thighs for only a moment. I lingered too long at the fountain, dipping my fingers into the water, circling, stroking as though I were already playing with myself.

But I never looked to see if he was there.

I didn't need to.

My body burned for him, every nerve aching, every breath a reminder of how close I had come to giving in. But I held it tight, the hunger, the ache. I wanted to see how long he could stand it.

Maui had stripped me. Maui had filled me.
But now Maui would teach me how to tease.

By afternoon the torches were extinguished, the fire circle erased by tide. A buffet had been laid in the gardens — platters of roasted fish, sliced fruit dripping with juice, sweet rolls glistening with honey. Guests drifted half-naked between tables, leis and laughter swaying in the heat.

And there he was.

I slowed my steps, pretending to study the food, but my eyes were on him. He looked refreshed, his hair tied back loosely, his chest glistening with a sheen of oil. Women leaned in when he spoke, men laughed at his words, and yet his gaze found me the moment I entered.

So I teased.

I chose a mango slice, lifted it slowly to my lips, sucking the juice with a soft moan. I let it drip down my chin, catching it with a fingertip, then slipping the finger into my mouth. My eyes flicked to him, just long enough for him to see, before I turned away.

I bent low to reach for another plate, robe falling forward, breasts almost spilling free. Then I straightened, smiled at nothing, and walked out into the garden.

But he didn't follow.

I lingered near the fountain, trying not to show my disappointment. The sound of water was joined by something else — low, urgent moans, groans, the unmistakable rhythm of bodies colliding. My pulse quickened.

I crept toward the foliage, careful, silent. And then I saw.

He was there again. But not with her.

Two other women straddled him at once — one riding his cock, the other grinding against his face. Another man knelt behind, fucking into a third woman while she sucked greedily at his cock. Their bodies tangled, slick, obscene. The air was thick with the smell of sex, the sound of flesh, the chorus of their cries.

I pressed myself to the stone, thighs trembling. My hand slipped beneath the lei, finding my cunt already slick. I rubbed hard, fast, unable to stop myself. Watching him move, watching his huge cock vanish into her, into the other, then the other, one cunt after another, watching his tongue shine with another woman's wetness — it undid me.

And then he looked up.

His eyes found mine in the shadows. He saw me rubbing myself, saw the hunger written across me.

This time, he didn't falter.

He smiled — slow, knowing — then turned his head away, burying himself back into the women, thrusting harder, groaning as though I wasn't even there.

My clit throbbed under my fingers. My cunt clenched with need. But his smile had burned itself into me.

He knew I ached for him.
And he wanted me to ache longer.

I came quietly in the shadows, my body shaking, my eyes never leaving him. I wiped my cum drenched fingers on the stone, trembling, furious, desperate.

This was a new game.

And I was already losing.

✦✦✦

Maui
Chapter Seven

The card had lain on my bed all afternoon, ignored while I teased myself with fruit and the man in the gardens. I had almost forgotten it, until at 10pm, the servants came with torches, guiding us toward the cliffside.

Tonight's game was the cave.

The air inside was damp and heavy, alive with echoes. Stalactites dripped from above, sharp teeth glistening in the firelight, while stalagmites rose from the floor like stone cocks, slick with spray. Mats of woven reeds had been laid between them, but the stone itself was the stage.

We were twenty again. Women lined one side, men the other. All garlanded, all naked, cocks already thick, cunts already wet. The smell of the sea mixed with musk, sweat, arousal.

The cave swallowed us whole.
Damp, echoing, alive with the drip of water. The stalactites above shone wet in the torchlight, their sharp tips glistening. Below them, the stalagmites rose like cocks of stone, jagged and merciless.

The rules were spoken, slow and clear:
The women will squirt to anoint the stalactites. The drops will bless the men. Then the women must ride the stone, no matter its hardness, no matter its cut. The men must hold back until their partner cries her climax. Only then may they spill their seed — not into her, but onto the stone itself.

My cunt clenched at the words, fear and heat tangled together.

We knelt beneath the hanging stone, spread wide, fingers already working. The men lay beneath us, cocks jutting, waiting for the first drop to fall. The cave filled with wet slaps, with women moaning and rubbing, chasing the spray.

I rubbed my clit, circling faster, hips jerking against my own hand. My thighs trembled, the ache too sharp, and then it burst from me — a hot rush, spraying upward, splashing the stalactite above. My breath caught as the drops gathered, then fell, thick with my wetness, splattering across a man's cock below. He groaned, hips jerking, but he did not stroke. He had to hold.

The ritual was only half begun.

The stalagmite waited.

I straddled it slowly, lowering myself onto the cool, ridged point. The first touch made me flinch — sharp, rough, not smooth like flesh but hard, unyielding. When I sank deeper, the stone scraped the lips of my cunt, dragging them raw, forcing me wider than I wanted to go.

I gasped — half pain, half heat. The stone hurt. Its edges bit into me. But that was the rule. I had to ride it.

I ground my hips, back and forth, the friction tearing at my tender flesh. Pain lanced through me, then shifted into something else — a dark pulse of arousal, sharp enough to make me moan. My clit caught against a ridge, sparking heat even as it stung. I bucked harder, my thighs shaking, juices spilling, slicking the stone.

The man beneath me groaned, his cock twitching, leaking pre-cum onto his belly. His hands clenched at his sides, his chest heaved, but he did not stroke. He held, fighting every instinct, every need, waiting for me to break first.

The pain built, unbearable. The stone bruised me, scraped me, marked me. And yet I ground harder, desperate to end it, desperate to climax so he could be free. I cried out, nails clawing the rock, hips jerking wild, until finally the wave tore through me.

I screamed as I came, my cunt pulsing against the unyielding stone, soaking it with my release.

The man roared then, seizing his cock, stroking furiously. He fought to the edge, then spilled over the stalagmite, thick ropes of cum streaking down the stone, mingling with my wetness. His seed glistened in the firelight, dripping to the floor of the cave.

Around us, the air shook with the same — women screaming in pain and ecstasy, their thighs streaked with scrapes and juices; men grunting as they fought their own release, some near breaking with the effort of holding back. When their women climaxed, they erupted at last, spraying seed across jagged stone, their cries echoing in the darkness.

The cave drank it all. Cum and squirt running down the stalagmites, pooling at their bases. The sound of moans and groans mixed with sobs, with ragged gasps, with the wet slap of flesh against rock.

By the end, every woman was trembling, thighs raw, lips swollen, some streaked with blood as well as cum. Every man shook from the effort of holding back, cocks red and sore from the strain.

I collapsed against the stone, breathless, cunt throbbing from pain and climax both. My thighs burned, my nipples ached, my body wrecked.

Across the cave, I glimpsed him. His hair plastered with sweat, his cock shining with cum, his body heaving with the release he had fought so long to contain. For a moment, his eyes found mine — not smiling this time, but dark, hollowed out, ruined.

And I knew Maui had changed the game again.

This wasn't just pleasure.
This was endurance.
This was pain made holy.

When it was finally over, we were led silently from the cave. No laughter, no chatter, just the shuffle of exhausted bodies across the sand. The fire had long burned down, and the moon watched us like a witness.

My thighs ached with every step. The raw sting of stone scraped between my lips, the bruises pressing sharp with every movement.

My cunt still pulsed with aftershocks, but it was no longer pleasure — it was soreness, swollen flesh rubbed too hard, too long.

When I reached my villa, the door was already open. Inside, the air was fragrant — hibiscus, sandalwood, eucalyptus. A bath had been drawn, the water steaming, scattered with petals. Bottles of oil and small jars of lotions lined the edge, their labels marked in both English and French: *Soothing. Antiseptic. Healing.*

The staff knew.
They always knew.

I let the lei slip from my shoulders, sticky with sweat and seed. My body was streaked with salt and stone dust, thighs sticky with my release, skin blotched with red scrapes.

I lowered myself slowly into the bath. The first touch of heat made me flinch — my cunt stung, my cuts burned — but soon the warmth seeped in, easing the ache, soothing what the game had taken.

I leaned back, letting the water cradle me. The petals clung to my breasts, floated against my thighs, their softness a cruel contrast to the rawness beneath.

I reached for one of the jars, dipping my fingers into the cool salve. The scent was sharp, medicinal, not like the perfumes of the day. I spread it carefully between my legs, onto the cuts along my thighs, the stings along my lips. It burned at first, then cooled, a steady calm seeping in.

I sighed, closing my eyes.

They had hurt me. The stones had hurt me. And yet the game had made me climax harder than I had thought possible. The ache between my thighs was punishment and reward in one.

And as the bath soothed me, another ache stirred — not the cuts, not the bruises, but the hunger.

Him.

Even in pain, I wanted him.
Especially in pain.

The water rocked gently, petals drifting, and I let myself float, half-healed, half-ruined, knowing Maui would demand more when the sun fell again.

I had just closed my eyes when I heard it — a faint knock. Not the heavy knock of summoning, not the staff's clipped knock of service. A softer sound, almost secret.

When I rose from the bath, water dripping from my skin, I found the envelope slid just inside the door. No seal. No markings. Only a single sheet of thick paper folded in two.

Tomorrow rest day. Fountain. Midday. Come alone.

My heart thudded.

It wasn't written in the elegant hand of the Palace's invitations. This was rougher, darker, rushed. But the meaning was clear.

Him.

The one whose eyes had burned through me in the cave. The one who had watched me in the shadows, smiled while I came for him, and turned away only to make me ache.

He wanted me.

I held the note in my wet hands, drops blurring the ink, and for the first time since the Crimson Key was placed into my possession, I felt the rules shift. This wasn't ritual. This wasn't dictated by cards and servants and masks.

This was his choice.
And mine.

Midday by the fountain.

I pressed the note to my chest, water soaking it through, my body still raw and tender from the stone. My cunt pulsed at the thought of him — not in a circle, not in a cave, but alone, his mouth, his cock. Ooh his cock, his hands only for me.

But the ache of the cave still lingered, reminding me of Maui's cruelty. Could this be a trap? Could the note itself be part of the game?

The thought made me shiver.

But it didn't matter.
I would go.

✦✦✦

Maui
Chapter Eight

Morning came too soon.

The light through the shutters was soft, golden, but I felt anything but soft. My thighs still burned with the memory of stone scraping flesh. My cunt was swollen, sore, my clit tender to the touch. When I shifted beneath the sheets, I winced — then sighed, because even pain now felt like a promise.

The note lay on the table, ink smudged where my wet fingers had touched it. *Fountain. Midday. Come alone.*

I read it again and again as I bathed, as I oiled my bruises, as I dressed my sores.

I should have rested. It was a rest day after all — no cards, no games, no torches or drums. But my body refused stillness. Every touch of oil on my breasts made my nipples stiffen, every careful sweep of lotion over my thighs made my cunt throb, aching to be filled.

Him.

The man whose eyes had followed me through every moan, every orgasm, every shadow. The man who had fucked others while watching me, made me come in silence while he spilled into their mouths.

And now, he had asked for me.

I paced the room, robe slipping from one shoulder, then the other. My mind spun with questions. Would it be only him? Would she be there too — the first woman from the cave, the one whose cunt had already swallowed him? Was it a trap, another cruel twist of Maui?

I pressed my fingers against my tender cunt through the thin silk, testing the soreness. A sharp sting made me hiss, but the sting melted quickly into heat. My body betrayed me, wetness slicking my fingers even as I winced.

I was bruised, but I was ready.

By mid-morning, I couldn't sit still. I tried to read, the words swimming on the page. I tried to eat, but fruit slid down my throat without taste. I stood before the mirror, adjusting the lei around my neck, parting the robe so that it barely hid my breasts, barely covered my thighs. If he wanted me — truly wanted me — I would make him ache as I ached.

The sun crept higher. My pulse quickened with every shadow that moved across the floor.

Midday was coming.

And with it, him.

✦✦✦

Maui
Chapter Nine

The sun was high when I reached the fountain, the water glittering, the air thick with jasmine. My pulse raced as I approached, certain I would see him there waiting.

But I wasn't alone.

Three other women stood in the shade, silent, eyes lowered. Their bodies were bare but for leis of white flowers, their breasts rising and falling with the same anxious breath I felt in my chest.

Confusion prickled through me. Who had brought them? Who had summoned us? The note had said 'come alone.'

No one spoke.

The only sound was the trickle of the fountain until footsteps broke the silence. A servant appeared, carrying a velvet pouch and a card. His face was blank, expressionless, as he bowed and unfolded the message.

The servant's voice carried above the fountain, sharp and deliberate:

'Four women. Four rings. The ocean will decide. Each woman will take a golden ring and push it deep into her cunt. Once the ocean has swallowed them all, you will enter waist-deep. You may use only your mouths, your tongues, your bodies. The last woman still retaining her ring shall be named the victor."

The gold glistened in his palm — four wide bands, heavy, smooth, obscene. One by one, he placed them in our hands. The others wasted no time. They spread their thighs, moaned softly, and pushed the rings inside, their cunts swallowing the metal whole.

When it was my turn, the heat of the sun had warmed the gold. It burned slightly as I pressed it between my lips, stretching me wide. My walls clenched against it, trying to resist, but I forced it deeper, inch by inch, until it sat lodged, heavy, deep inside me.

We walked together to the sea, silent but trembling, our bodies marked by salt and bruises from the cave. The water rose cold against our thighs, then our waists. The rings shifted deep within, and each of us clenched hard, desperate to hold.

The servant raised his hand.
"Begin."

Chaos erupted.

One woman lunged at another, dragging her under, forcing her thighs apart. She dove between them, mouth wide, tongue stabbing, desperate to pry the ring loose. The victim screamed into the water, legs thrashing, cunt clenching tight to hold.

I felt hands seize me — sharp nails against my hips. A head pushed between my thighs, mouth latching, tongue plunging. I cried out, the intrusion hot and desperate, my walls fighting to keep the ring lodged. She licked furiously, her tongue curling, scraping, trying to hook the edge of gold.

"No!" I gasped, shoving her head down, grinding my cunt against her face, smearing myself over her nose to suffocate her. She fought back, sucking, pulling, making me spasm so hard the ring threatened to slip. I clenched until my thighs shook, sweat and seawater streaming down my body.

I countered. Diving forward, I forced myself between another woman's legs. My tongue stabbed inside, slick and hot, her cunt clamping around me, walls twitching in panic. I tasted her salt, her juices, felt the hard edge of the ring deep within. I curled, hooked, tugged. She bucked, trying to crush my head between her thighs, but I bit gently, pulled, and felt the ring begin to slide.

She screamed into the water, body convulsing, and when she surfaced it was gone. 'Fuck…No!' She shouted— her cunt empty, her chance lost.

The servant's voice rang out over the waves.
"One is fallen. Three remain."

The sea grew wilder, our bodies thrashing harder. I was attacked from both sides — mouths sucking at my cunt, tongues spearing inside, trying to pry my ring loose. I clenched until I cried, tears mixing with saltwater, every muscle straining. My thighs shook, my cunt burned, but still I held.

I lashed out, forcing one of the women under, grinding my cunt onto her face while I dove at the third. My tongue speared her cunt, curling deep, tasting her moans. She writhed, her ring shifting dangerously close to my lips. I sucked hard, pulled, and with a violent thrust of my tongue, it slipped free.

She broke the surface screaming, 'Nooo….' empty, defeated.

"Two remain."

It was her and me. The last.

We circled, breasts rising with each ragged breath, thighs trembling with exhaustion. My cunt throbbed around the ring, every wave threatening to pull it free. Her eyes were wild, lips parted, chest heaving.

She lunged. Our bodies crashed together, water splashing high around us. Her mouth forced between my thighs, tongue stabbing, relentless. I screamed, clamping hard, grinding against her face, my nails digging into her scalp. But she didn't stop — licking, sucking, pulling.

I shoved her under, dove onto her, buried my tongue deep into her cunt. She convulsed, walls trembling, the ring slipping. I bit lightly, tugged, twisted my tongue, and then — yes — it came loose, spilling into my mouth like treasure.

I surfaced, gasping, triumphant, the last ring clamped between my teeth. She floated back, sobbing, empty.

The servant raised my arm declaring.
"The victor."

My cunt still clenched around its ring. I was the last. The winner. The one who had held on when all others had been forced open.

The ocean lapped against my thighs, cool and cruel, as I realised — victory didn't ease the ache. My cunt was raw, my body ruined, but the hunger in me only burned hotter.

✦✦✦

Maui
Chapter Ten

The servant took my hand. My thighs still trembled, cunt raw from clenching, body shaking with exhaustion. Salt and bruises covered me, my nipples sore, my clit swollen. And yet I followed.

He led me away from the beach, past the rocks, deeper into the cliffs where the torches burned lower, where the air grew thick with musk and shadow.

At last, a cave.

And inside, him.

He was waiting, naked, cock already thick and hard, glistening in the torchlight. His eyes locked on mine, and for the first time there was no crowd, no other women, no rules but us.

My breath caught. My cunt clenched painfully around the last ring still lodged deep inside me.

He came forward, slow, steady, and caught me before I could collapse. His hands were warm, his touch steady. He laid me down gently on a bed of woven mats, petals scattered over them, as though the cave itself had been prepared for this moment.

I winced when my thighs spread, the soreness too sharp. But he reached for a small vial, clear oil glistening on his fingers.

When he touched me, it wasn't rough.
It was soothing.

He smoothed the oil over my swollen lips, slow and careful, working it into every bruise, every scrape. The burn eased, coolness spreading, my breath shaking with relief. His eyes never left mine, and for the first time, I felt cared for rather than used.

Then his mouth descended.

His tongue parted me, soft at first, tasting, teasing. Then deeper, firmer, pressing against the walls of my cunt that had held the ring so tightly. My body arched, torn between soreness and hunger, the sting of raw flesh giving way to the throb of arousal.

He licked deeper, curling his tongue, searching. I moaned, hips jerking, my cunt trembling around him. And then he found it.

The ring.

His tongue hooked the edge, teasing it free, tugging carefully until the metal shifted, slid, and finally spilled out into his mouth. He raised his head, lips glistening, the golden ring between his teeth.

I gasped, trembling, tears stinging my eyes.

He placed the ring beside me on the mat, then lowered himself again, his tongue claiming me once more — but this time with hunger. Lapping, sucking, thrusting deep, driving me higher, pushing me past soreness into pure heat.

I clutched his hair, hips grinding against his face, moans echoing off the cave walls. My cunt pulsed, wetter, looser, aching for his cock.

But still he teased. Still he licked, deeper and harder, until I screamed, climax tearing through me in waves.

When I fell back, shuddering, he rose over me, his cock pressing heavy against my entrance. My lips were slick with oil, cum, and his saliva, ready despite the ache.

This time, when he pushed inside, it wasn't pain I felt. It was surrender.

At last, he was mine.

At last, I was his.

When he pushed inside me, it was as though the ocean itself split me open. My cunt, swollen and sore, clung to him hungrily, greedily, the ache drowned in the sheer size and fullness of his cock.

I cried out, nails raking his back, thighs wide as he sank deeper, deeper still, until there was no space left between us. He groaned into my ear, the sound thick, primal, his chest slick with sweat as he began to thrust.

Slow at first. Careful. Testing.
Then harder. Rougher.
Like he had been waiting all along.

My cunt gushed around him, slicking his cock, the oil and my juices mixing as he pounded into me. Each stroke drove the soreness away, replacing it with fire, heat, raw hunger that left me screaming.

“Harder,” I begged, hips lifting, breasts bouncing with every thrust. “Take me harder.”

He did.

He flipped me onto my knees, grabbed my hips, and rammed into me from behind. My cry echoed off the cave walls, my hair sticking to my face, my ass stinging from the slap of his hips. I shoved back against him, grinding, demanding more. His cock stretched me, slammed deep, battering the ache into oblivion.

I came again, soaking him, my cunt pulsing, milking his cock as he roared. But he didn’t stop.

He pulled out suddenly, my cunt dripping, and shoved me onto my back. His cock pressed against my mouth, thick and glistening. I opened wide, gagging as he thrust, my throat swallowing his length. His hand tangled in my hair, holding me down, fucking my face until tears streamed down my cheeks and spit poured from my lips.

When he pulled free, gasping, I thought he would spill — but no. He flipped me again, spreading my ass wide, pressing the head of his cock against the tight ring.

I froze, gasping. “Yes—”

And then he pushed in.

Pain seared through me, then melted into heat as he stretched me wide, his cock burying itself in my ass. I screamed, clutching the mat, body shaking as he fucked me there, relentless, claiming me in every hole. My cunt dripped down my thighs, pulsing, empty but aching, while his cock drove into my ass harder, harder, until I broke, climax ripping through me with violent force.

He didn't stop. He spun me, lifted me, carried me onto his lap. I straddled him, cock impaling me once more in my pussy, bouncing on him, riding hard, tits slapping against his chest as we moaned together. His hands clamped my hips, guiding me faster, harder, until we were both nothing but sweat, cum, and sound.

"Now," I gasped, nails digging into his shoulders. "Fill me. Everywhere. I want it all."

He roared, slammed deep, and erupted. Hot cum spilled endlessly into me, filling my cunt, my ass, spilling across my stomach as he pulled out to paint me. Ropes of white glistened on my breasts, my lips, my thighs.

I collapsed onto him, body wrecked, dripping with his seed, every hole used, every ache replaced with raw satisfaction.

At last.
After all the games, the rules, the rituals—
This was ours.

The cave fell quiet at last.

My body lay wrecked across his chest, my cunt dripping with his huge load, my ass aching, my breasts sticky with his cum. My thighs still trembled from the pounding, every hole filled, every nerve spent.

And yet, in the silence, he held me.

Not rough. Not demanding. Just his arms around me, his chest warm against my cheek, his hand stroking my hair as if I hadn't just been fucked to ruin on the mats. His cock, still thick, rested against my thigh, twitching now and then with the last echoes of his release.

I sighed, eyes fluttering closed. For the first time since Maui, since any of the cities, I felt something softer than ritual.

"You were always going to win," he murmured, lips brushing my temple.

I stirred, half-asleep, half-alert. "What do you mean?"

His fingers traced my sore thigh, circling the bruises, smoothing oil into my skin. "The rings… the others never had a chance. It was arranged. From the start, the last woman standing would be you. The final ring was never meant to leave your body until I took it."

I blinked up at him, heart pounding. "Arranged? By you?"

He smiled, faint and secret, his eyes glinting in the torchlight. "By me. By the Key. By both. Does it matter?"

I wanted to ask more, to press, but his lips silenced me. Soft, unhurried, his kiss tasted of salt and sweat and something darker — knowledge I hadn't been given yet.

My body, sore and sorely used, melted into him anyway. Because for the first time, I wasn't just a player in Maui's games.

I was his.
And he had chosen me.

The cave echoed with the hush of the ocean outside, the faint drip of stalactites, the sound of his breath in my ear. And in that moment, despite the pain, despite the bruises, I wished the day would never end.

By the time I was led back to my villa, the torches along the path had burned low. My body ached with every step — holes stretched, lips sore, thighs trembling from the strain. His cum still clung to my skin, sticky on my breasts and belly, dried at the corners of my lips.

And yet my chest was light, almost floating.

I sank into the sheets, staring at the ceiling, unable to close my eyes. The memory of his touch replayed over and over: the way he had smoothed oil into my bruises, the way his tongue had taken the final ring, the way his arms had wrapped around me when it was over.

It had not been just another game. I knew that now.

Who was he?
How had he arranged it?
And why me?

I had come to Maui expecting more of the Key's cruelty — the endless rituals, the endless hunger. And instead, I had found him. Not just his cock, not just his mouth, not just the way he had filled me in every hole until I screamed — but the way he had cared for me afterwards.

That was what undid me most.

I touched my sore lips, pressed my thighs together, and sighed.

Tomorrow was the last day. No card, no ritual, no instructions. Just silence. A day for rest, for packing, for preparing for the flight that would take me away.

But sleep didn't come easily. Because even as my body healed, my mind stayed with him — the man who had broken the rules, and made me crave him more than any game could.

✦✦✦

Maui
Chapter Eleven

The last day passed in silence.

No card.
No ritual.
No sign of him.

I stretched out by the pool with a book open in my lap, sunlight flickering over the pages, but I read nothing. My body was healed enough to move without flinching, though soreness still lingered faintly between my thighs. The ache was not of pain now but of absence.

My eyes scanned the grounds over and over. Every servant's face, every guest's body — I searched for him in the line of a shoulder, in a stride, in the tilt of a head. Nothing. He had vanished, as though the cave had swallowed him whole.

By late afternoon, my bags were already packed for me. The soft knock at my door came, and a servant bowed, wordless, waiting. It was time.

The farewell was unlike anything I had seen before.

The staff gathered at the entrance to the resort, dressed in linen whites, flowers in their hair. One by one they placed garlands over my shoulders until my chest was heavy with petals. They hummed a low song, a rhythm that rose and fell with the ocean behind them. Their eyes were calm, solemn, as though they were not just seeing me off, but cleansing me of what had happened here.

I bowed, murmured thanks, but my throat tightened. Every glance I gave the line of faces was another silent hope: 'was he there?'

He was not.

The car door shut with a soft thud, sealing me into leather and silence. The driver said nothing as we pulled away, the resort shrinking behind us.

The road hugged the cliffs, the ocean flashing silver beneath the fading sun. I leaned against the window, the air heavy with salt, every curve of the road pulling me farther from him. My fingers twisted in the petals of the leis, crushing them until their scent filled the car — sweet, intoxicating, too much.

Could he still be here? Could he be watching me even now, hidden in the shadows, letting me go but holding me in ways I couldn't see?

The airport rose like another world: white concrete, glass, the bustle of travellers dragging cases, voices loud and ordinary. I walked through it like a ghost, my clothes neat, my hair brushed, my face composed. No one saw the bruises beneath, the soreness still pulsing between my thighs.

The other passengers glanced at me without knowing. Men checked me with casual interest, women noted my dress or shoes. None of them knew that only hours ago I had been filled, stretched, covered in cum. None of them knew the ring he had taken from my cunt with his tongue still burned in my mind.

I boarded with them, took my seat among them, carried my secret into the sky.

As the plane lifted, the island fell away beneath the clouds. I pressed my forehead to the glass, searching the land and the sea one last time. Was he still there? Would I ever see him again?

The leis around my neck wilted, petals browning at the edges. I held them tighter anyway, as though they might keep me tethered to him, to Maui, to the cave where he had chosen me.

And though I was leaving, though the plane carried me farther with every second, I could not shake the truth:

The other passemgers would go home with suntans, souvenirs, memories of cocktails and beaches.

But me — I carried something darker, heavier, a secret they would never touch.

And it was mine alone.

✦✦✦

Maui
Epilogue

Home.

The silence of my own rooms felt almost unreal after the noise of the island. No sea, no drums, no moans echoing through caves. Only the dull tick of the kitchen clock, the hum of the fridge, the ordinary stillness of walls I knew too well.

I dropped my suitcase by the door, kicked off my sandals, and paused.

There it was.

An envelope.

Unstamped, unmarked, lying on the doormat as though it had fallen from nowhere. My pulse quickened. The Key's envelopes always came the same way — cream, plain, heavy paper. But this one was different. The flap bore a wax seal, deep crimson, pressed with a mark I couldn't make out.

I left it.

I forced myself to. I carried my bags to the bedroom, unpacked slowly, folded clothes, put the leis in the bin where their petals crumbled to dust. I bathed, washing the last salt from my hair, then brewed coffee and sat at the kitchen table with the cup warm between my palms.

Only then did I break the seal.

The card inside was heavier than the others, the paper rich and textured. The handwriting was not elegant like the Palace summons — it was bold, personal, unafraid.

You were more than I imagined.
Thank you for your presence in Maui.
Thank you for being such a great lover.
And thank you for being you.

I read the words twice, then three times, my hands trembling.

"I hope you will accept your next invitation when it arrives. Acapulco expects obedience. I demand it. And you know my demands are never without pleasure."

Beneath the lines, one final phrase, written smaller, almost like a whisper on the page:

'*What opens without a key, and closes without a lock?*'

I stared at it until the letters blurred. A riddle. A message. A key within the Key.

I pressed the card to my chest, my coffee cooling, my pulse hot.

Who was he?
How had he done this?
Why did I still ache for him? And why did I already know I would go?

The End

Prologue
Acapulco

The rain had followed me down Bond Street, streaking the windows with silver, but inside the boutiques the air was warm with perfume and promise.

Fifty-eight years old, I thought, running my fingers over a rack of dresses. Too old for some of this, perhaps. But then, had I not proven to myself in Dubai, Rome, Marrakesh and Maui, that my body could still be worshipped? Still be tested? Still be taken?

I lingered over silks and satins, letting the fabric slide through my fingers like a lover's touch. A sliver of crimson lace caught my eye, cut daringly low at the breast. I slipped it from the hanger and held it against myself in the mirror. It clung beautifully to my waist, but the plunge at the neckline — was it too much? Was it too young?

I almost put it back. Almost. But then I imagined 'Him.' Imagined his eyes tracing down that neckline, his hand following after. My nipples hardened even in the fitting room, betraying my hesitation. I bought it.

Next came a black slip dress — simple, elegant, cut to skim my thighs. Not girlish, but bold. With heels, it would lengthen my legs, remind me I was still dangerous. I chose it without doubt.

For the heat, I allowed myself gauzy skirts, thin straps, sheer blouses that revealed just enough. At my age, the game was not in pretending to be younger. It was in wearing what whispered confidence, what dared him to look closer.

By the time I left with bags heavy on my arms, I had built a wardrobe not for Acapulco's sun, not for its strangers — but for him. Every piece chosen in the hope that when his eyes fell on me, he would know I had dressed for him alone.

The flight was long, my body restless, my mind circling the same thought: 'would he be there?'

When at last the wheels touched down in Mexico, the cabin filled with heat that London had long forgotten. The air smelled of spice and salt, thick enough to taste. Outside, the sky blazed orange as the Pacific swallowed the sun.

The Crimson Key had brought me here.
But it was not the Key I craved.

It was him.

And if he was waiting in Acapulco, I was ready.

Acapulco
Chapter One

The car slid out of the airport into streets that felt nothing like Maui.

Maui had been soft: the hush of waves, the quiet murmur of servants, the whisper of palms. Acapulco struck me hard in the chest with its noise. Horns blared, laughter spilled from open bars, street vendors shouted their prices in rapid Spanish. Neon signs flickered even in daylight, fighting with the burning sun for attention.

Through the tinted window, I watched men pushing carts piled with fruit, women balancing baskets of flowers, children darting barefoot between cars. Music pounded from somewhere — drums, bass, voices raised in celebration, or was it protest? It didn't matter. Everything here seemed louder, faster, hotter.

I pressed back into the leather seat, the bags of silk and lace resting beside me, and felt my pulse quicken. I had dressed for him, shopped for him, imagined him. But Acapulco was already testing me differently.

We wound upward through the hills, the city falling behind, replaced by steep roads clinging to cliffs. The Pacific spread out below in sheets of silver and fire, the sun sinking toward it. For a moment I closed my eyes and tried to recall Maui — the stillness of the caves, the private laughter by the fountain, the way he had soothed me with oils before he entered me.

But the memory was fragile against the chaos outside.

Children's voices chased the car until the road climbed too high for them to follow. Dogs barked, motorbikes roared past, a man shouted something crude that made the driver glance at me in the mirror, then quickly away.

And then, suddenly, silence.

We passed through tall iron gates that groaned open at our arrival. The noise of the city fell behind, replaced by the sigh of the ocean below and the faint rustle of palms. The road curved one last time, revealing the hotel clinging to the cliff

The hotel loomed above me like something carved out of another century. Not sleek glass, not light or modern — but heavy, rooted, colonial. Its whitewashed walls were broken by wooden shutters, its balconies trimmed with wrought iron that curled like vines. A dozen torches stood ready along the entrance, their iron cages waiting for fire.

Inside, the air was cooler but no less heavy. Dark wood panelled every wall, polished until it gleamed in the lamplight. Oil paintings of hunting scenes stared down from gilt frames. The carpets were thick and patterned in deep reds and golds, muffling every step.

It felt like stepping into a gentlemen's club — the kind whispered about, the kind where power was exchanged in cigars and handshakes. The scent of leather and polish mingled with something faintly musky, as though too many secrets had been kept in these rooms for too long.

Maui had been ritual, primal, open to the sky and sea. Acapulco was different. Acapulco whispered of rules, of history, of traditions that would not be easily broken.

A servant in a white jacket guided me through the lobby, his eyes respectfully lowered. Men in linen suits lounged in deep armchairs, glasses of brandy in their hands, while women in silk gowns sat close enough that knees brushed. No one looked at me directly, but I felt every eye.

The corridor stretched long, lined with carved doors. When the servant stopped and opened mine, I stepped into a room that was no less opulent. A four-poster bed with heavy drapes. A writing desk with brass fittings. An armoire tall enough to swallow me.

The balcony doors were open, letting in the roar of the ocean.

And there, on the pillow, lay the card.

The Key had arrived with me.

✦✦✦

Acapulco
Chapter Two

The card lay on the pillow, the black velvet ribbon tied tight around it. My hands trembled a little as I pulled it free, the paper thick, the writing precise.

Tonight's game begins at midnight. You are to dress only in what is provided. You will be summoned when the bell sounds.

Beside the card lay a box, its lid sealed with wax. I broke it open and found lace and silk folded carefully within — stockings, suspenders, a bra so sheer it was almost nothing, a thong threaded with pearls.

I lifted each piece slowly, holding it against my skin. Black lace over my breasts, transparent enough to see the dark circle of my nipples. Pearls against my fingers, cool and obscene. The suspender clasps clicked as though they had been made for me alone.

For a moment, I laughed softly. It was not so different from the bags I had carried with me from London. The Key knew what I was. It knew what I had bought, what I had craved.

I stripped and dressed before the mirror. One by one, I tried each piece, watching myself change. The stockings gripped my thighs, the pearls pressed against my cunt with every movement, the bra made my breasts seem fuller, more demanding.

And yet — it was too neat. Too arranged.

I laid the Key's offerings across the bedspread, black lace spilling like shadows against the white sheets. Sheer bra, pearl thong, suspenders that would cling and command. Beautiful, yes. Erotic, certainly. But they weren't mine.

I turned instead to my suitcase and drew out the slip I had chosen a few days ago, the one I had bought with him in mind. Claret silk, cut low and narrow, thin straps sliding easily from my shoulders. It poured down my body like molten fire, hugging the waist, skimming my thighs.

In the mirror, I slipped it over my skin and let it settle. My nipples pressed against the silk, already tight. The neckline plunged low enough to reveal the valley between my breasts, the colour so bold it dared anyone to look away.

Still, something was missing.

I rolled on a pair of hold-up stockings, sheer as smoke, the deep lace bands gripping high on my thighs. I smoothed my hands slowly up each leg, watching how the fabric blurred my skin yet somehow made it seem more naked.

And then — the heels. Claret stilettos, the exact shade of the slip. Sharp, defiant, impossible to ignore. When I stood, the heels arched my back, pushed my breasts forward, lengthened my legs until I looked — not fifty-eight, not thirty-eight, not any age at all — but timeless.

I walked across the room, each step a click of authority against the wood, the silk of the slip whispering at my thighs. I felt dangerous. Alive.

The Key could dress me in its lace and pearls if it wished. But this — this was me.

Claret. Bold. Chosen.

When the bell tolled midnight, I would not be summoned like a doll dressed by others. I would step into Acapulco's games as the woman I had decided to be.

The time had come. A single, deep sound that rolled through the corridors like thunder.

The servant led me into the grand hall. The air was thick with polish, musk, and history, the high ceiling lost in shadow. Dark wood and towering bookshelves lined the walls, but in the centre, the feast glistened — fruit, meat, wine, all laid out like an offering.

And then I saw them.

Every guest. Every body. All dressed identically in sheer lace and pearls the Key had sent. They looked like an army of shadows — bound by uniform, stripped of individuality.

All but me.

I stood in claret silk, sheer stockings, and claret heels. The only splash of colour in a sea of black. Every head turned. Every eye judged.

The host's voice rose above the silence. Deep, rich, impossible to ignore.

"One among us has forgotten obedience. The Key provides, and she refuses. The Key commands, and she chooses."

A low murmur rippled through the hall, like the rumble of a storm. My breath caught.

"Then let her learn," he said. *"She will not eat tonight. She will be eaten."*

The words struck me like a lash.

Hands seized me, not cruel but firm, guiding me back against the long table. The claret slip was pulled up to my waist, baring me to the hall. My heels scraped against the wood as they spread my legs wide.

The first mouth descended — hot, hungry, merciless. A tongue drove deep, sucking, lapping, pulling gasps from my throat. Fingers pried me open further, pushing fruit into my cunt, slices of mango and orange shoved inside until the juice ran sticky down my thighs. Another mouth followed, devouring me, sucking the fruit from my cunt and chewing it before the crowd.

Laughter, moans, whispers filled the hall.

Hands tugged at my breasts, fingers pinched my nipples hard, lips bit at them until I cried out. Wine was poured over my chest, running down for others to lick away. My claret slip was soaked, clinging, ruined.

I was passed from mouth to mouth, cunt to tongue, fruit to lips, until I was shaking with humiliation and need. Every guest took a turn. Every mouth fed. Every eye devoured.

The host's voice rose again, sharp with command.

"And now she must give back what she has taken."

Cocks were freed, hard and waiting. My mouth was filled, then another cock pressed against my lips before the first had finished. Hot cum spilled across my face, my chest, my thighs, mingling with wine and fruit juice until I was sticky, dripping, trembling.

The hall roared with release. Women straddled men and came screaming, men groaned and spilled cum into eager mouths. I was dragged from one to the next, a feast made flesh, punished for daring to stand apart.

When it ended, I sagged against the table, legs trembling, silk ruined, hair wet with sweat and seed.

And still, from the far end of the hall, the host's eyes lingered on me.

"You are claret tonight," he said, almost softly. *"But next time, you will be black."*

The game was over.
The punishment had only begun.

I stumbled back to my suite, my heels dangling from my fingers, the claret slip torn and sticking wet to my body. My thighs ached, my breasts throbbed, my clit was raw. The scent of sex and fruit clung to me as though it had seeped into my skin.

The bath was already drawn — hot, steaming, laced with oils. I let the ruined slip fall to the floor and lowered myself in. The sting of the water against my swollen cunt made me hiss, but slowly it turned soothing, easing the ache, washing away the stickiness of cum and wine.

I closed my eyes and tried to steady my breath. The hall still swam in my head: the mouths, the hands, the host's voice. And beneath it all, the ache of wondering if he had watched, if he had touched, if he had judged me.

A sound cut the silence.

Soft. Deliberate.

Paper sliding against wood.

I froze, water lapping at my skin, and looked toward the door.

A towel clung to me as I stepped dripping from the bath. My bare feet left prints across the wooden floor as I bent, lifted the envelope from where it had been pushed under.

Not sealed. Just folded.

The handwriting was sharp, angled, unlike the elegant script of the Key's cards.

Claret was beautiful on you.
But claret also bleeds.
The question is… will you bleed for me again?

My breath caught.

It was not the Key's voice. Not the host's. This was different. More intimate. More dangerous.

I clutched the towel tighter around me, the words burning in my hand.

Him. It had to be him. The man from Maui, the one who had arranged it so I would win, the one who had licked oil and seed from my body as though I were sacred.

And yet — the script was harsher. The tone sharper.

Was it him?
Or someone else, hiding behind his shadow?

The card trembled in my fingers.

Acapulco was louder, harsher, unrelenting. And perhaps — it was already turning me against myself.

Acapulco
Chapter Three

I slept little.

The words on the card seemed to glow in the dark beside my bed, sharper than the cut of any lash. *Claret was beautiful on you. But claret also bleeds.*

I turned it over and over in my hands, comparing it to the cards I had received in Marrakesh, in Maui. The Key's script was elegant, measured, the kind of hand that brooked no question. This was not the same. This was jagged, intimate, a hand that wanted to dig beneath the skin.

'Was it him?'

The thought circled like a fever.

I had come to Acapulco for him, for his cock, his mouth, not for the games. I had told myself the truth in London as I slid silk and lace into shopping bags: I wanted his eyes on me, his hands on me, his cock inside my wet cunt. I had pictured it on the flight — romantic, inevitable, private. A secret apart from the Key.

But the Key was never designed for secrets.

The Key was designed for spectacle. For obedience. For games.

And I already knew — my arrival was confirmation enough — that I could not step aside, could not opt out, could not wait for him in quiet corners. I would participate. I would submit. Whether he revealed himself or not, whether he had written the note or it was another hand playing with my mind, I was caught.

Still, I obsessed. Clit tingling just at his thought.

I laid the cards beside each other, tracing the shapes of the letters with my finger. The angle of the "C" in Claret, so much sharper than the soft curl of “Cave” in Maui’s note. The almost violent slash of the “B” in Bleeds.

If it was him, he had changed.
If it was not, then someone else knew me too well.

I pressed the card to my lips, tasting the ink, breathing the words into me. My cunt clenched, aching.

The Key had stripped me bare in the hall, fed me to mouths, to cocks like I was nothing but meat. And still, I wanted him. Still, I clung to the fantasy that he might be different.

But Acapulco was not romance.
Acapulco was punishment.
And the Key would not allow me to forget it.

Acapulco
Chapter Four

The morning light fell pale through the shutters, striping the floor with bars of gold. I rose early, though I had hardly slept. My body still ached from the night's humiliation, my skin marked where mouths had pulled, where fingers had gripped, where seed had dried.

But it wasn't the soreness that drove me from the bed. It was the card. The sharp, slanted script that I still half-believed was his.

I wrapped myself in a light robe, slipped on sandals, and began to walk the corridors.

The manor was larger than it had seemed on arrival, a warren of carved staircases and endless wood-panelled halls. Each corner revealed another painting — stern men in uniforms, women in gowns, saints staring down with sorrowful eyes. The air smelled of polish and age, as though nothing had changed here in a hundred years.

I lingered by the library. Floor-to-ceiling shelves filled with leather-bound volumes, their spines cracked, their titles faded in gold. The silence was heavy, broken only by the tick of a grandfather clock. I imagined him here — leaning against the shelves, a book in his hands, waiting for me to notice.

But the room was empty.

In the courtyard, sunlight poured onto stone warmed by centuries. Servants moved quietly, their faces lowered, carrying trays of fruit and wine. I studied each of them, hoping for a flicker of recognition, a glance that lingered too long. None came.

By midday I had drifted into the garden — a maze of palms and bougainvillea, fountains trickling into marble basins. I walked slowly, touching the flowers, pretending to admire them, but all the while scanning, searching.

Every man I saw, I compared to the memory of him. The line of a jaw, the width of shoulders, the way a hand curled around a glass. None were him.

And yet, I felt him. I felt watched, measured, as though behind one of the shuttered windows, eyes followed my every step.

By late afternoon, I returned to the great hall. It was empty now, the tables cleared, the air still scented faintly of wine and musk. I stood at the centre, where they had spread me open the night before, and let my hands drift down over my thighs. My cunt clenched at the memory. My humiliation still throbbed — but so did my desire.

Was he here, watching even now?
Or had I imagined it all?

When I returned to my suite, another card awaited me.

This one in the Key's elegant script.

Tonight, obedience will not be asked.
It will be taken.

My breath caught.

Acapulco was not going to let me play hide-and-seek.
It was going to make me kneel.

✦✦✦

Acapulco
Chapter Five

The servant came for me just before midnight. He did not lead me toward the great hall, where I could already hear the muffled laughter and gasps of other guests, but down a narrow corridor lit only by torches.

At the end of it, a door waited. Heavy oak, carved with strange designs I could not place.

Inside lay the chamber.

Dark wood. Iron hooks fixed into the walls. Chains that rattled when the door closed behind me. And in the centre, draped across a chair, the costume.

The maid's dress weighed on me like a sentence. Thick cotton, high-necked, long-sleeved, pooling to the floor. It scratched my skin, clung in the heat, and turned every breath shallow. By the time the apron was tied around my waist, I already felt bound, smothered, silenced.

The card's words burned in my mind: *You refused what was given. Tonight, you will serve.*

The door opened.

They came in groups — men and women, naked, glistening, cocks already hard, cunts already wet. Their eyes locked on me, and I felt my cunt clench beneath the suffocating layers of cloth.

The first pulled me to my knees. My skirts fanned around me, my apron brushing the stone floor. His cock was thick, heavy, and he thrust it straight into my mouth without hesitation. My lips stretched, my throat gagged, the fabric muffling my gasps. He gripped my head hard, fucking my mouth until drool soaked my chin and dripped down into the apron.

Before he finished, another came behind me. My skirts were heaved up, my ass bared, and a cock slammed into me. The fabric pressed down on my back, heavy and suffocating, as I was fucked hard and deep. The weight of the dress trapped the heat until I was drenched in sweat, my breasts sticking to the bodice, my cunt flooded with every brutal thrust.

Then another cock pressed at my ass. I gasped, muffled by the cock still filling my mouth, as he forced himself in, stretching me wide, the pain searing, the fabric trapping every cry. I was double-filled, pounded from behind, gagged from the front, my body used like a vessel.

I came, hard, choking on it, cunt clenching, ass burning, drool and tears soaking the apron.

But there was no pause.

Hands hauled me up, bent me over a bench. The skirts were spread wide across my back, heavy, sticky now with seed. A woman climbed onto the table, her cunt pressed to my mouth. I licked desperately, tasting her wetness, sucking her clit while another cock hammered into me from behind. She screamed above me as she came, flooding my mouth, smearing her juices across my face.

Men surrounded me. Cocks slapped my cheeks, my breasts, rubbed against my ass. Hot cum spurted across my bodice, soaking the stiff cotton until it clung wet to my nipples. Another load hit my face, dripping down, streaking the high collar. My apron was stained with seed and saliva, dripping onto the stone floor.

They took turns. One in my cunt, one in my ass, one in my mouth. Then they changed, another pushed in, another used me. I was never empty, never free. My body convulsed with orgasm after orgasm, my cunt clenching until it hurt, my throat raw from swallowing, my ass stretched until I thought I would tear.

Women climbed over me, sitting on my face, smearing their wetness across my lips, tugging my nipples hard through the fabric. My breasts were pinched, bitten, twisted until I screamed into their cunts.

Men grunted, spilling inside me, pulling out to paint my body with cum that soaked into the heavy dress.

Hours passed. I lost count of how many.

The dress grew heavier with every release, soaked with sweat, wine, spit, and cum until it dragged at my shoulders, stuck to my thighs, clung suffocatingly between my legs. The apron was no longer white but stained a dark, filthy grey. My hair clung to my face, wet with sweat and seed.

And still they came.

On my face, in my mouth, between my tits, across my ass. The chamber floor was slick with their spend, the air thick with sex. My body shook with exhaustion, yet they wrung orgasms out of me again and again, until I was raw, sore, and trembling.

At last, when the final cock spilled across my back and the final woman came on my tongue, I collapsed to the floor. My skirts spread around me like a shroud, soaked and stinking of sex.

The servant stepped into the chamber, his voice cold, almost gentle.

"Now you understand. Disobedience is not a choice. It is a cost."

The others left, silent. I was alone, dripping, broken, bound in cloth that felt heavier than chains.

The Key had punished me.
And I knew — Acapulco had only just begun.

✦✦✦

Acapulco
Chapter Six

I woke late, the curtains drawn, the room heavy with stillness. My body ached in every joint, my cunt sore, my ass raw. When I shifted, the phantom weight of the maid's dress seemed to cling to me again, heavy, suffocating, reeking of what they had spilled into me.

I lay still, staring at the ceiling, and let the memories play.

The black hall of Marrakesh. My shame carried like a banner through the souk. The warehouse of shopkeepers, their seed drying on my skin as I walked through the airport. I had told myself then — 'stick to the rules and all will be fine.' The Key did not forgive indulgence. The Key punished arrogance.

And yet last night, I had broken that vow.

I had chosen claret over black. My colour, my will, my defiance. And the Key had answered with humiliation worse than Marrakesh. Not in spectacle, not in public, but in cloth. They had buried me in fabric until I was nothing but sweat, spit, and cum.

The disgust rose fresh even now. The dress had clung to me like skin, soaked in filth until I could no longer tell where my body ended and punishment began. Every inch of me had been taken, stained, smothered.

And still I had come. Again and again, until my body betrayed me.

I turned onto my side, clutching the sheets, and whispered aloud — to the room, to myself, to the Key.

"No more."

I would obey.

For the rest of Acapulco, I would follow every card, wear every garment, submit to every demand. No more defiance. No more claret.

And when the last game ended, when Acapulco released me, then I would rethink. The final city — Tokyo — loomed in my mind like a shadow. Could I endure it? Could I surrender again?

I pressed the sheets tight around me and closed my eyes.

One thing I knew:
I would not break the rules again.

✦✦✦

Acapulco
Chapter Seven

The card came at dusk, slid beneath my door as the candles were being lit in the corridors outside.

Tonight, you will not be played. You will observe.

I read it twice, tracing the familiar script with my fingers. Relief stirred — and suspicion with it. In Marrakesh, in Maui, in Acapulco's chamber, the Key had never let me rest. Why would it now?

Still, I obeyed.

At midnight, I was led to another wing of the manor, my heels echoing softly against the old tiled floor. The gallery lay ahead, long and high-ceilinged, with carved balconies overlooking a circle of cushions below. The air smelled faintly of oil and smoke, the heavy sweetness of candles burning in iron holders.

The other observers gathered with me — men and women already half-naked, their eyes shining with hunger. Cushions were laid out for us along the railing, thick and deep, as though we were meant not just to sit, but to recline, to surrender.

I settled against the cushions, my slip sliding loose at the straps. My body still ached from the punishment of the night before, but the sight below soon overwhelmed it.

On the floor, the players assembled. Naked, blindfolded, their hands bound behind their backs with silk cords. Servants positioned them in pairs and triads, mouths forced to mouths, cunts lowered onto faces, cocks pressed between lips.

And then the game began.

The first sound was a moan — long, low, helpless. It was followed by another, sharper, then the wet suck of lips taking in a cock, the slurp of tongues against cunts. A wheel of bodies moved beneath us, each one unable to guide, only to receive.

The gallery grew silent at first. All of us watched, our breath caught, our thighs clenching. Then — a hand slipped across my leg. A woman to my left, her eyes locked on the sight below, her fingers stroking slowly up my thigh until she brushed the silk between my legs.

I gasped, and she smiled without turning her head.

To my right, in the shadows, a man pressed closer. His cock was huge, already hard, brushing against my arm. Without words, I curled my fingers around him, stroking slowly, the heat of him pulsing against my palm.

Below, the cries rose higher. Blindfolded mouths gaped open, cocks erupted across chests, women squirted onto faces they couldn't see. The wheel turned, moans spilling into moans, until the hall itself seemed to vibrate with sound.

Around me, the gallery had dissolved into its own frenzy. Observers kissed hungrily, hands roaming over bodies, clothes abandoned. A woman knelt between my thighs, slipping the silk of my slip up, her tongue sliding over my cunt until I arched against the cushions. I gasped into the mouth of the man beside me, his tongue pushing into mine as I stroked him harder.

Someone else's hands found my breasts, pulling the straps down, squeezing, pinching, biting until I cried out. Seed spurted across my chest, dripping down, while the woman's tongue lapped greedily at my cunt.

I lost myself in the chaos. One moment filled by a cock in my mouth, thick and relentless, the next moaning against a woman's clit as she straddled my face. My hands never stopped — stroking, cupping, grasping, spilling seed over thighs, licking it from fingers, sharing it in kisses.

Everywhere, the gallery echoed the wheel below. Moans on moans, cries on cries, wet flesh against wet flesh. The air was thick with sex, the floor slick with sweat, the cushions stained with seed and juice.

When I finally came, it tore through me in waves, my cunt clenching hard against the tongue still buried there, my mouth filled with another's cum. I screamed into the mess of it, body jerking, hands clawing for more.

But the frenzy did not stop. Orgasms came like firecrackers — one igniting the next, bodies shaking, spilling, consuming each other until no one knew whose mouth, whose cock, whose cunt they had.

By the time the final moans drifted into silence, the gallery was a ruin of bodies. Limbs tangled, hair damp, chests heaving, seed streaking skin and fabric alike.

Below, the players sagged against each other, blindfolds wet, mouths swollen, their bodies spent.

Above, I lay trembling, the slip twisted and soaked, my thighs wet, my face sticky with seed and sweat.

I had been told to observe.
And I had.
But Acapulco had ensured that observation was its own form of surrender.

Back in my suite, the silence pressed down thick as velvet. I stripped away the slip, sticky with seed, and collapsed into the sheets. My body still trembled, my cunt sore from tongues and fingers, my lips swollen from cocks and kisses.

But in the haze of it all, one image refused to leave me.

The first cock I had taken in my hand.

Thick. Heavy. The girth filling my palm so completely I could barely close my fingers around it. Veins ridging up the shaft, pulsing under my skin, the head swollen and shining. The weight of it had thrilled me, a weapon alive in my grasp. His balls had been full and heavy, brushing against my wrist as I stroked him, promising a flood.

And when he had cum, oh God, when he had cum — the spurt had been violent, thick streams hitting my chest, my chin, dripping hot across my breasts until I was painted in him.

The memory alone made my cunt ache.

I slid my hand down, finding myself already wet, slippery from need. My fingers circled my clit, teasing slowly, while in my mind I pictured him again — his cock throbbing in my fist, the heavy weight of his balls slapping as he groaned, the way his seed had spilled without end.

I spread my thighs wider, pressing deeper, curling my fingers into myself, imagining it was his cock stretching me. Thick. Relentless. Filling me until I couldn't breathe.

I moaned into the pillow, grinding, my nipples hard against the sheets. My orgasm built fast, sharper than I expected, rushing through me in a hot, pulsing wave. I cried out as it broke, my body jerking, cunt clenching around nothing but my fingers, but in my head — in my head it was him.

I lay panting, hand still between my thighs, the sheets damp beneath me.

The gallery had been a frenzy, a storm of mouths and cocks and cunts. But this — this private hunger for one man, one cock — unsettled me more.

Because I wanted him again. Needed him.
And I didn't even know who he was.

✦✦✦

Acapulco
Chapter Eight

I could still feel him in my hand.

The thickness. The weight. The ridges of vein pressing into my palm. The swollen head leaking as I stroked him. The way his balls had dragged heavy against my wrist before he had erupted across my chest, marking me, painting me.

It had been him.
It had to be him.

I had fucked him in Maui. I had memorised the stretch, the girth, the way his cum poured like a flood. My cunt clenched even now at the memory, as though reaching for him again.

I knew him not by face, not by name, but by cock.

And Acapulco had shown him to me again.

I dressed lightly, ignoring the soreness between my thighs, and wandered the manor's halls. The corridors seemed endless, lined with portraits of forgotten men, the air smelling of polish and dust. Servants passed with their eyes lowered. Guests drifted in silks and robes, speaking softly in corners.

I searched them all.

Every glance, every body, I measured against my memory of him. Broad shoulders, greying hair, the way he held a glass, the curve of a hand. But I could not be sure. Not without seeing him stripped, hard, full, ready to spill.

I lingered in the courtyard, where fountains trickled and bougainvillea spilled like blood over the walls. I thought perhaps he would appear there, leaning in the shade, waiting for me as he had in Maui.

He did not.

I circled the gardens, the paths winding beneath palms and hibiscus. The heat pressed against me, sweat running down my back, my thighs sticky with the memory of last night's lust. Every archway, every bench, every shadowed alcove — I imagined him waiting, cock hard, ready to pull me into silence and fill me until I screamed.

But the gardens were empty.

By late afternoon, I returned to the gallery. It was quiet now, cushions straightened, railings wiped clean, the wheel of blindfolded bodies nothing but an echo. I touched the place where I had sat, where I had held him, and pressed my thighs together as my cunt pulsed again.

It was him.
It had to be.

But if it was, why did he not claim me? Why had he let me stroke him in shadow, cum faceless onto my breasts, then disappear again?

I returned to my suite with no answers, only need.

When I pushed open the door, another card lay waiting.

Tonight, you will not hunt. Tonight, you will be hunted.

I shivered.

If it was him, he would find me.

If it was not, then Acapulco was about to show me what being prey truly meant.

✦✦✦

Acapulco
Chapter Nine

The card's words haunted me as I dressed: *Tonight, you will not hunt. Tonight, you will be hunted.*

The servant collected me at midnight, his torch flickering as he led me through the manor's labyrinthine halls. I wore what had been left folded across my bed: a sheer black shift, light as smoke, clinging to my skin, leaving nothing hidden. My hair was unpinned, tumbling loose, my feet bare.

We stopped at a door I had never seen before — heavy oak, its iron handle shaped like a snarling lion. The servant did not meet my eyes as he opened it.

Inside was darkness.

The air smelled of wax and dust, of wood warmed by centuries. I stepped forward. The door closed behind me with a heavy clunk.

Silence.

For a moment, nothing. Then — footsteps. Soft. Careful.

My heart raced. I moved quickly, the shift clinging to my thighs as I slipped through narrow corridors I had not walked before. Arched ceilings, tall windows black against the night, staircases that spiralled downward into shadow. Every sound echoed — my own breath, the whisper of fabric, the creak of floorboards.

I was prey.

And I was being stalked.

The silence broke with the faintest of sounds — leather brushing stone, a breath released too quickly. I turned sharply, pressing against the wall, chest heaving. My nipples hardened against the thin fabric, my cunt already wet.

The hunt was as arousing as the promise.

I slipped into a smaller passage, lit faintly by torches. Shadows stretched long, curling into corners. I padded quickly, then froze — a figure loomed ahead, tall, broad, unmoving.

I spun, running back the way I came, my pulse hammering. Another figure emerged behind me. My bare feet slapped against the stone. The shift clung to me as though dragging me down.

Then — a hand. Strong. Seizing my wrist. Another arm circling my waist, pulling me back hard against a chest.

I gasped, twisted, but the grip was relentless. My back was pushed against the wall, the stone cold, my breath stolen from me.

And then I felt it.

Pressed against my thigh. Thick. Hard. Alive.

The cock.

The cock I had held in my hand in the gallery. The cock I had been split by in Maui.

Recognition tore through me. My cunt clenched violently, wetness spilling down my thighs. My body arched toward it, even as my mind screamed that I should resist.

A hand forced my shift up, baring my cunt to the cool air. Another hand clamped over my mouth, silencing my gasp.

And then he entered me.

Thick. Relentless. Stretching me wide until I cried into his palm. My body gave instantly, my cunt gripping him, sucking him deeper.

It was him.
It had to be him.

Every vein, every ridge, every thrust was memory. The heavy weight of his balls slapped against me, his cock pulsing as it drove into me harder and harder. The stone wall scraped my back through the thin fabric, but all I could feel was him.

He took me mercilessly — not tender, not slow. A predator claiming prey. His cock slammed into me until I thought I would split, my body convulsing with each thrust, orgasm clawing at me too quickly, too violently.

I came hard, my scream muffled by his hand. My cunt squeezed around him, milking him, begging for his seed.

He growled low against my ear, and with one final thrust he spilled into me. Hot. Endless. Flooding.

I shook against him, trembling, pinned by cock, by hand, by the sheer weight of being taken.

When he pulled out, his seed dripped hot down my thighs, soaking the stone beneath us.

The hand left my mouth.

But when I opened my eyes — he was gone.

Only the dark remained.

Only the ache in my cunt, the wet dripping between my thighs, the undeniable knowledge that it had been him.

And yet — no face. No voice. Only cock.

I leaned against the cold stone, legs trembling, my cunt dripping with the proof of him. The throbbing still echoed inside me, the heat of his cum slicking my thighs. I thought the hunt was over.

But I was wrong.

Footsteps. Not his. Not one pair — many. Slow, deliberate, circling closer.

The game was still in play.

What had just happened — that cock, his cock — had been something else. His own intrusion. His own claiming. The Key's game had not yet ended.

Shadows moved along the corridor walls. A torch flared. And then they came.

Three men, naked, hard, eyes gleaming. Two women behind them, breasts bare, lips wet as though already tasting what was about to happen.

I stumbled back, but there was nowhere to run.

They descended on me silently. My shift was yanked higher, my arms pinned above my head. A cock pressed into my mouth before I could protest, filling me, gagging me. Another slid into my cunt, pushing through the slick mess left by him, fucking me deeper, harder, my body forced open again.

The third gripped my hips, forcing my ass to spread, his cock pushing at me until I screamed around the one filling my throat. Pain flared, sharp, relentless — then gave way to shuddering heat as I was taken from every angle at once.

Hands clawed at my breasts through the thin fabric, fingers pinching and twisting my nipples until I cried out. A woman's mouth latched onto one, sucking hard, while the other knelt between my thighs to lick the cum that dripped out around the cock pounding into me.

I was prey. Prey split wide, filled, smothered, used.

They came in waves. One spilling across my chest, another into my throat, another deep into my cunt. When one cock pulled out, another replaced it, cocks hard and endless, mouths hungry. The women took their turns too — straddling my face, riding my tongue until they screamed, then holding me down so the men could fuck deeper, harder, rougher.

The shift clung to me, soaked with sweat and seed, my body burning beneath it.

I lost count of how many times I came. My orgasms ripped through me, raw, violent, helpless, until I was shaking, my thighs numb, my cunt aching.

The hunt did not end until every one of them had spilled — over my breasts, across my stomach, dripping down my thighs, pooling on the stone floor beneath me.

At last, they left me there. Used. Stained. The Key's prey, hunted and consumed.

I lay back against the wall, my body wrecked, my cunt still dripping with him and with them.

Two hunts.
One his.
One theirs.

And neither gave me peace.

I wandered, barefoot, through the narrow corridors, my thighs slick, my cunt aching, my skin sticky with seed. The stone walls twisted into a maze, one hallway bleeding into the next, I no longer knew where I was.

The air grew cooler. The silence deeper. And then — a doorway opened into moonlight.

I stepped through and gasped.

A clearing stretched out before me, hidden within the manor's labyrinth. Tall palms bowed over a pool of water fed by a trickling fall of stone. A freshwater lake, still and silver in the moonlight, its surface barely disturbed by the cascade.

Without thought, I stripped the soaked shift from my body. It fell heavy to the ground, stained with sweat and cum, an offering abandoned. Naked at last, I stepped into the water.

It was cold, shockingly so, and I shivered as it closed over my bruised thighs, my swollen breasts, my raw cunt. I sank deeper, ducking beneath, letting the water wash away the filth, the stink, the shame.

For a moment, I floated. Weightless. Free.

When I emerged, gasping, hair slick against my shoulders, I felt almost clean again.

Almost.

On the bank, beside my discarded shift, something had been placed.

A card. A small vial of oil.

I froze, water dripping down my skin. My heart thudded in my chest.

I emerged from the lake, body bare, wet in the moonlight. My fingers shook as I reached for the card.

The same elegant script stared back at me.

I saw you bathe.
The water kissed what I have already claimed.
Rub this into your skin, and know it is my touch you spread.
I will always find you, even when you do not seek me.

I held the vial to my nose. A rich, intoxicating fragrance spilled out — musky, floral, threaded with spice. My cunt clenched instantly, my clit tingled, the ache returning, the memory of his cock filling me still raw inside me.

It had been him. He had been here. Watching.

Watching me strip, watching me wade in naked, watching me wash myself clean of others while still belonging to him.

The oil glistened in the moonlight.

I pressed it to my skin, slicking my shoulders, my breasts, my nipples., my thighs, my cunt. The fragrance curled around me, warm, consuming, as though his hands guided mine.

And for the first time that night, I did not feel prey.
I felt possessed.

✦✦✦

Acapulco
Chapter Ten

The servants said nothing as they led me back through the labyrinth. Their torches flickered along the stone, their footsteps soft, their faces unreadable. I clutched the card in my hand, fingers trembling, the fragrance of the oil still clinging to my skin.

Back in my suite, I collapsed onto the bed, hair damp from the lake, thighs slick from the oil, the card lying open beside me.

I saw you bathe.
The water kissed what I have already claimed.
Rub this into your skin, and know it is my touch you spread.
I will always find you, even when you do not seek me.

I read it again. And again.

Every word pulled me deeper. He was everywhere now — in the corridors, in the gardens, in the shadows that crept across the ceilings. He was in the weight of the sheets against my breasts, in the pulse of my clit when I shifted my thighs.

He had become intoxicating.
An obsession.

I closed my eyes, the oil's fragrance surrounding me, and I saw him not as a faceless cock, not as the shadow in Maui, not as the hunter in Acapulco. I saw him as mine.

My partner. My lover.

It wasn't the games that haunted me now — not the wheel of blindfolded bodies, not the hunt, not the punishment in the maid's dress. It was him.

And not even him as he had taken me — rough, silent, hidden. But him as he could be.

I imagined us at breakfast, the ordinary kind, a small café tucked into some forgotten street. He'd reach for the sugar and brush his fingers deliberately against mine. He wouldn't look, not right away, but I'd feel the charge run up my arm, the kind that left my nipples stiff under my blouse. Later, he'd lean close to taste my coffee from my cup, his lips still wet when he placed it back down.

I imagined walking through a busy market, sunlight thick overhead, people pressing on every side. And suddenly his hand would slide into mine, not gentle but firm, a silent 'you're mine.' No one would notice, but I'd feel it everywhere — in the pit of my stomach, in the throb between my legs. He wouldn't let go until we'd turned a corner and he pressed me into a wall, just long enough to kiss me so hard the taste of spice and sweat blurred into him.

I imagined us at a dinner party — others laughing, drinking, oblivious — while his hand slipped beneath the tablecloth. His fingers would part me, stroke me, tease me until I squirmed and bit my lip to keep from moaning. And when I thought I'd burst, he'd withdraw and raise the same fingers to his mouth, licking me clean before joining the conversation as though nothing had happened.

Even ordinary nights at home filled my fantasies. He'd read while I pretended to watch television, and then, without warning, he'd press his hand to the back of my neck, tilting me into a kiss that left me dizzy. His cock would already be hard, tenting his trousers, and he'd unzip himself, sliding inside me while we were still on the sofa, still half-dressed, his thrusts slow, claiming, never in a hurry.

Little gestures. Small moments. But they pierced me deeper than the games.

Because they weren't about rules, or cards, or punishments. They were about him choosing me, in silence, in shadows, in the everyday.

And the more I imagined, the more dangerous it became.

He wasn't just part of the Key anymore.
He was becoming my world.

Sleep carried me under, the card still on my bedside, the oil still fragrant on my skin.

And then he was there.

Not faceless this time, not shadow. He was presence, power. His hand gripped my hair and pulled my head back until I gasped. A leather collar clicked shut around my throat, the weight of it pulling me down. I was his.

Chains hung from the walls. He fastened my wrists, spread me wide, my nipples straining, my cunt exposed and glistening in the candlelight.

"Mine," he said. Just one word, but it burned through me.

He struck my breast, sharp, stinging, making me cry out. Then again, harder. My skin flushed red beneath his palm, my nipples swelling, aching for more. I begged without words, writhing against the chains, desperate to be touched, to be used.

He didn't wait. His hand slid down, fingers plunging into my cunt, stretching me open. His thumb ground against my clit until I sobbed, begging, trembling.

Then he withdrew, leaving me empty, slick, needy.

"On your knees."

The chains released, and I dropped instantly, without thought. My mouth found his cock as though it had always belonged there. Thick, veined, pulsing. I swallowed him, deeper, deeper, until he filled my throat, choking me, tears streaming down my cheeks. He held me there, his cock lodged in my throat, my nose pressed against his body. I struggled for breath, and still I wanted more.

When he pulled free, I gasped, drool streaking my chin. He wiped it with his cock and smeared it across my lips.

"Good girl."

He bent me forward, pushing into my cunt hard, relentless, his balls slapping my thighs. The sting of his strikes still burned on my skin as his cock drove me into the floor. I cried out, each thrust breaking me further open, each stroke pulling me deeper into him.

And then he flipped me, spread my legs wide, and pressed his cock into my ass. Pain flared sharp, but I welcomed it, begged for it. "Yes—yes, please, fuck me, take me, use me." He filled me until I thought I would split, then drove harder, punishing thrusts that left me sobbing, gasping, desperate for him never to stop.

Every command, I obeyed. Every strike, I craved. Every filthy act, I gave myself to.

I was nothing but his vessel, his toy, his slave. And the more he degraded me, the more I wanted him.

He finished by grabbing my hair, forcing me to look up at him, told me to open my mouth as his piss cascaded down my throat, spraying my checks, forehead, nose and tits, then almost immediately his cum spilled across my face, hot, endless, painting me in him. I licked it from my lips, swallowed it eagerly, smiling even as it dripped from my chin.

"Whatever I ask," he murmured, cock still twitching against my cheek, "whatever I want, you will give."

"Yes," I whispered, voice hoarse, tears still wet. "Always. Anything."

In the dream, I meant it.

When I woke, trembling, my sheets were wet, my thighs slick. My body throbbed with the aftershocks of orgasm.

And in my heart, I knew: I would do it all awake.

Not because the Key demanded it.
But because he did.

✦✦✦

Acapulco
Chapter Eleven

I woke with a start, the sheets damp beneath me, my skin clammy with sweat. My heart thudded as though I had been running. For a moment, I didn't know where I was — Acapulco, the Key, the games — or the dream.

The dream.

I pressed a hand to my face, and shame burned hot.

I had dreamed of him binding me, striking me, humiliating me until I cried. And I had begged for it. Begged. I had swallowed his filth as though it were wine, welcomed every punishment, offered every hole.

Even now, awake, my cunt clenched at the memory.

I turned in the sheets, disgust curling in my chest. What kind of woman dreamed of that? What kind of woman wanted to be broken, degraded, owned?

I told myself I hoped he wasn't like that in truth. That in reality he would be tender, gentle, a lover who could soothe as much as he could claim. That my dream was just the Key's corruption, not him.

But something deeper whispered otherwise.

Because when I thought of him — the cock I had known in Maui, the cock I had stroked in Acapulco, the cock that had hunted me in the corridors — my cunt warmed again.

A part of me craved him to be exactly as he was in the dream. Demanding. Cruel. Merciless.

Because only then could I surrender fully.

I sat up, pressing the heel of my hand between my thighs, hating myself for the slick heat I found there. My body betrayed me, and worse, it told me the truth I couldn't admit aloud:

I wanted him not in spite of the darkness.
I wanted him because of it.

The dream clung to me like a bruise, deep and sore. Even after bathing, even after scrubbing myself until my skin tingled raw, I could not wash it away.

The images returned again and again — the collar at my throat, his hand striking my breasts, his cock choking me until tears streaked my cheeks. And worst of all, the way I had begged for more.

I wanted to believe it was only a dream. Only a fantasy twisted by the Key. But what if it wasn't? What if that was who he truly was — not saviour, not lover, but a man who would use me until I was nothing?

The thought left a cold weight in my chest. For the first time since Maui, I found myself almost hating him.

So I asked the servants to take me out into the town.

The car wound through Acapulco's streets, the world outside bursting with colour and noise. Market stalls spilled with bright fabrics, painted masks, fruits piled high and glistening. The air smelled of lime, grilled meat, sea-salt. Children darted through alleys, their laughter sharp as bells.

I walked among them, wrapped in a light dress, sunglasses hiding my eyes. A servant lingered always a step behind, unobtrusive but watchful. A bodyguard, I realised, though dressed as staff.

I tried to focus on the normal.

I bought trinkets: a carved wooden bird, a silver bracelet shaped like waves, a shawl of turquoise silk. I tasted sweet bread dusted with sugar, let the juice of a mango drip down my wrist. I bartered half-heartedly, laughed politely, let myself pretend I was simply another tourist passing through.

And for a while, it worked.

The dream faded to a dull echo. My steps grew lighter, my smile more real. I breathed in the scent of flowers spilling from clay pots, the brine of the ocean drifting in from beyond the cliffs. I let the colours distract me, the noise overwhelm me.

But then — a glance.

A man in a doorway, watching. Not remarkable, not unusual. But the way his gaze lingered, steady and unreadable, sent a shiver up my spine.

Was it him?

I turned quickly, forcing myself back into the press of the market, back into colour and chatter and life. But no matter how many stalls I passed, no matter how many bracelets I slipped over my wrist, the shadow of him followed.

By the time I returned to the manor, arms full of souvenirs, the dream had shifted again. From guilt, to fear, back to the quiet throb of wanting.

I hated him for what he was in the dream.
And I craved him for it all the same.

✦✦✦

Acapulco
Chapter Twelve

The card had said only: *No games tonight. Food, wine, and company.*

I felt a strange relief when I read it. Relief, and perhaps a flicker of disappointment. After the dream, after the hunt, after the day in town, my body still overflowed with need — but my mind longed for stillness.

The great hall was transformed. Chandeliers cast a mellow glow, candles softening the shadows. Long tables glittered with silver platters and crystal glasses: roasted meats fragrant with spice, bowls of mango and papaya, baskets of breads still warm. Decanters of deep red wine glowed in the candlelight.

The guests wore silk and linen, elegant but revealing. Men in open shirts, their chests bare beneath the fabric. Women in gowns slit to the hip or falling from one shoulder, breasts half-exposed, skin glowing with oil. No one was fully dressed. No one was fully naked. It was decadence made into clothing.

I entered cautiously, shawl draped around me, and was greeted with warm smiles and raised glasses.

"Ah, Marrakech," a voice said as I passed. I turned to see a woman with sharp cheekbones and eyes lined in kohl. She tapped her glass against mine. "I remember your face. You were there, weren't you?"

Heat rushed to my cheeks. I nodded, trying to mask my reaction.

She smiled knowingly. "The night of the crosses. Half the hall could hardly walk afterwards. I still see the bruises when I bathe." Her laugh was low, dark, amused.

'Had she remembered I refused that game? Was she toying with me?'

Across the table, a man leaned in. His accent was Eastern European, his eyes playful. "Rome," he said simply, as if offering me a confession. "The labyrinth of mirrors. You remember? Everyone inside their own reflection, never knowing who was real."

I swallowed, my throat dry. "I remember," I whispered. I had not seen him there, but now the fragments connected — the glint of his hair in candlelight, the curve of his shoulders in the shadows.

"And Dubai," another guest chimed in, a woman in a silk gown the colour of emerald. "The pool of pearls. How many were spilled in the water that night? How many swallowed whole?" She laughed, tilting her glass to her lips.

I listened, drank, and joined where I could. For the first time, I did not feel like an outsider — not entirely. These people had bled, groaned, cum and cried in other cities just as I had. The Crimson Key was bigger than me. Bigger than Maui. Bigger than Acapulco.

And yet, in their words, I caught something else. A glance that lingered too long. A pause before laughter. A shadow behind the sparkle of memory.

It wasn't only me who carried scars.

Later, I found myself seated beside a man I thought I recognised. His eyes were steady, his voice quiet. "You were in Rome," he said, as though it were a certainty.

"Yes."

He leaned closer. "Do you ever wonder if the games are truly random? Or if someone always chooses for each of us?"

My pulse quickened. His question dug too close to my own obsession. I looked away, sipping my wine.

Around me, the night blurred into laughter, food, flirtation. Guests touched casually, a hand lingering too long on a thigh, lips brushing a shoulder. Some drifted into alcoves together, their whispers softening into moans.

I left before the wine emptied, before the laughter grew careless.

From my balcony, I could still hear the faint notes of a violin, the murmur of voices. The night was alive below me, but I wrapped my shawl tighter and turned away.

There had been no games tonight.

And yet, in every word spoken, in every look exchanged, I felt the Key's shadow.

No games, the card had said.

But there were always games.

✦✦✦

Acapulco
Chapter Thirteen

The card was waiting when I woke, tucked into the folds of my shawl.

One more day. One more night.
Prepare yourself for the piñata.

I stared at the words, my breath shallow. The piñata. In childhood, it was laughter, colour, sweet prizes spilling to the ground. But in Acapulco, under the Key, I knew it would be nothing innocent.

The pool was cool, the tiles warm beneath my bare feet, the sun pressing down like gold. I thought the last day might be peaceful. A day around the pool of stillness before the final night.

But he appeared.

At first, I thought he was harmless — a man in his late fifties, broad-shouldered, balding and a smile that was too quick, too eager. He drifted near my lounger, wine glass in hand, asking questions that had no weight: 'where are you from? how are you enjoying Acapulco? have you played many of the games?'

I gave polite answers, my shawl drawn close, my eyes on my book. But he lingered.

Hours passed, and still he was there. Moving when I moved, leaning in too close, his laughter forced, his gaze crawling over me in a way that soured the heat of the day.

"I'm not interested," I said finally, sharper than I intended. But he only smiled wider.

By late afternoon, I'd had enough, my skin prickled not from the sun, but from the weight of him. He was relentless, like a wasp that couldn't be swatted.

I left the pool early, retreating through the corridors, my sandals clicking against the tiles. I locked my door, my heart pounding, pressing my back to the wood as though he might still be outside.

I thought of him, the one I wanted, the one I feared. The difference between them was a knife's edge — one I felt in my body, but not yet in my mind.

✦✦✦

Acapulco
Chapter Fourteen

The lanterns glowed low, shadows swallowing the great hall. Chains rattled, ropes swayed from beams. The card had promised *The Piñata.*

We were blindfolded one by one, strips of black silk tied firm across our eyes. My breath came shallow, every sound sharpening — the shuffle of feet, the creak of rope, the soft groans of bodies already being secured above.

Then something was pressed into my hand. A switch — smooth wood wrapped in leather at the tip. I swallowed hard. Around me, others shifted, gripping their own weapons.

A drumbeat began — slow, steady, commanding.

On the first beat, I swung. The switch met flesh with a sharp crack. A gasp rang out — high-pitched, feminine. The sound shot straight to my cunt, heat blooming as I realised I had struck a woman's breast.

Another beat. Another swing. This time a grunt, low and guttural, unmistakably male. The switch had landed across a cock or thigh, and the man moaned as though pain and pleasure had fused into one.

The air filled with the symphony of it: cracks of leather, cries of surprise, groans of hunger. I swung again, and again, each blow finding new flesh — nipples stiffening, cocks swelling, cunts growing wetter with every strike.

Someone struck me too, the lash snapping across my hip, the sting sharp and sudden. I gasped, half in shock, half in pleasure. Blindfolded, there was no defence, no anticipation — only surrender.

The beat quickened.

Cries turned into moans. The air thickened with the smell of sweat, musk, arousal. Flesh slapped against flesh as the bound guests began to grind, to thrust, to rub themselves raw against rope and air, desperate for release.

I struck harder, surer now, aiming low. My switch met the thick length of a cock, and the man's cry broke into a groan as his cum spurted hot, dripping down his thighs.

A cheer rose. A climax. The piñata had been broken open.

Others followed. A woman squealed as lashes rained across her breasts, her juices spilling down her legs. Another man shouted, hips jerking as his cock erupted, painting his stomach. Each orgasm was met with applause, with laughter, with the pounding rhythm of the drum.

I was wet beneath my slip, my nipples straining, my cunt aching to be struck, filled, used. The sting of leather on my own skin mixed with the thrill of striking others — of breaking them open, of coaxing out their treasure.

Blindfolded, lost in heat, I didn't know where the next blow would land. A cunt? A cock? A breast? A thigh? It didn't matter. Every cry fed the fire in me. Every moan made my clit throb harder.

By the time the drum slowed, the hall reeked of sex — sweat, cum, the copper tang of blood where lashes had broken skin. Bodies hung shuddering in their ropes, seed and wetness glistening in the candlelight.

The first part of the game was over.

The piñatas had been struck, and they had spilled themselves for us all.

The blindfolds were removed.

The hall shimmered with heat and sex. Guests sagged in their ropes, dripping, trembling, spent. The floor was slick with seed, with wetness, with the perfume of arousal and pain. Applause faded into silence, then into a hush that settled like smoke.

The servants cleared the ropes quickly, efficiently. Harnesses were unbuckled, bound bodies gently carried away, leaving the space in the centre bare.

And then they brought him in.

The man from the pool.

Naked, dragged by two attendants, his wrists bound behind him. His eyes darted, his mouth worked soundlessly. He looked nothing like the smug figure who had lingered by my lounger, smiling as though I were his prize. Now he was prey, and the hall was the hunter.

They fastened him to a wooden contraption — a frame that rotated slowly, exposing every inch of him. His chest, his thighs, his cock, his back. Vulnerable. Defenceless.

The drumbeat began again.

But this time, no blindfolds.

A servant stepped forward with a whip — not the thin switches from before, but a heavy, braided lash, thick enough to tear. The crack split the hall. The man cried out, twisting in his bindings.

Another crack. His chest. Then his thigh. His cock jerked in fear.

The whip sang across his flesh, strike after strike, the sound brutal, the welts rising angry and red. His cries echoed against the high ceilings, but the guests did not laugh this time. They watched in silence, glasses in hand, faces unreadable.

I couldn't move. My body trembled, my cunt wet in spite of the horror curling in my chest.

Only I knew why.

Only I knew what he had done — the pool, the hours of pestering, the way he ignored every 'No!'

Was this his punishment? Was this for me?

I searched the shadows at the edge of the hall, half-believing, half-hoping. Was He here? Watching me watch? Had He seen the man that day, had He arranged this, had He whispered to the Key that arrogance deserved blood?

The whip cracked again, this time across the man's back. Flesh split. Blood trickled, glistening dark in the candlelight.

Gasps rose from some of the guests. Others touched themselves quietly, as though cruelty itself was enough to stir their lust.

The man sagged, his head falling forward, his groans turning into broken whimpers. Still the lash fell. Again. Again. Until his body was striped with welts and red.

Finally, the drum slowed. The contraption spun one last time, deliberate, displaying his ruined flesh to every guest.

Then the servants wheeled him away into the shadows, his cries fading, his body gone.

The silence that followed was suffocating.

I sat frozen, my heart hammering, my cunt throbbing, my mind reeling.

The Crimson Key did not forgive disobedience.
And perhaps neither did He.

I didn't know if He had been there. I didn't know if He had ordered this.

But I felt His hand in it.
And I knew — He had seen me.

✦✦✦

Acapulco
Chapter Fifteen

I returned to my suite unsteady on my legs.

The echoes of the whip followed me through the corridors, sharp in my ears, sharper still in my cunt. The man's cries, the crack of leather, the final sag of his body before the shadows swallowed him — it played again and again, as if burned into my skin.

My hands shook as I undressed. I wanted to wash, to scrub the night from me. But when I opened the bathroom door, I stopped.

A card lay on the counter.

Not slipped beneath the door. Not left on the bed. Placed where only I would find it, where I would see it before I touched the bath.

I picked it up with trembling fingers.

The Key sees. The Key knows.
You were right to refuse him.
Not all punishments belong to you.

No signature. No mark. Only the faintest trace of fragrance — the same oil that had been left by the lake, the scent that clung to Him.

He had chosen. He had judged. He had punished.

I had told myself he was just another guest, a man lost in the games like me. But no. He had influence. He had power. Perhaps even control.

The thought thrilled me. And terrified me.

If he could bend the games themselves, what else could he command? The servants? The cards? The guests?

And then came the darker questions.

Was I the only one he watched? Had I been singled out from the start? Or was I one of many?

Were there others, women in other cities, who felt his eyes on their skin, who dreamed of him, who carried his scent on a secret card? I had seen him with other women in Maui. Did he spread his attention like the Key spread its games, or had he truly chosen me?

My mind spiralled, drowning in the thought of him.

I imagined him with another — his cock inside a stranger, his lips pressing words of control into her ear, his hand writing messages like the one I now held. My cunt clenched at the image, a hot stab of jealousy burning through me.

I wanted to be the only one. His obsession, his choice, his prize.

And yet… wasn't that part of his power? That I could never know. That I could never claim him. That I could only surrender and hope he would keep looking at me, keep wanting me, keep punishing me when I strayed.

The card trembled in my hands. I pressed it against my lips, then lower, against my damp cunt, letting the paper grow wet with me.

I whispered into the dark:

"Who are you?"

No answer came. Only the silence of the suite, heavy and suffocating, broken by the faint thrum of the ocean against the cliffs.

But I knew he had heard. Somewhere, somehow, he always did.

That night, sleep did not come easily. The card lay on the bedside table, its words etched into my mind. My body ached, my cunt slick even after a long bath, but my thoughts circled endlessly.

Was he protecting me? Punishing the man from the pool because he had seen what I endured?
Or was he controlling me? Marking me as his possession, reminding me that every move I made was under his gaze?

The questions tangled into knots as I drifted at last into uneasy sleep.

And then he was there.

Not in the shadows this time. Not a faceless presence. Him. Strong, towering, his eyes unreadable. His hand against my throat, not cruel, but claiming. His body pressing mine into the mattress, my legs spread helplessly beneath him.

"Mine," he whispered against my ear, and the word sank into me like heat.

I wanted to fight. I wanted to yield. Both at once. My dream-body arched, my cunt wet, my clit aching as his cock pushed inside me, thick and relentless. Every thrust blurred the line between protection and possession — between being cherished and being owned.

In one moment, he held me tenderly, shielding me from unseen threats. In the next, he was merciless, fucking me so hard I screamed, his grip firm, his pace brutal.

The dream shifted, flickered. I was tied, blindfolded, whipped — yet at the same time I was cradled, kissed, soothed. Both truths at once, both unbearable and irresistible.

And still, through it all, I was wet.

I woke gasping, the sheets damp, my cunt throbbing as though he had been there in the flesh. One hand slid between my thighs before I could stop it, fingers circling into my cunt. Sliding in and out, in and out faster until my hands became a blur. The other hand on my clit, thumb circling then grinding at it, viciously faster and faster both hands working my body into a trembling frenzy. My orgasm ripped through me fast, violently, raw, leaving me shivering, whispering his name into the dark though I didn't even know it.

When I lay back, fully spent, the card on the table seemed to watch me. His words echoed still:

Not all punishments belong to you.

But the arousal belonged to me.
And it was his doing.

I drifted back into a restless sleep, cunt still slick, clit throbbing, body still aching, knowing Acapulco had marked me forever.

✦✦✦

Acapulco
Chapter Sixteen

I woke early, restless. My suitcase was already packed, my shawl folded neatly at the foot of the bed, but my body refused to calm.

My flight was at one o'clock. *One o'clock.* That meant leaving the manor no later than eleven if I were to reach the airport, check in, pass through security. I knew the routine; I had done it a hundred times before.

But the clock crept past ten, and still I had not been called.

No knock at the door, no servant appearing with the usual gentle, "Señora, the car awaits." Nothing. Only silence, only the distant echo of the waves against the cliffs.

By half past ten, my nerves were raw. I paced the suite, my heels tapping across the tiles. "Ridiculous," I muttered. "Absolutely ridiculous. They know my flight. They must know."

At quarter to eleven, my irritation swelled into anger. "I'll be late," I hissed aloud. "Missed flights, new tickets… chaos."

Eleven came and went.

Still, no one came for me.

By half past eleven, I was nearly trembling. I pictured the lines at the airport, the stares, the endless waiting. I pictured the humiliation of explaining myself, of standing there in crumpled clothes while the eyes of other passengers glarred.

I wrapped my shawl around me and marched towards the door, ready to find someone, anyone, to demand answers. My hand touched the brass handle —

And then, at last, a knock.

"Your car is ready, Señora," came the soft voice of a servant.

I bit back my anger, though it seared me still. It was already midday. I would be late. I gathered my hand bag, my patience stretched thin, and followed them through the hushed corridors.

Outside, the staff were waiting. They stood in two neat lines on either side of the gravel path, bowing slightly as I passed. It was a farewell as formal as it was unsettling — eyes lowered, hands folded, their silence heavy.

I gave them no smile. I was too agitated. My mind spun with the time, the minutes lost, the thought of boarding gates closing before I arrived.

The car door shut behind me, and we pulled away. The engine hummed. The city's outskirts unfolded, crowded streets, horns blaring, the colours of Acapulco rushing past the window.

By now it was twelve. Only one hour until departure. My fingers drummed against my knee, my irritation rising with every turn of the wheel. "This is madness," I muttered. "Absolutely madness."

And then the car veered off.

Not towards the main terminal. Not towards the queues of passengers.

Down a narrow road, away from the noise, towards a quiet hangar tucked behind the airport buildings.

The gates opened without question. And there it was.

A private jet. Gleaming white against the tarmac, its nose pointed towards the runway, its steps lowered, attendants waiting at the base.

My anger dissolved, replaced in an instant by shock, then awe.

The car slowed to a stop. One of the attendants bowed. "Señora, your aircraft awaits."

The words hit me like a wave. 'My' aircraft. Not a commercial flight. Not a missed check-in. A jet waiting only for me.

I stepped out, the hot air curling around me, the sound of the engines faint but steady. The smell of jet fuel. The attendants smiled warmly with their uniforms sharp, blowing in the wind, their manner deferential.

I climbed the steps slowly, my hand brushing the polished rail. Inside, the cabin was cool and hushed, the air scented faintly of leather and champagne. Cream seats, polished tables, crystal glasses. A silver bucket cradled a bottle already beaded with condensation.

I sank into the seat, my breath shallow.

Of course.

It had been Him.

This was no accident, no courtesy of the Key alone. This was His touch, His power, His arrangement.

My irritation was gone, replaced by a pulsing warmth between my thighs. He had delayed me deliberately — made me doubt, made me fume — only to reveal what had always been waiting.

Not a punishment this time. A gift.

The jet belonged to me. And to Him.

The aircraft lifted from the runway with barely a shudder. The city of Acapulco slipped away beneath the clouds, replaced by endless blue sky.

The cabin was silent save for the soft hum of the engines. An attendant appeared almost at once, bowing lightly before setting a tray before me.

Champagne fizzed in crystal. A silver dome was lifted to reveal delicate slices of fruit — mango, papaya, pineapple — glistening with juice, arranged like jewels. Another plate followed: warm bread, butter whipped soft, and thin slices of smoked salmon with capers and lemon.

The cutlery gleamed. The napkin was pressed linen, folded with precision.

I ate slowly, tasting each bite, though my mind was elsewhere. Even the food felt like Him — chosen, placed, orchestrated for me.

As I sipped champagne, another attendant approached. In her hands was a gold tray, polished so bright it caught the light like fire. Upon it lay a long, velvet jewellery box, deep burgundy in colour. Beside it, a cream card.

She bowed, placed the tray carefully before me, and withdrew without a word.

My breath caught.

The jewellery box was cool beneath my fingertips. I opened it slowly. Inside lay a necklace of heavy gold, delicate and brutal all at once. The chain was thick, unyielding, but at its centre hung a small key-shaped charm — wrought so finely it gleamed like it had been cut from sunlight.

My hands trembled as I lifted it.

The card was handwritten, the script precise, slanted, unmistakably His.

Every lock has its key.
Every woman her chain.
You wear this for me now.
And for me alone.

I pressed the card to my lips, my cunt throbbing, my chest tight. The necklace glinted in the cabin light, weighty in my hands. I clasped it around my neck.

It was not just jewellery. It was a collar. His mark. Proof that even thousands of feet above the sea, even as Acapulco disappeared behind me, I belonged to Him. I leaned back into the cream leather, the chain heavy at my throat, the champagne sweet on my tongue, and whispered into the silence:

"Yes."

✦✦✦

Acapulco
Epilogue

The flight was smooth, silent, unreal. By the time I stepped back into my own house, it was as though Acapulco had been a fever dream.

I unpacked slowly, each garment folded, each trinket placed aside. I bathed until the scent of salt and sweat was washed from my skin. The gold necklace lay against my collarbone, cool and heavy, catching the bathroom light. I did not remove it.

I thought I would sleep.

But when I stepped into the hallway, there it was.

An envelope. Not posted, no stamp, just lying on the doormat as though it had slipped beneath the door in silence. The paper was thick, cream, sealed with wax pressed into the shape of a key.

Beside it, a black box tied with crimson ribbon.

My throat tightened. My cunt throbbed.

I carried them into the sitting room. I poured a brandy, before I dared break the seal.

The card inside was simple.

Welcome home.
You pleased me in Acapulco.
Now you are ready for Tokyo.

My breath shook. My eyes dropped to the box.

I untied the ribbon slowly, my fingers trembling, and lifted the lid. Inside lay a kimono, silk — the colour of midnight — folded with impossible precision. A robe, light as air, so soft it seemed to slip through my fingers like water.

Beneath it, another card, smaller, handwritten in the same slanted hand.

Wear this when the Key calls again.
Tokyo is waiting.
So am I.

I pressed the silk to my cheek, my cunt tightening, my heart aching.

It was no longer a choice.

Acapulco had changed me. He had marked me. And now Tokyo awaited.

I closed my eyes, the robe cool against my lips, the necklace heavy at my throat.

"I'll come," I whispered into the silence. "I'll always come."

The End

Tokyo
Prologue

The card had never left my side. Nine months had passed since Acapulco, and still I found myself twirling it between my fingers, its cream surface softened, its wax seal half worn from the hours I had handled it.

Welcome home.
You pleased me in Acapulco.
Now you are ready for Tokyo.

Nine months. The longest silence since the Key first entered my life. Long enough for the fever of obsession to cool. Long enough for the feel of His cock to blur around the edges, the thrill of His control softened by the simple rhythm of ordinary days.

For weeks, I had convinced myself I was free.

I told myself the games had run their course, that Acapulco's punishment had been enough, that the Key had demanded everything it could. I told myself that I didn't need Him. That I had outgrown Him.

And yet, the card never left me.

It sat on my desk while I slipped into the pages of whatever book I was reading, laid beside my cup of tea as though it belonged there. Always present. Always a weight.

Now, with my ticket to Tokyo confirmed, I sat staring at it, asking myself questions I no longer knew how to answer.

Did I still want this?

Did I still need it?

The truth was uncomfortable. The months of distance had eroded some of the urgency. The memory of His voice, His touch, His cock, Oh his cock, His punishment — it had grown hazy, as though part of a dream. The lust that had once consumed me was no longer burning so brightly.

But it was Tokyo.

The final city. The final keyhole waiting for me to turn.

To stop now, after everything, would be foolish. Cowardly. To have endured Dubai, Rome Marrakesh, Maui and Acapulco — only to falter at the last door — would make a mockery of everything I had given, everything I had endured.

I traced the edge of the card with my thumb. Sakura season. That was no accident. The blossoms were already in bloom. I could see them in my mind: soft pink, fragile, falling almost as soon as they opened.

They would not just decorate the games. They would be the games.

A shiver ran through me. Doubt and desire knotted together in my belly.

The truth was, I wanted to know. I had to know. Who He was. Why He had chosen me. Whether He would still be waiting in Tokyo.

The card lay on the table, the wax seal catching the light.

With a sigh, I reached for my passport.

"I'm going," I whispered to the empty room. "One last time."

✦✦✦

Tokyo
Chapter One

The flight to Tokyo seemed endless. A blur of recycled air, plastic trays, dimmed lights. I half-watched films I couldn't follow, read the same page of my book three times, and dozed in fits that left me more tired than before.

But I wasn't restless because of the flight. I was restless because of Him.

Nine months. The longest silence.

The hum of the engines was steady, hypnotic, pressing down on me as the hours dragged. The cabin was dim, passengers lost in films or sleep, the aisle lights a soft glow.

I lay beneath the thin airline blanket, restless, eyes fixed on the screen in front of me but seeing nothing. My book lay abandoned in the seat pocket. My wine glass empty. Nothing held me. Nothing but Him.

Nine months of silence. Nine months of replaying Acapulco's departure in my head — the private jet, the champagne, the velvet box on a gold tray. The necklace, heavy around my throat, His mark.

And then, nothing.

Until now.

I pressed my thighs together, the ache unbearable, the Key's return cutting me open with need. His face I never had. His voice, faded now. What was left was the memory of His cock.

Thick. Veined. Heavy in my hand, stretching me until my body burned with it. That impossible fullness, that brutal possession. The way I had known in that moment no other man would ever compare.

My cunt clenched hard. I shifted under the blanket, my hand sliding lower, the movement so small it would look like nothing at all. My fingertips pressed against the fabric of my knickers, and a tremor ripped through me.

I closed my eyes, pretending to rest. My mouth parted, breath shallow. I traced the wet heat through the cotton, the outline of my swollen lips, pressing harder as the ache swelled.

Images filled me. His cock in Acapulco. His cock in Maui. That weight, that thickness, ramming into me until I screamed. My cunt gripping it, desperate, starving.

My fingers slipped under the waistband, and I touched bare skin. Slick already, soaked with nine months of waiting. I circled slowly, then faster, biting my lip to keep from gasping.

The engines roared louder in my ears, or maybe it was my pulse.

I rubbed, harder now, my cunt pulsing, the wet sounds muffled by the blanket. My hips lifted slightly, my thighs tightening around my hand. I thought of Him pushing me back into this seat, unzipping His trousers, forcing His cock into my mouth with all the power He carried.

I was shaking. The orgasm hit sudden, sharp, making me shudder silently under the thin cover. My body convulsed, my cunt squeezing tight around nothing, my lips parted in a voiceless cry.

I pressed my hand harder to stifle the spasms, my knickers soaked, my thighs trembling.

The plane flew on. Everyone slept. No one saw.

The shudders slowly left my body, leaving me damp beneath the airline blanket. My hand was still wet between my thighs, my knickers sticking to me, my cunt throbbing even as the orgasm faded.

For a moment, I closed my eyes and let the bliss wash through me.

And then the doubt came.

Nine months.

Nine months since Acapulco, since the necklace, since that final card that had promised Tokyo. And yet, here I was — on a commercial flight like any other passenger, not a private jet with champagne and gold trays. No gift waiting, no subtle reminder of Him. Only a ticket booked in my name and a destination printed on a card.

Perhaps that was all He ever intended.

Perhaps I had been nothing more than one of many women — chosen, tested, used, then discarded for another.

The thought cut deeper than I expected.

I tried to push it aside, but questions pressed harder than the memory of His cock. Would He even be in Tokyo? Had He moved on? Would I recognise Him if He was there? Of course I would if He gave His cock to me.

Or had I built Him up so completely in my mind that He was no longer a man at all, but an obsession?

I shifted in my seat, wiping my hand discreetly on the blanket. The air felt suddenly colder, thinner, the hum of the engines sharp in my ears.

No. I told myself firmly. This was not about Him. It was about the Key. About the games.

The Key had always been the centre. The card, the invitation, the rules.

It was Tokyo I was flying towards, not Him.

I forced myself to breathe, to picture the cherry blossoms drifting down in temple gardens, to imagine the rituals and games waiting there. If He was gone, if He had chosen another, then at least I still had that.

And perhaps that was enough.

I tightened the blanket around me, staring out at the endless dark sky.

But deep inside, the truth gnawed.

It was never enough without Him.

Tokyo
Chapter Two

The wheels hit the tarmac with a heavy shudder that jolted me from shallow sleep. The cabin lights flicked on, blinds raised, and the dull grey of morning spilled through the windows. Japan.

Narita Airport unfolded in glass and steel, precise and gleaming. Passengers stirred, stretching limbs, gathering bags with the quiet efficiency of people who belonged here. I sat still for a moment, clutching the card in my bag, my heart tightening with every breath.

Nine months of waiting, and now Tokyo.

The jet bridge hummed as I stepped onto it, the air cooler, fresher than I'd expected. A faint scent of disinfectant mingled with roasted coffee from a kiosk nearby. Everything seemed sharper, tidier, even the footsteps echoing along the corridors.

Immigration moved quickly. Polite bows, no unnecessary words. My passport stamped with a thud that felt almost ceremonial. The officer's eyes lingered for a second too long, and I wondered absurdly if he knew — if somehow the Key marked me in ways others could see.

I collected my case from the carousel in silence. Around me, families reunited with laughter, businessmen strode with purpose, tourists clutched guidebooks and cameras. I alone carried the weight of the Key, a secret no one could guess.

In the arrivals hall, a cluster of drivers held white boards with neat black names. I searched them, pulse racing. For a moment, my throat dried — had He sent no one? Was I truly alone this time?

Then I saw it.

A single word, handwritten in elegant brushstrokes.

Key.

No name. No explanation. Just the word that bound me.

The man holding it was dressed in a black suit, his bow precise. He asked for my passport. I passed it to him reluctantly. He returned it with another polite bow, his eyes lowered. A servant, nothing more. He lifted my case without another word and gestured toward the sliding doors.

The air outside hit me fresh and cool, carrying the faintest trace of cherry blossoms from somewhere beyond the concrete. Petals were already in my mind, drifting like whispers into the games to come.

I followed him into the waiting car, my heart pounding.

Tokyo had claimed me already.

The car pulled away from Narita with a smooth hum, its interior hushed, cocooning me from the clamour of the airport. The driver said nothing. No conversation, no explanation. Just a polite nod in the mirror before his eyes returned to the road.

At first the motorway stretched straight and wide, lined with service stations and billboards in Japanese, trucks and taxis rolling steadily beside us. Beyond, I glimpsed the suggestion of Tokyo's vast sprawl, shimmering on the horizon like a promise of neon and noise. But we did not go that way.

Instead, the driver veered toward quieter routes, the roads narrowing, winding through small towns where tiled roofs and corner shrines stood between convenience stores and rice paddies. I pressed my forehead to the window, watching schoolchildren in neat uniforms, elderly couples tending garden plots, the ordinary life of Japan unfolding in quick snapshots as we passed.

The further we drove, the softer everything became. Hills rose around us, clad in cedar and pine, the air sharp with green. Cherry trees lined the road in bursts of pale blossom, petals drifting across the windscreen like soft rain.

And then the towns thinned, replaced by silence.

Shrines appeared tucked into forest glades, crimson torii gates bright against stone lanterns. A hush descended that felt older than the road itself.

The driver turned onto a gravelled lane bordered with bamboo. The world outside grew stiller with each bend. Time seemed to fold, every sound absorbed into the hush of the forest.

And then, at last, it appeared…

The temple rose from the hillside like a vision from another age. Dark cedar beams gleamed as though polished by centuries of hands, their weight supported by pillars thick as tree trunks. The tiered roofs curved into the sky with sweeping grace, tiles glinting like scales in the soft morning light.

Gold accents edged the eaves, catching every flicker of sun, while carved dragons and lotus flowers coiled around the wooden frames as though alive. Wide stone steps led up toward a veranda lined with paper lanterns swaying gently in the breeze, each one painted with characters I couldn't read but felt sure were prayers.

It was not a hotel, not even a sanctuary for guests.

It was a place of worship.

A place where pleasure and punishment might both be cloaked as ritual.

My breath caught in my throat. The air smelled faintly of incense and cherry blossoms, sweet and heavy, as though the temple itself exhaled it.

The car drew to a stop at the foot of the steps. Attendants in silk robes stood waiting in a neat line, their heads bowed, their movements so precise they seemed choreographed. One stepped forward, sliding open the door, and bowed deeply before offering his hand.

I stepped out onto the gravel, the crunch sharp beneath my heels. For a moment I simply stood, staring upward at the palatial temple, the sheer weight of it pressing down on me.

If Acapulco had been opulence, Tokyo was power.

And it was about to claim me.

✦✦✦

Tokyo
Chapter Three

The attendants bowed as I followed them through wide wooden corridors, the air cool and scented with incense and cedar. Our steps made no sound on the polished floors. On either side, rice paper screens glowed softly with light, shadows shifting faintly behind them — lives, secrets, whispers.

At last, one of the servants slid a door aside and gestured for me to enter.

My chamber was a different world.

The space was elegant in its restraint, pared back to only what was needed. A low futon, its white bedding crisp and precise. A single lacquered chest in the corner. A delicate scroll painting of plum blossoms hung on the wall, the brushstrokes so fine they seemed to breathe.

Sliding doors opened onto a private garden no larger than a courtyard. Stone lanterns stood among raked gravel, patterns curling in perfect spirals. A narrow pond rippled softly, the flash of koi carp gliding beneath the surface. Two bonsai trees framed the space, their miniature branches sculpted into living art.

I stood at the threshold, drinking it in. The quiet was profound, the sort that pressed itself into your chest until you had no choice but to breathe slower. It felt less like a room and more like a meditation.

But I knew better.

This was not simply a sanctuary. It was a stage. Every detail, every shadow, every ripple in the pond had been chosen for me.

An attendant placed my case carefully beside a chest, bowed, and slid the door closed behind him without a word.

I was alone.

Alone, and already claimed.

I stepped out into the garden, crouched at the edge of the pond, and let my fingers trail through the water. The koi scattered in flashes of orange and gold. For a moment, I thought of the flight, of the necklace, of Him. Was He here, within these walls, or had He sent me again only to watch from a distance?

A petal drifted from the bonsai and landed on the water's surface, trembling before it sank. My cunt tightened with a sudden, inexplicable ache.

This was Tokyo.

And it promised not punishment, but romance.

✦✦✦

Tokyo
Chapter Four

I must have drifted off after unpacking, because when I opened my eyes the lanterns outside glowed soft against the paper screens and the air smelled faintly of incense. My futon was still warm, my body heavy with the ache of travel and memory.

Something lay on the floor by the door.

Another card.

Slipped silently beneath the rice paper, as all the others had been before.

My fingers trembled as I picked it up. The brushstrokes were beautiful, more art than words, and yet the message was clear.

Tonight you will wear what I gave you. The silk is yours to carry, but never yours to keep.

I knew instantly what it meant. The kimono He had sent me months ago, folded carefully among my things. Sheer silk, colour of midnight, so light it clung to my skin and revealed everything it touched. I had tried it on once, at home, in secret. It had made me feel exposed, trembling, utterly His.

And now, tonight, it was to be worn.

I bathed quickly, dried myself, and slipped into the silk. It floated against me like a whisper, every curve of my body visible beneath it. I tied the sash loosely, the fabric falling open just enough to show the swell of my breasts, the soft line of my stomach, the neat trim of my cunt.

When the attendants came for me, they did not let me walk. They lifted me, carried me in silence through the corridors, the night air cool against my bare legs as we passed into the temple grounds.

Lanterns lined the path. Petals fell in soft showers from the cherry trees above. The sound of water trickled from a hidden fountain, mingling with the low murmur of voices.

They set me down at the steps of a shrine.

And there, I saw them.

Other guests.

Men and women alike, the women all wearing the same sheer kimono, identical in cut and colour to mine. The silk floated around them, concealing nothing, every body laid bare beneath its veil. The sight took my breath, not because of their nakedness, but because of the sudden, sharp realisation.

I was not the only one.

He had given them this too.

The Key. The silk. The invitation.

For months I had held to the belief — or the hope — that I was special, singled out, chosen. And now, standing in the glow of lanterns among others draped in the same fabric, I felt the first stirrings of doubt.

Had He whispered to them too? Had they felt His cock inside them, the way I had?

The shrine bells chimed, low and resonant, cutting through my thoughts. The attendants guided us forward, side by side, as the ritual began.

And though my cunt ached with arousal, though my skin burned beneath the silk, I could not silence the question beating in my chest.

Was I ever His?

Or was I only one of many?

The shrine doors opened with a long, low creak, the sound of wood and age. Lanterns glowed softly within, paper panels painted with mountains and flowing rivers. The air was heavy with incense — cedar, sandalwood, and a sweetness I couldn't name, something floral, almost intoxicating.

We were guided inside and placed in a circle on low cushions. Twenty of us — ten men, ten women — wrapped in sheer silk that clung to our skin. The fabric hid nothing. Every curve, every swell, every damp shadow was on show.

Then they entered.

Twenty Japanese men and women in silk robes of pale cream, their movements slow and deliberate, eyes lowered in reverence. Each bore something in their hands: a bronze mirror, a fan, a lacquered box, a carved idol, a scroll tied with red silk. Artifacts from shrines and history, gleaming under the lantern light. They set them gently on the stands before us, bowing low, then knelt behind the guests.

The hall grew quiet. I heard only the faint crackle of incense and the soft rustle of silk being lowered as the first vial of oil was uncorked.

Warmth spilled across my shoulders in a slow, deliberate pour. Thick and fragrant, it rolled down between my breasts, slicking my skin. Strong hands smoothed it into me, wide strokes across my collarbones, down the slope of my arms. Another pair of hands joined, softer, a woman's touch — tracing circles over my chest, pausing just long enough at my nipples to make me gasp.

The oil smelled faintly of yuzu and cedar, the scent sharp and bright in my lungs. Fabrics joined the touch, strips of silk drawn across my slick skin, sliding over my breasts, my belly, the inside of my thighs. The combination of warmth and cool, of firm pressure and delicate caress, was almost unbearable.

Around me, the same ritual played out. Men groaned softly, their heads tipping back as hands massaged oil into their thighs, their cocks swelling visibly beneath the sheer fabric. Women sighed, bodies arched as breasts were cupped, stroked, kissed through oil and silk.

It was not hurried. Every movement was slow, reverent, as though each body was being prepared for worship. My skin tingled, alive, every nerve singing. By the time the hands slid down to my stomach, massaging slow circles just above my mound, my cunt was wet enough to soak the silk.

When the first mouth touched me, I almost cried out.

Soft lips pressed to the back of my neck, then my shoulder, a kiss that lingered. Fingers spread my thighs wider, oil-slick hands parting my folds with patient care. Then a tongue — slow, deliberate, tracing me from base to tip, circling my clit before pulling back.

I trembled, my breath breaking.

And then the silence shattered.

One cry became another. A woman moaned loudly, her kimono already shoved aside, her breasts pulled into a man's mouth. A man groaned, jerking his hips as two attendants stroked his cock with oiled hands. The stillness cracked open, the air filled with panting, sighs, gasps.

The attendants shed their robes. Naked bodies moved among us, mouths to nipples, tongues to cunts, cocks sliding into waiting mouths. I cried out as fingers pressed inside me, curling just right, while a woman's lips sealed over my clit and sucked until my hips bucked.

The shrine dissolved into an orgy.

Silk fell open, kimonos discarded. Oiled bodies writhed on the tatami, men pumping into cunts, women grinding faces, mouths moving from cock to cunt to nipple. The sound was overwhelming — wet, slick, desperate.

And then the artifacts were lifted.

The bronze mirror was carried forward, its polished face gleaming in the lantern light. A woman was pulled to her knees before it, her cunt already dripping as she rubbed herself against its cold surface. A man beside her grunted, stroking his cock faster until thick ropes of cum spattered the bronze, streaking across her belly.

A lacquered box followed, its lid opened as though waiting. I pressed forward, guided by unseen hands, until my cunt was poised above it. The woman who had been licking me pressed harder, her tongue relentless, until the orgasm broke and I squirted across the wood, fluid running into the grooves of its carvings.

One by one, artifacts were christened. Scrolls unfurled, stained with slick. Carved idols stroked by cocks until seed dripped down their faces. A flute filled with hot streams of cum, its lacquer glistening. Fans unfolded and sprayed with cunt-juice, handled like holy relics.

By the end, every piece shone wet, transformed into something alive with sex.

Forty bodies writhed in the shrine, covered in sweat, oil, and seed. My cunt throbbed, my thighs slick, my nipples aching from mouths that would not let go. The room smelled thick of sex, incense buried beneath the heat of it.

And through the blur of it all, through the haze of bodies and blossoms drifting in from the open doors, I thought of Him.

Had He sent them all?

Had He sent me here only to realise I was one of many?

Or was He still watching, waiting, somewhere in the shadows — just for me?

✦✦✦

Tokyo
Chapter Five

The attendants guided me back along the silent corridors, their steps so quiet I almost doubted they were there. When they slid open the rice paper door and bowed, I stepped alone into my chamber, the air cool and scented faintly of the oils still clinging to my skin.

I let the kimono slip from my shoulders, the silk falling soundlessly to the tatami. My body was glistening, my thighs sticky, the faint ache between my legs a reminder of how many mouths, how many hands, how many cocks had claimed me tonight.

And yet… it was different.

I sank onto the futon, knees drawn up, arms wrapped around myself. My mind replayed the evening in fragments: the slow press of oil on my shoulders, the reverent kiss on my neck, the way every caress felt like worship. Nothing brutal, nothing humiliating.

And still, when I thought of Him, I remembered something else.

The way He had once held me so gently, as though I were porcelain, before thrusting into me hard enough to steal my breath. The way His tongue had teased me until I whimpered, only to follow with deep, merciless strokes of His cock. The way He could take me from softness to savagery in a single heartbeat.

I pressed my hand between my thighs, finding myself wet again despite the soreness. My body remembered Him — the extremes, the opposites. The tenderness that lulled me, the rawness that consumed me.

Tonight had not been His. It had been ritual, sacred, collective. Beautiful in its way.

But only He could give me both.

The Key was His. The romance, the brutality, the silk, the seed — all Him.

And I longed for Him, more than ever.

Sleep did not come easily. My body was exhausted, sore, spent from too many mouths, too many hands, too many cocks — and yet my mind spun in restless circles. I lay on the futon, the scent of oil still clinging to my skin, the whisper of silk still in my ears.

When at last I drifted, He came to me.

Not in tenderness, not in blossoms. But in the way I had always known Him best.

Brutal.

The dream pulled me back to Acapulco, to that night when I had imagined Him as a shadowed figure, using me without mercy. Only this time it was sharper, clearer. I felt His weight pinning me down, His breath hot against my ear, His cock slamming into me hard enough to make me cry out.

I whimpered beneath Him, my arms stretched, my cunt filled to breaking. His rhythm was merciless, every thrust driving deeper, harder, until I could no longer tell if it was pain or pleasure splitting me apart.

Around us, others watched, but I didn't care. There were cocks in my mouth, hands pulling at my breasts, tongues lapping at the slick pouring from my cunt. But they were nothing.

Because none of them were Him.

Only when His cock was inside me did I feel complete.

He whispered something — I couldn't catch the words, but the tone made me shiver. Possession, command, hunger. I opened for Him, wider, always wider, willing to take whatever He wanted to give.

And still I wanted more.

The dream blurred, His thrusts growing faster, his cock pounding me into the futon until I came screaming, squirting around Him, begging for release. His seed flooded me, hot and heavy, and I moaned His name — though I didn't even know it.

I woke shaking.

The futon was damp beneath me, my thighs slick with the evidence of my dream. My cunt clenched, empty, aching for Him.

Tonight I had been taken by many. But none of them were Him.

And the craving was unbearable.

✦✦✦

Tokyo
Chapter Six

The knock was soft, almost apologetic. When I slid the door open, a tray had been left on the tatami: a lacquered box with breakfast.

I carried it to the low table by the window and unwrapped it carefully. Rice, pickles, grilled fish, miso soup, a small bowl of fruit arranged like petals around a single strawberry. Simple. Elegant. Perfect.

And yet I ate with no appetite.

There was no restaurant here, no dining room, no gathering of guests. Only solitude. The temple seemed built for silence, as though every corner whispered: *reflect, wait, endure.*

After breakfast I walked the gardens, barefoot on the cool stones, the cherry blossoms drifting like pale snow onto my hair and shoulders. Carp glided lazily in the pond, their mouths opening and closing as if chanting something I couldn't hear. I sat beneath a bonsai, its twisted branches centuries in the shaping, and opened a book I had packed. I read the same line ten times before I realised I hadn't absorbed a single word.

Because I was waiting.

For Him.

Every shadow along the corridor, every rustle of silk, every reflection in the pond — I searched them all for a glimpse of Him. Would He appear suddenly, as He had in Maui? Would He watch from afar, as He had in Acapulco? Or would He never come at all, leaving me only the memory of His cock, the ghost of His hands, the ache of craving?

The hours passed with maddening slowness. The temple gave me peace, yes, but not the peace I wanted. I wanted Him. I wanted to feel Him inside me, even once, even briefly, even brutally.

But day gave me nothing.

And so I returned to my chamber as the lanterns were lit and the shadows lengthened, knowing that if He came at all, it would be with the night.

And with the games.

As dusk settled, the silence of the temple deepened. I lay on the futon staring at the ceiling beams, the faint smell of cedar drifting in from the garden. My body was restless, shifting under the thin blanket, my cunt throbbing with an ache that no amount of stillness could soothe.

The soft scrape of something sliding across the floor snapped my head around.

Another card. Another parcel.

I didn't move straight away. I stared at them as if they were a trick. My chest tightened, the memory of every other note flooding back: Marrakesh's promises, Maui's riddles, Acapulco's punishments. Always the same — words that teased, garments that bound, instructions that controlled.

At last I picked up the card.

Blossoms fall only once. Tonight you must wear the petals that will not last.

I sighed. The script was beautiful, delicate. But I was tired of poetry.

I wanted Him.

The garment was folded carefully in a lacquered box, tied with pale silk cord. I undid it slowly, my fingers trembling more with anger than anticipation. Inside lay another kimono finer than the last — sheer, embroidered with scattered pink blossoms. Beautiful, yes. Fragile, yes. But it wasn't His cock.

I pressed the fabric to my face, breathing in its faint fragrance. My body burned hotter for it, but the fire had nothing to do with silk.

All I wanted was to feel Him again.

The thickness of Him stretching me wide. The heat of Him spurting endlessly inside me, across my breasts, dripping down my thighs. The way His rhythm had once broken me apart, gentle one moment, brutal the next.

No more riddles. No more garments. No more patience.

I wanted Him.

And as I laid the kimono out before me, readying myself for the night, I could only hope — pray — that tonight would finally give Him back to me.

✦✦✦

Tokyo
Chapter Seven

The bells rang, low and deliberate, summoning us to the great hall. My body was wrapped in the blossom kimono, its sheer silk floating around me, clinging to my skin where heat already gathered.

When I entered, I gasped.

The long tatami tables had been removed. In their place lay bodies.

Naked attendants stretched across low platforms, men and women alike, their skin gleaming with oil, their bodies covered with dishes of food. Bowls of rice balanced on flat stomachs. Slices of sashimi arranged across breasts. Pomegranates and figs nestled between thighs. Grapes dangled from nipples. Rolls of sushi lined the ridges of cocks.

The guests filed in silently, twenty of us, dressed in the same sheer blossom kimonos. We were guided to our chosen places, men led toward female attendants, women toward male. I was placed before a young man whose chest rose and fell steadily, his eyes closed as though already surrendered.

The signal came not in words but in music. A single note from a flute, drawn out until the hall filled with its tremble.

Then we began.

I leaned over him, the silk of my kimono brushing his skin, and picked a grape from his chest with my lips. He shuddered, his breath catching. I let my tongue linger on his nipple, tasting salt and oil, before moving lower to pluck a slice of sashimi from the flat plane of his belly.

Around me, the hall filled with wet sounds and sighs. Women licked fruit from cocks, their hands already stroking shafts hard beneath the plates. Men teased breasts with chopsticks before lowering their mouths to suck and bite gently, coaxing moans. Food disappeared quickly, replaced by tongues and fingers.

I cupped his cock, not big in length but rock solid, heavy and warm, slipping the sushi roll from it with my lips. He groaned, his hips lifting, his cock swelling fully in my hand. I stroked slowly, letting oil slick my palm, and bent to take him into my mouth. He tasted of salt and citrus, the remnants of fish and the rawness of flesh. I sucked, my tongue circling the head, while my other hand cupped his balls, rolling them until he whimpered.

The flute gave way to drums — soft at first, then faster. The signal was clear.

Release.

The attendants were no longer still. They groaned, arched, spread their legs, their hands finally touching us in return. The guests abandoned the pretence of dining. Nipples were pinched, cunts fingered, cocks stroked. The hall filled with moans, groans, the wet slap of flesh.

The young man beneath me came first, spilling hot cum into my mouth, his body trembling under my hands. I swallowed greedily, licking every drop from his cock, the taste thick and musky.

Then I lay back, my kimono falling open, and let two attendants take me. One sucked my nipples until they ached, the other pushed his fingers deep into my cunt, curling until I cried out. I came over and over, my thighs slick, my cries lost in the cacophony around me.

Soon there was no order, no pairing. Guests fell upon one another, attendants now summoned away, the hall alive with writhing bodies. Women rode men's faces, men thrust into mouths, cunts and asses filled and emptied again and again. Sweat dripped, cum spurted, blossoms scattered across oiled skin.

It was indulgence, pure and unashamed.

And yet—

As I lay gasping, a cock still twitching between my lips, I knew.

None of them were Him, Again!

The thickness, the length, the heat of endless release — I craved only His cock, His seed. And it was not here.

Not tonight.

✦✦✦

Tokyo
Chapter Eight

The knock woke me before dawn. A tray was left outside again, the same quiet ritual of rice, pickles, fish, and fruit. I carried it in and set it down, but my appetite was gone.

I was tired. Not in my body — the games had always demanded that — but in my spirit.

It all felt empty now.

The shrine, the feast, the endless mouths and hands. Bodies had pleasured me, cocks had filled me, but none of it mattered. None of it was Him. I craved His cock, His brutal rhythm, His hot release spilling inside me. Without that, the rest was meaningless.

Tomorrow I would go home.

I wasn't going to waste this last day locked in my chamber, waiting for another card with another cryptic message. So when the offer came — a car to the city — I accepted.

The drive took me away from the temple's stillness into the pulse of Tokyo. By the time we reached Shibuya, the contrast was dizzying.

The crossing was alive with movement, hundreds of bodies weaving past one another with a grace that looked like chaos from above. Neon lights flickered even in daylight, signs screaming colour and promise in every direction. The air was thick with roasted meat, fried batter, perfume, exhaust fumes.

I walked. Slowly at first, then with purpose.

I drifted into shops, running my hands over silk scarves, lacquered hairpins, paper fans painted with blossoms. I tried on a dress I knew I would never wear, just to feel the fabric against my skin. I bought a small wooden box carved with cranes, no idea what I'd use it for, only that I wanted it.

Lunch was simple — noodles steaming in a bowl, broth rich and salty. I slurped like everyone else, unashamed, the taste warming me more than the touch of any mouth had last night.

Later, I found a coffee shop tucked into a narrow side street. Wooden walls, soft lighting, the faint hiss of milk steaming behind the counter. I sat by the window with a dark roast, watching Tokyo move around me.

Students laughing as they spilled out of a record shop. Salarymen in dark suits bowing to one another. Couples walking hand in hand, their gestures shy but sure.

I had been here before, years ago, on business trips. I had thought then that Tokyo was overwhelming. Now, after Marrakesh, Maui, Acapulco, even the temple itself — it felt comforting. A reminder that the world was still real, still ordinary.

And yet, as I stirred my coffee, I couldn't silence the ache.

He had vanished again.

Had He moved on to someone else? Were there other women in other temples, other kimonos, other cards slipping under doors?

The thought stung, but I forced it away. I was here, in Tokyo, and for one day at least I would not spend it wishing for Him.

Tomorrow I would leave.

But tonight…

Tonight would still come.

✦✦✦

Tokyo
Chapter Nine

I had just finished my coffee when he approached.

Tall, silver grey-haired, dressed simply in a shirt and trousers that did nothing to hide his presence. His eyes held mine as though he already knew me. There was nothing forward in his manner, nothing pushy — just an ease, a confidence that unsettled me.

"Do you mind if I join you?" His English was broken but clear, with an accent I couldn't quite place.

I nodded before I could think.

We spoke lightly at first. About the city, about the chaos of the crossing, about how Tokyo never seemed to sleep. He was a stranger, yet the rhythm of his words was strangely familiar. I found myself leaning closer, drawn in by the warmth of his voice.

When the conversation turned to drinks, I let him lead me down a narrow street to a quiet bar. Lanterns glowed red above the doorway, and inside the air was heavy with whisky and low jazz. We sat close, too close, his knee brushing mine. Each time it did, my cunt throbbed, slick with a heat I tried to ignore.

Then he spoke of the love hotels.

"You've seen the signs, haven't you?" he asked, his lips curling into a faint smile. "The neon, the hearts. Couples slip inside for a night—or an hour. Privacy, no questions asked. Tokyo's secret indulgence."

I swallowed hard, the image burning into me. Neon-lit windows, curtained rooms, strangers giving in to lust high above the streets.

I should have left. I should have returned to the temple for the final night. But when I reached for my phone, my driver had already been summoned away.

It was just him and me.

"Come," he said softly, leaning close enough for his breath to touch my ear. "I'll show you."

The words were simple. But they were familiar. Too familiar. My heart jolted, my body shivered.

We walked together under the neon glow, the signs flashing their promises of *whatever the Japanese characters read.* He guided me into one without hesitation, past the unmanned desk, into a room lit softly with paper

The door clicked shut behind us, and the room seemed to exhale. A wide bed stretched before me, white sheets tucked smooth as silk, a mirror hung above it. Paper lanterns glowed from the corners, casting everything in a soft golden haze.

I turned to face him, my heart hammering.

He was already undressing, each movement slow, deliberate, as if he knew I would savour every second. His shirt slipped from his shoulders, revealing a chest I had only dreamed of. Broad, lean, cut with strength. Then his belt loosened, trousers falling away, and there it was.

My breath caught. My cunt clenched.

His cock.

The thickness I had longed for. The length that haunted my sleep. The weight I had craved for nine long months.

It was Him.

I dropped to my knees without thinking. My lips parted before I even touched Him, and when the head of His cock brushed against my tongue, I moaned so loud it shocked me.

The taste. The salt. The heat.

I wrapped my hand around the base, barely able to close my fingers, and guided Him deeper into my mouth. He groaned above me, low and rough, one hand slipping into my hair, holding me steady as I sucked Him slow and deep.

I wanted every inch. I needed it.

I gagged, tears pricking my eyes as He pushed further, His cock thick against my throat. I didn't care. I wanted to choke on Him, to drown in Him. My cunt was dripping already, wetting the silk of my skirt, but my mouth was greedy, desperate, insatiable.

"Good girl," He murmured, His voice exactly as I remembered — that perfect blend of praise and command.

The words made me shudder, my nipples hardening, my thighs trembling.

I pulled back, saliva glistening from my lips to His cock, and stroked Him hard and fast, my eyes never leaving His. "Nine months," I whispered, my voice breaking. "Nine months I've needed this."

He didn't answer. He pulled me up, turned me, and pushed me onto the bed.

I landed on the sheets, breasts bared, thighs spread. He loomed above me, His cock heavy against my belly as He pressed down, kissing me hard, tongue thrusting into my mouth the way His cock had just thrust into my throat.

Then, there He was. For nine months, where I had craved Him to be, inside me, I screamed in ecstasy.

It was like being split open, stretched to the edge of pain. My cunt clamped around Him, slick and tight, the months of longing crashing into one shattering moment of fullness.

He fucked me hard. Brutal, relentless, each thrust pounding deep, hitting that place no other cock had ever reached. The bed shook, the mirror above us catching the sight of my body jolting with every stroke, breasts bouncing, mouth open in a cry.

I clawed at Him, nails raking His back, begging for more even as my body buckled beneath Him. He gave it — more, harder, faster — until I came screaming, squirting across His cock, soaking the sheets.

But He didn't stop.

He flipped me, pulling me onto my knees, my face pressed to the pillow. He took me from behind, His cock slamming into me so deep I thought I might break. I sobbed into the sheets, my cunt clenching, my ass twitching with every thrust. His hand came down hard across my hip, holding me in place, owning me completely.

"Mine," He growled.

"Yes," I gasped, tears spilling. "Yours. Always."

Another orgasm tore me apart, violent, unstoppable, my body shaking as cum gushed down my thighs. He pulled out suddenly, stroking His cock hard, and with a roar He came — hot endless ropes of seed splattering across my back, my ass, my hair. I collapsed forward, panting, trembling, soaked in Him.

For a moment, silence. Just the sound of our breathing, the faint hum of neon through the window.

Then He pulled me up, turned me, and kissed me again. Not brutal this time, but soft. Tender.

The extremes. Always the extremes.

I lay against Him, His cock still twitching against my thigh, His cum dripping from my skin, and I knew: no matter what the games were, no matter how many mouths, hands, or cocks I had taken, only His ever truly mattered.

Only Him.

Steam curled into the air as He turned on the bath. The room filled with warmth, the scent of cedarwood soap drifting between us. He led me by the hand, as though I were fragile, lowering me into the water. My body shivered at the heat, muscles sighing with relief.

He joined me, sliding in behind me, His chest against my back, His arms circling my waist. I closed my eyes as His hands moved slowly, tenderly, stroking my skin as if memorising every inch. He dipped a cloth into the water, smoothing it over my shoulders, down my arms, across my breasts. My nipples hardened again, sensitive, aching, but His touch was unhurried, reverent.

When He reached between my thighs, I gasped. His fingers traced me softly, parting my lips, stroking gently through the soreness of being taken so hard. I relaxed into Him, tilting my head back onto His shoulder, letting Him care for me in a way no other ever had.

"You're worried," He murmured against my ear.

I swallowed, my body trembling at His voice. "I should be back. At the temple. They'll expect me for tonight's game—"

"They won't," He said, calm, certain. "It has been arranged."

The words sank into me like warmth into the water. Of course. Always. He was the Key. He moved the games, the rules, the cards. He was behind everything.

His hand slid lower, oil slicking His fingers now as He stroked me more firmly. My thighs opened, my hips lifting in the water. I moaned, clutching at His arm, His cock already hard again pressing into the small of my back.

"I've needed you," I whispered, almost breaking. "For so long."

"You have me," He answered simply.

He turned me then, lifting me effortlessly from the bath, water streaming down my body, and laid me across the cool sheets of the bed. He oiled me carefully, affectionately, rubbing it into my skin until I glistened. Over my breasts, my stomach, my thighs. His hands strong, His touch slow, lingering.

Then He spread my legs and slid into me once more.

The stretch was just as shocking, just as overwhelming. His cock filled me again, deep and merciless, driving me to sobs as He thrust hard, fast, unrelenting. I clung to Him, nails scoring His back, crying out His name though I still didn't know it.

And as He pounded into me, His lips found my ear.

"These," He whispered, each word a thrust, "are the final moments we will have together."

My breath caught. My body tensed around Him.

"No—" I gasped, shaking my head, tears spilling. "Don't—"

He silenced me with His mouth, kissing me hard as His cock drove deeper, faster, until my resistance broke and I shattered around Him. My orgasm ripped through me, violent and raw, squirting over His cock, soaking the sheets again. He groaned, pulling out, stroking hard until He erupted, spilling hot and endless cum across my belly, my breasts, my throat.

I lay beneath Him, covered in His seed, sobbing not from pain but from the unbearable mix of pleasure and loss.

Because even in the throes of ecstasy, I knew.

This was the last time.

I lay still, my body trembling, His seed cooling on my skin. The sheets were damp, tangled, the air heavy with sex. He sat beside me, silent, stroking my hair, my cheek, as if calming a wild animal. I closed my eyes, wishing I could freeze the moment, trap it, live forever in this single breath between us.

But I felt it slipping.

He stood, dressing slowly, each movement as deliberate as undressing had been. I watched, wordless, the ache in my chest deeper than the ache in my cunt. I wanted to beg Him not to leave, to demand that

He stay, but I already knew — it would mean nothing. He had already told me: these were the final moments.

When He leaned over me, fully dressed once more, I braced for emptiness. Instead, His lips brushed my ear, and in that low, steady tone that always commanded me, He gave me not an order, not an explanation, but a rhyme:

"A blossom falls, yet leaves its trace,
A fleeting kiss, a soft embrace.
Though seasons change, one truth holds true—
No other soul will be as you."

My throat tightened. Tears blurred my vision.

By the time I opened my eyes, He was gone.

Only the words remained, echoing in me like a bell, filling me with both unbearable sadness and a strange, aching pride.

I was His. Always had been. Always would be.

But never again in flesh.

✦✦✦

Tokyo
Chapter Ten

The car was waiting in the shadows of the love hotel's hidden car park, its black paint glinting faintly beneath neon. The driver said nothing as I climbed in. The door closed with a soft thud, and we slipped silently back through the streets of Shibuya.

The car slid silently out of Shibuya, its tinted glass shutting me off from the noise, the people, the neon chaos. Yet I couldn't look away.

I pressed my cheek to the window, watching the colours smear into liquid ribbons — pinks, reds, greens, the kanji signs flashing promises of love, lust, escape. Even at two in the morning, Tokyo pulsed with life. Lovers holding hands at crossings. Girls laughing in too-high heels. Men leaning against glowing vending machines.

Nine months I had dreamed of Him. And tonight, beneath those same neon lights, I had found Him again.

My body still pulsed with it. My cunt was swollen, tender, still slick from the last time He had filled me. My breasts tingled where He had pressed His lips. My skin smelled faintly of cedar from the bath, but underneath, I swore I still carried the musk of His seed.

The city blurred past, but inside the car I was cocooned in silence. I whispered His rhyme again and again under my breath, as if repetition might anchor me:

A blossom falls, yet leaves its trace…

When the car turned from the city roads onto the dark, tree-lined path to the temple, my stomach clenched. I wasn't ready.

But the temple was ready for me.

Lanterns flickered low along the eaves, soft pools of amber light marking my way. My sandals tapped quietly against the stones, the only sound in the stillness. Inside my chamber, the air smelled of incense and clean tatami.

I stopped dead.

Everything was immaculate.

The futon smoothed flat. The low table polished. The paper doors drawn straight. My bags packed neatly, tied with cords, waiting by the door.

It was as though I had already gone.

I undressed slowly, my skirt falling in a soft heap, and stepped into the bath. I washed quickly, my hands scrubbing away the sweat, the oil, the sex — but never quite washing Him from me. He was in my skin now, my breath, the hollow of my chest.

When I stepped back into the chamber, towel loose around me, I noticed it.

On the pillow of my futon lay a box. Small, lacquered, sealed with a wax crest I hadn't seen before.

Beside it, a card.

Do not open until you are in the sky.

My throat tightened. I traced the wax seal with trembling fingers, but I didn't break it. I couldn't.

I slid into bed, the box cool against my palm, the card burning against my chest.

Sleep would not come.

I lay staring into the dark, replaying every moment of the night. The love hotel. His cock. His hands in the bath. His words — tender, final.

By the time dawn paled the rice paper doors, my eyes were still open.

The box waited.

And tomorrow, so would the flight.

✦✦✦

Tokyo
Chapter Eleven

The knock came at dawn.

A tray was waiting outside my chamber, as it always had been. Rice, miso, pickles, a slice of grilled fish, a small bowl of fruit. My last breakfast in Japan. My last breakfast within the Key.

I carried it to the low table and sat cross-legged before it, the steam rising into the cool morning air. I ate slowly, mindful of every taste. The salt of the soup, the sweetness of melon, the bitter edge of green tea.

It was ritual. It was farewell.

I touched the necklace as I ate, fingers tracing the heavy gold key that still hung around my neck. He had never asked for it back. Perhaps that was the point. It was mine now, to wear always, to carry like a brand or a blessing.

I closed my eyes and thought of Him.

The love hotel. His cock. The way He had filled me until I screamed. The way He had oiled my body with such tenderness, then whispered the rhyme that broke me:

A blossom falls, yet leaves its trace…

My body clenched at the memory. My cunt still ached from Him, still swollen, still bruised, as though marked from within.

And yet it was not pain I carried with me, but presence.

The presence of knowing I had been chosen. That I had been His — for a time, at least.

When the tray was empty, I rose and dressed. My travel clothes had been laid out already, pressed and neat. The temple seemed to breathe silence all around me, as though it too were waiting for me to leave.

The walk across the courtyard was dreamlike. The koi pond was still, the bonsai precise and perfect, the air filled with nothing but birdsong. No staff. No guests. No sign of the life that had pulsed through these walls just nights before.

Only me.

The car waited at the gate. The driver bowed once, silent, and opened the door.

I slipped inside. My bags had already been taken. The temple gates closed behind us.

As the road carried me away, I pressed the gold key to my lips, eyes burning, heart heavy.

No private jet this time. No champagne. No Him.

Only the necklace around my throat, and the memories — of Him, of His cock, of the love that was never mine to keep.

The Key had ended.

But I would carry it always.

The hours slipped away above the clouds.

The hum of the engines was constant, the cabin dimmed, other passengers sleeping under thin blankets. I sat upright, my book open in my lap, unread. My mind was not in the words.

It was still with Him.

The rhythm of His thrusts. The scent of cedar oil and sex. The feel of His cock, thick and deep inside me, stretching me open one last time.

I shifted in my seat, thighs pressing together. Even now, high above Siberia, I ached for Him.

And then I remembered.

The gift.

The small black box, sealed with wax, waiting in the pocket of my handbag.

Do not open until you are in the sky.

I reached for it, fingers brushing the lacquered lid. Heavy. Solid. A weight as real as His hand on my throat, His cock in my cunt.

For minutes I stared at it.

I could hear Him in my head. That low command, that certainty. I could almost see His eyes watching me even now, expecting obedience.

But I did not open it.

Not this time.

I slid the box back into my bag, tucked it deep beneath my scarf, and rested my hand against the gold key at my throat instead.

He was not mine.

And I would not let Him own me forever.

The plane rocked gently. The woman in the seat beside me stirred, sighed, and went back to sleep. Around us, life carried on.

And I sat still, awake, the unopened box resting heavy in my bag.

I returned to the book. This time relaxed and able to take in the words.

My final secret.

✦✦✦

Tokyo
Epilogue

The Box

The house was silent when I stepped inside.

No envelope on the mat. No invitation on the table. No perfume of incense lingering in the air.

The Crimson Key was finished.

I unpacked slowly, methodical, folding clothes, stacking shoes, rinsing the scent of Tokyo from my hair. On the dresser, the gold necklace caught the light, heavy and eternal, mine to keep.

But the box weighed more.

Black. Lacquered. Sealed with wax.

I set it on the desk and stared at it, and stared at it, for a long time.

I could open it now. I could finally find out everything. Perhaps even the truth of how it all began.

Instead, I turned away.

Not everything had to be His.

I slipped the box into a drawer, turned the key, and locked it with a soft click.

The Key had changed me. The Key had consumed me. The Key had given me Him, and taken Him away.

But this last secret — this last choice — was mine, all mine.

'He was the Key. The games, the journeys, the punishments, the romance — all Him. A gift I could wear, but never own. A cock I could feel, but never keep. A love I could taste, but never hold. And like the Sakura, He had been mine only for a season.'

The End

www.ingramcontent.com/pod-product-compliance
Lightning Source LLC
Chambersburg PA
CBHW030340310726
48979CB00001B/115